MOVING VIOLATIONS

McGee Mathews

First paperback edition April 2019

ISBN 978-1-0907-9742-1 (paperback)

DEDICATION

For Chris.

You start walking your way, I'll start walking mine.

CONTENTS

ACKNOWLEDGMENTS

I wrote my first novel thirty years ago and rewrote it for almost five years. The last paper copy is gone, the computer files incompatible with any current machinery. The universe is better for the loss of that effort, but it did teach me a great deal about myself. For over twenty years my wife has nudged me to consider writing again, like water torture but well intended. Thank you.

None of us write alone, and I would not have taken another shot at writing without the love and support of the Tuesday night Skype group: Claire Britain, Anna Riley, and CJ O'Hara. I remain grateful for you helping me to learn and polish the craft, reading my best and worst efforts, and whispering to keep going because it's a process.

My friends who took the time to beta read literally cross the country: Tigger Redwood, Sherri A. Dub, Helen Hall, Karena Chambers, Heather North, and Andrea Smith. It takes a village, and your insights helped me as a writer and more importantly as a person. Thank you for your friendship.

Those in the writing field who lifted me up are led by Cherry Adair and her Plotting by Color and the Butt In Chair Challenge. She is a treasure for the romance community. Harper Kincaid, Mary Boland-Doyle, M. Jane Collete, Rhiana Caley, and all the other classmates, you don't know how close I was to tossing in the towel when you brought me into your fold.

CHAPTER 1

Amy Gilbert swung the bat, the yellow rubber softball recoiled with a metallic clink against the gleaming blue aluminum. The evening air was warm for a Michigan spring, and without any breeze, the humidity was crushing. Wisps of dark hair escaped her ponytail and stuck to her forehead. Sweat seeped around the stitches of her batting glove. Willing to do, or spend, whatever it took to break her batting slump, she eyed the next roll of the pitching machine arm and watched the yellow ball arch to the batter's box. Her feet slid on the concrete and another ball flew foul.

Robin Barberg spit out a sunflower seed shell. "You're dropping your shoulder."

"Am not." She now regretted letting Robin talk her into another evening apparently wasted at the batting cages. The problem was her old bat, not her swing.

"You are too, and you're not turning your hips soon enough."

Amy turned to look at Robin. They'd been best friends since they met in middle school. "Are you going to keep hassling me?"

"It's my job to call you out on your shit. Hands across first, then rotate with the swing." Robin popped a seed in her mouth. "Ball."

"What?" And then the rubber ball hit Amy on the back. "Son of a bitch, that was a ball! I thought pitching machines were supposed to throw strikes."

Robin spit out a shell. "Nope. There's a ball once in a while. You don't want to get in the habit of hitting every pitch."

Amy turned just in time to hit the next pitch, sailing the ball right back at the machine.

"You'd be out; can't hit it to the pitcher. Have you been golfing?" Robin accused her.

"No, well, just the driving range with Cheryl." Amy watched the next hit fly in an arc over the machines.

"Cheryl at the car dealership or tight skirt Sheryl?"

Amy turned to face Robin. "Dealer Cheryl. Just work stuff."

"Says you. She's hunting after you." Robin picked a piece of shell off her tongue. "Are you out of quarters yet?"

"I have enough for one more round." Amy dropped the coins into the blue box, and when the indicator glowed inside the plastic bubble, she pushed the round start button. The machine across the concrete lot made some clicking noises, and the arm rotated and pitched the ball. Amy swung and whiffed the ball.

"Now you're stepping too far back. Will you stop trying to crank it and just hit the damn ball?" Robin popped more sunflower seeds in her mouth.

"Your spitting is almost worse than the cigarettes."

"My new lady wants me to quit. It's killing me."

Amy leaned back as the pitch arrived, popping the ball in a solid hit. "The redhead or the basketball player?"

"Both of them." Robin laughed. "Neither. She's a new waitress."

"You shouldn't date at work. It gets too messy." Amy grinned at her friend.

"Easy for you to say." Robin stuck out her tongue. "Besides how would you know? You work with all family."

Amy laughed. Robin worked as a cook at Denny's, and Amy had worked at the Gilbert and Son family garage since she was old enough to see over the hood of a car. Her grandfather started the station some fifty years ago. "Yeah, I really would be kissing my sister." She made a barfing face. She chipped a ball over the machine. "I must say that some pretty fine-looking ladies bring their cars into the shop."

"Yeah, yeah, but you won't actually talk to any of them. I really think you need to get back on the horse. Put yourself out there. Start looking. The right person could be right in front of you and you wouldn't notice."

Amy shrugged. "I don't have the moves like you do. I think I should take it slow."

Robin said, "I saw Deb at the Lounge last weekend. She didn't frickin' wait."

The breakup had not been mutual and Amy was still wounded. "Shit, she didn't wait until we broke up."

"Now she's playing for Emily's team. They might beat us with her bat."

Amy slung her bat in the bag and ripped off her glove. "Are you trying to encourage me, because right now it seems you are already blaming me for the loss we haven't even had yet."

"Hey, I just want you to get your head clear. You just need to hit a single and I'll clean it up."

"Just don't pass me on the baseline. This ankle is still bothering me."

"If you'd wear shin guards or something you wouldn't keep getting hurt." Robin opened the door to the batting cage as Amy stepped toward her. "Or you could bend your ass over and use the fucking mitt to catch the ball."

Amy grabbed Robin and rubbed her head. "Noogies. Thanks, I needed some company."

Robin laughed. "Always. I'm supposed to meet someone. I can cancel. Let's get some nachos. I'm buying."

"Nah, I have to get to work early or my dad will lose his shit. Go have fun. I'll see you tomorrow."

Amy sat her gear bag in the back of her Jeep, unlatched the door, and slid into the seat. She put the clutch in and let the vehicle roll forward until it just touched the bumper of Robin's new sports car, a 1986 yellow Corvette.

"If you hit my frickin' car, I'm going to kick your ass." Robin glared as she unlocked her door.

Amy gave her the finger, and cranked the key, popped it in reverse and squealed the tires out of the parking lot.

Robin screamed, "Asshole."

Amy gunned the engine at the gate when Robin finally got to the exit of the park. Robin just waved as she peeled out and left Amy sitting at the curb. Amy smiled. She and Robin met during a victorious dodge ball game in gym class. They'd been competing with and against each other ever since. No one would describe Robin as refined, but she was good people. When she heard that Amy and Deb split up, the first thing Robin did was to borrow a truck and help Amy move into her house that very night.

Amy smacked her steering column. She had been with Deb for almost three years, she was sure she was 'the one' but Robin had never liked her, considering her snobbish. One thing was for sure, the game tomorrow was going to suck. Amy pulled into the driveway between her parent's house and the Gilbert and Son Garage and killed the engine. She could see the television glowing in her parent's family room from the driveway.

Banging the screen door open, Amy entered the kitchen and lifted the lid to the crockpot on the counter. "It's just me, Ma."

Her mom called from the living room, "If you're here only for the food, use a plastic bowl. You have too many of my dishes already."

Amy scooped several ladles of chili into a glass bowl. "Okay. Good night mom, I'm heading over. See you in the morning."

"Good night, honey. And bring the bowl back clean."

Amy crossed the lawn and climbed back into her Jeep. She drove down the block and around the corner to Robin's house and turned off the key. Balancing the chili bowl, she unlocked the back door to the American four-square style house, cleverly named for the four-square floor plan of both the first floor and the second floor. It wasn't ideal living so close to her parent's place, but Robin's rent was cheap and she could maintain her delusion of maturity. She could also score food if she could catch her parents' meal times. She made pretty good money but was usually broke, and moving back home would have been a full step backward in her journey in adulthood. Her striped cat greeted her with indifference, remaining prone on the kitchen table.

"Good evening. Sorry to disturb your siesta." She grabbed Meow and headed up the stairs.

Amy moved around the few boxes in the spare room with her foot, dropping the cat onto the highest, placing the bowl on the lowest. She sat on the folding chair and flipped on the TV. Deb may have all the furniture, but she owned the electronics. A low hum filled the room as the surround sound speakers came to life. Amy scarfed the chili while watching MTV. Maybe she should just skip the game tomorrow. It was bad enough to deal with the sympathetic looks of the women on her team without knowing they would rather still have Deb on their roster. Well, at least her bat. Amy reached into the nearby mini fridge and took out a Bud Light. Twisting it open, she flicked the top toward the trash bin, hearing a satisfying plink as it hit.

After finishing the beer, she wandered into the bathroom for a shower in the Chicago tub with a curtain strung around a circular shower rod. The hot water came in intermittent waves, like her anger and her resolve. She scrubbed the dust out of her hair, deeply breathing the fresh scent of the soap. She left her clothes on the floor and slid between the new, fresh sheets. Meow sat on the foot of the bed like a sphinx and stared at Amy.

"Hey, if we were still at Deb's you'd be banned to the kitchen. You are not sleeping on the other pillow."

Meow seemed to understand and curled into a ball. Amy stared at the ceiling, listing to the clinks and knocks of the hundred-year-old house. She thought about Deb, the softball game tomorrow, and then back to Deb. The ticking of the clock eventually sent her to a restless sleep.

CHAPTER 2

Amy stepped into the shower, too impatient to wait for the hot water. She shivered as she shampooed her hair. Life was pretty much what you made it. And she hadn't made it anywhere. The only job she'd ever had was working for her dad. The water gurgled and a hot blast steamed into the tub. Amy leaped out before she was scalded.

She dressed into her uniform of gray cotton pants and a button-down shirt to match. The shop logo was okay, but wearing her name on her chest seemed unnecessary in a six-person garage. It made her feel like a teenager working at McDonald's. It was Dad's rule, and everyone followed his rules. She pulled on her favorite boots, finally broken in to the point the leather was soft across the top of her foot, and also the point at which the soles had lost most of their tread.

"Meow. Be a good girl." Amy skipped down the stairs with a light step, and in less than a minute was parked at the rear of the shop. She crossed the parking area and entered the back door of the garage.

She passed through the body shop and spotted her sister and her brother-in-law. "Hi Olivia. Yo Donny. How are two of my favorite people this fine morning?"

Olivia stopped sanding. "Well aren't you in a good mood?" She pushed a stray strand of reddish hair from her forehead.

"Aimster. Glad you could find the time to join us." Donny already had a paint suit on. Olivia had excellent taste. He was a gorgeous man. His azure eyes sparkled over his sculpted, dark beard.

"Doesn't take me as long to get my work clothes on," Amy said.

Don said, "Admit it. We look good." He waved his hand down his body, his muscular frame evident under the thin fabric.

"Dad's gonna be pissed that you're late again," Olivia warned.

"I've got a good feeling about today." Amy kept walking. "See you at lunch?"

She took the long hall along the parts storage room and opened the door that led into the main garage area. The ceiling was two stories, with open metal roofing visible between the girders. Eight stalls were arranged with four on one side, three on the other, and a tire mounting stall tucked in a corner.

The quiet was broken as her sister cranked an air tool. "Good morning!"

Amy waved. "Another day in paradise."

A Ford Lincoln sat in her preferred stall. She picked up the work order on her toolbox. Brake job. She kicked in the lift arms, engaged the hoist, and watched the car rise toward the ceiling. At a comfortable height, she stopped the movement and selected a socket for the air wrench. She had just taken off the last nut on the first wheel when her dad came up.

"Morning, Sunshine. You skipped the bagels your mom brought in. Do you want any coffee?" Frank was still managing the garage, although he was nearing sixty-four. His silver hair was still combed into a pompadour, thick and full. His blue eyes matched the sky.

Amy grabbed the tire and pulled it from the axle, dropping it to the ground with a bounce. "Nah, I just want to cruise through the day."

"Fine. More for me," Frank said. "I got a guy coming to look at the shop later, try not to tear up the place too much."

Amy cursed under her breath. She watched her dad walk off,

a slight limp on the left side, the remnants of a car crash years before. Maybe it was best to just sell the place. Maybe she could get out of turning wrenches. Everyone in her immediate family still worked there, and truth be told, could do every job related to automotive work. Her youngest sister Tina, the book worm, stood changing the oil on a small Toyota truck. Her mom ran the office with all the paperwork. Dad did whatever needed to be done, but he was slowing down. It had been a family business since grandpa opened the gas station in the thirties. Grandpa was the first Gilbert, and her father was the first Son. They phased out the fuel tanks before regulations demanded they pull them out of the ground and replace them. Although now focused solely on auto repairs, to Amy the shop would always be where she was closest to her grandfather. She could almost sense him, a rag in his back pocket, pumping gas, wiping windows and shooting the breeze. *Could he really have been gone fifteen years now?*

Her mom stuck her head out from the office window. "Amy, phone call."

Amy cursed again, wiped her hands and headed to the office. "Hello?"

The familiar voice said, "You took my jumper cables. They were in the garage."

"I did not. I work in a fucking garage. Why the hell would I need your jumper cables? Stop calling me at work." She slammed the phone down. "Ma, don't bother me if Deb calls. I told you."

"Excuse me, how am I supposed to keep all your friends straight, Miss Social Butterfly." Her mother stacked some papers with an indignant look. "I have enough to do without screening your calls."

"You know darn well Deb was my girlfriend."

"I thought lesbians stayed friends." She picked up her bagel. "That's what they said on Oprah."

"I don't have time for this." Amy strode back to her bench. At her station, she cranked up the radio and heavy rock blared out across the garage.

The rest of the day was uneventful, and Amy clocked almost ten hours on an eight-hour shift. That was her dad's latest brainstorm. Instead of paying them all hourly, they went by the Chilton manual for the time that it should take for any given job. Should was the keyword. It was her personal goal to beat the time, but it didn't always go that way. Today no bolts were frozen needing to be torched off, no screws stripped into place, and all the parts she needed had been delivered on time. She passed through the body shop, now empty, two cars sitting taped and ready for the morning. She slid into her Jeep with little energy for the night to come.

Amy circled the long way for the drive to Robin's house, her heart pounding thinking about the evening. Usually, she looked forward to games, but today scenarios of confronting her ex ran through her head. *Am I angry? Or hurt? Lost. Dammit.* She climbed the stairs as Meow ran between her legs like a ninja assassin. Amy stripped and dropped the greasy items into the separate laundry basket for work clothes and stepped into the bathroom in her underwear. She picked up the clothes abandoned yesterday and flicked them toward the clothes basket. *Two points.* She looked at her image in the mirror. Dark hair without much style. No reason to fuss with hair going into a ponytail all day. *Maybe shorter?* Her eyes were the same as her mother, dark brown. Olive complexion, which was weird as everyone else in her family was lighter. *Maybe the milkman really is my father?* She flexed her arms, she didn't need the gym thanks to hours turning wrenches, but on occasion, she would run. She turned to consider her backside. Yeah. She looked pretty good for just past thirty.

A few hours in the sun, and she'd be dark. She put on a bikini and took a towel downstairs. She stopped in the kitchen and tossed a few beers into a cooler, and headed out to the backyard. She flipped the towel out and laid down, adjusting her Walkman on her head. The days before the spring solstice were her favorite, long evenings of daylight, but not scorching.

She jumped when the cold water hit her back. "Damn it, Barberg."

Robin laughed. "You move pretty quick for an old woman." Robin hosted Amy's thirtieth drunk fest this year, and Amy was already planning for when Robin turned 30 in a few weeks. Amy had a deposit on a keg of beer and had a hot lead on a stripper that dressed like a cop.

"You scared the shit out of me." Amy put her sunglasses back on her face. "Asshole. You want a beer?" She opened the cooler and pulled out a long neck.

"Just one, I got shit to do and those Mothers Against Drunk Drivers billboards are up all over town. Personally, I think I drive better after a couple beers because I focus."

Amy said, "No, no you don't. Remember the time you hit the curb and I had to get you a new rim. You'd only had like three beers all night." She stood up, collected her now wet towel and the empty cooler.

Robin followed her up the stairs. "I like how you've decorated the place. What do you call this? Urban poverty meets almost living at Daddy's?" Robin sat in the second lawn chair. "I got an extra chair in the garage if you want it. Meow looks uncomfortable on that box there."

"Yeah, that'd be cool." Amy handed Robin some Pringles from the top of the mini fridge. She wiped her face with a Kleenex. "I need a shower before the game."

"Because you got to look good when Deb gets there. Make her regret dumping you. Don't wear your pink compression shorts, they make your ass look huge."

"No danger of me getting a fat head around you," Amy said.

Robin chuckled. "Just helping you out." Robin looked at her watch and popped up out of the chair. She turned as she headed out the door. "I gotta get some bubble gum before the game. You need anything?"

"Nope."

"Thanks for the beer."

"Don't tip at red lights," Amy said.

"Won't need to. This soldier is down." She put the bottle next to the recycle bin and knocked on the door jam as she left the room. Amy opened a box and shifted clothes around until she located the black shorts. She put on her softball uniform and surveyed her image in the mirror. Not too shabby. She picked up her car keys and then changed her mind. She snagged the key fob with the rabbit's foot that held her motorcycle keys. She threw her cleats in her gear bag. She took a deep breath and marched to the carport between the garage and house.

CHAPTER 3

Amy climbed on the motorcycle with a moment of hesitation. It was true that if she got banged up during the game, it would be harder to drive home on the bike than in her Jeep, even with the stick shift. When she rode the motorcycle, she had a certain confidence and a sense of adventure. She pulled on the helmet and tugged the strap through the D ring. Deb loved this bike. Amy smiled. All the more reason to ride it. She pulled out the foot and kicked the engine to life. With a quick twist of the throttle, she was off and flying out of the driveway, her ponytail flapping on her back.

The shifter felt odd with only tennis shoes on. She usually wore long pants and leather boots to ride, but she didn't want to change at the ball field. At the traffic light, she revved the engine at a kid on a crotch rocket. He smiled. When the light turned, she headed left, cutting off an old man driving a Pontiac. She was halfway down the block before the car even made it into the intersection.

Nearing 50 mph, she worked the brakes, leaned hard and skidded into the parking lot, gravel flying up behind her. At the back diamond, she pulled up and parked next to Robin's car.

"If that thing starts smoking and gets oil on my car, you're dead to me," Robin said. She put her hands on her hips. In her full softball uniform, she looked quite intimidating. At five-eight, she wasn't that tall, but she was built solid. "I'm not kidding,

Amy."

Amy flipped up her visor. "It purrs like a kitten." She took a metal plate from her pocket, let the rope unwind, and slid it under the foot peg to keep the kickstand from sinking into the soft ground. Wrapping the rope over the handlebar, she pulled off her helmet. "Looks like Coach is geeked up."

A small framed woman was pacing back and forth across the dugout, flipping through the rule book. Her blond hair was short and curled slightly around her ears.

Amy hung her bag on the chain link fence with a carabiner. "What's up, Coach?"

"The roster is supposed to be frozen after the second week. And they added Deb yesterday, citing some player that dropped out. All I'm saying is that every team will swap around all season every time some couple splits up; no offense." Gail slapped the book closed. "I'm calling Hank tomorrow. I want Ida on our roster if that's how they want to roll."

"We got enough to play?" Robin dropped her bag on the ground, slid it open and picked up her mitt. She leaned her bat against the dugout fence.

"Yeah, Julie will be here in about fifteen. I called her yesterday."

Amy smiled. Julie worked at Deb's office, and Coach knew it would piss her off to have her show up at the game. "Thanks, Gail."

"Oh, shoot, don't thank me yet. If you don't hit the dang ball first pitch, I'm benching you." Coach Gail picked up a clipboard and headed out of the dugout.

Amy and Robin were tossing throws to warm up when Deb arrived. She walked past them, her cigarette hanging on her lip as she fooled with her gear bag. Amy fired an atomic ball to Robin.

Robin shook her mitt, gave Amy a stern look and tossed the ball back. "Harness the rage, girlfriend, harness the rage."

When they sat on the bench, Amy noticed Deb jog to second base. She knew if she kept her sunglasses on much longer, she wouldn't be able to see as the sun continued down. For now, she could watch without people knowing if she was watching pitches or her ex.

Julie hit an easy fly that dropped just in between the two out-fielders and trotted to first. You could count on a hit, she just wasn't running. Linda took it to a full count before blasting a shot that skipped just out of the reach of the shortstop.

The coach stopped Amy. "Just hit the dang thing. Doesn't need to go to Mars. Robin will clean it up, so get ready to run." She patted her arm.

Amy stepped into the box, and as she was getting into position, the ball whizzed into the catcher's mitt.

Strike.

She stepped out of the box and glared at the pitcher, who just smiled. *If that's how you want to play it.* She balanced the bat and stepped into the box. The next pitch was so far outside the catcher couldn't pull it in. Amy stepped out and looked at Coach Gail. She made a little swinging motion with an imaginary bat. No walks.

Amy stretched her neck, then stepped in, and a ball flew past her knees causing her to jump back. She took two steps toward the mound before she heard Robin from the On-Deck circle. "Hold it, slugger. She's not worth it. Just hit the ball."

She took a deep breath, leveled the bat, and stepped in the chalk box. The next pitch was just a little outside. She stepped forward to reach it and hit the ball full force. It almost hit the pitcher in the head as it flew over. Amy started to run toward first and saw the coach point so she ran wide and headed for second. The shortstop was standing on the bag, so she threw back and slid, sending up a cloud of dust.

Gail screamed, "Come on ump, that was a fake tag."

Amy stood as the ball went home. The third base coach held her hands up to hold her. Julie scored with Linda right behind her.

Coach clapped. "Way to turn it, ladies. Come on now. No outs. Let's hustle. Watch on second, now, tag up on a fly."

Deb stood near the bag, her hands on her hips. She flicked her mitt up as the ball came. She tossed the ball to the pitcher. Deb looked right through her.

Amy smacked the dust off her pants while looking at Deb. She debated between begging Deb to reconsider and just leaving the field. Her mind was not on the game when she heard Robin yelling, "Move your ass or I'm pushing you home."

Amy hustled around third, skidded over the home plate and Robin came right behind her. Slapping high fives, they headed to the bench.

The scorekeeper leaned close to Amy. "You almost stepped on the plate at-bat, you could have been out." She sat upright. "Hon, that was a hell of a hit, but I'm telling the coach to put in a sub. You're distracted. You're going to get creamed out there. Here, take this clipboard and keep a double book. Or doodle. I don't care."

Robin sat a cooler next to Amy. She opened the lid and pulled out a beer in a little foam wrapper. "It's called a koozie. Keeps your pop cold."

Amy smiled and took the beverage. By the end of the game, all the beer was gone, and Amy suddenly needed to go to the restroom before they slapped hands. Coach Gail wouldn't be happy, but she just couldn't do it. She paced in the damp restroom shed until she was sure that most of the players were already gone.

Amy walked to her bike, strapped her gear bag on, and didn't bother to take her cleats off. She straddled the seat, holding her helmet.

Julie came by. "Hey, we're going to the Lounge if you want."

Robin answered, "See you there." She opened the trunk and put her gear in.

"Surprised you can fit the bag in that trunk." Amy stood back up and propped her helmet on the sissy stick. "Robin, can I ask you something?"

"Always. What's up?"

"Did it seem like Deb noticed me at all?"

Robin put a hand on her car door. "And why in the hell would I pay attention to that little bitch? She did you a favor, and if I wasn't your best friend, I'd be dating you already. It's going to be okay. It will. Maybe not tomorrow. Or next week. But it will be."

Amy's throat tightened and her heart started to race. She pressed her lips together so they wouldn't shake. Robin could be an ass, but she also sometimes knew just what to say. She stared at the bugs flying around the park lights. "Thanks, bud. Why don't you go on? I need a little time."

"See you there?"

"Yeah." Amy rubbed at the corner of her eyes and sighed.

CHAPTER 4

Molly Gorman put down her Coke when the call came in about a nuisance in the park. She cranked the engine, flipped on the blue lights, and hit the gas pedal. The Chevy Caprice was still so new it smelled weird; there were certainly perks of being the boss. She'd been interim police chief for almost a month, the first woman to hold the job in Diamond Lake. Her grandfather had been the chief of police for over twenty years. That helped her seal the deal. Her uncle being on the city council didn't hurt, either. A little nepotism canceled the discrimination against women. And she was a damn good cop.

She pulled into the park, circling around the back lot where only one car remained. She had seen it earlier. Probably wouldn't start. She swung around the back, and as the lights swept the field, she saw the problem.

Some lunatic was riding a motorcycle around the softball fields while standing on the foot pegs. No helmet. Not wanting to startle the fool, she slowed the car, hoping the lights would be enough to catch his attention. If not, she'd have to use the siren, and that might cause a wreck. As she reached the last parking spot near the field, the motorcyclist showed no signs of stopping. She flipped the switch and a loud bwap, bwap rang across the fields.

As she predicted, the driver jumped, lost his footing, and

slammed hard onto the seat. The bike teetered wildly but didn't go over completely. At least he had the sense to stop the bike and get off.

Molly flicked off the siren, popped on the spotlight and focused on the driver. To her surprise, it was a woman in a softball uniform. She hesitated, then called in that she didn't need backup. As she got out of the car, she grabbed her baton and slid it in her belt.

The dirt crunched under her feet as she walked the familiar diamond, this was the first time in her work uniform and not cleats. She got close.

"Jesus, what the hell?" she muttered to herself. She recognized the woman. She played for Gail's team. Molly noted that her uniform sported some dirt streaked down the left leg. Must have slid.

"Dude, you scared the fucking shit out of me," Amy called out, wobbling back and forth as she spoke.

Great, Molly thought to herself. *She's probably drunk.* "Do you have a license on you? The park is closed after dark."

"Do I need a license to drive on dirt? Because I'm not on the road." Amy put her hands on her hips.

"You drove it here. And helmets are required." Molly crossed her arms. She was not in the mood for a hard time.

Amy looked at her closely. "You play shortstop for Nancy, don't you? I hope you shoot better than that throw to first. You almost broke my fucking ankle." She began to laugh.

Molly bit her tongue and hoped her blush didn't show in the dark. *Who should be asking questions?* "Ma'am, have you been drinking this evening?"

Amy stopped digging in her gear bag and handed Molly the wallet. "Yes. I have. And again, I repeat, I'm not on a public road."

Molly would normally ask the person to take out the license, but she sensed it would only provoke more hostility. She was starting to regret turning down backup. She opened the wallet and saw the image and the name *Amatta Gilberta*. "You play for Gail?"

"Yes, I do." Amy leaned back and screamed, "When I'm not benched because Deb is playing for the other team and making me lose my fucking mind!" She collapsed to the ground, kneeling, and sat back on her feet. Tears began to roll down her face.

Molly considered the situation. By the book, she should tag her and put her in jail to sober up. The list piled up fast: no helmet, reckless driving, trespassing, drunk driving. The blow limit was .01 and most women did that with two drinks. She looked at the woman on the ground. "You stay here, and I will be right back."

Amy didn't answer.

Molly trotted to her squad car. She picked up the mic and called out her license numbers. It came back clean.

She stood and closed the door. Regardless of what she did, Amy shouldn't be riding that bike. She walked toward the figure now sitting on the motorcycle. "I'm going to have to ask you to get off the bike."

Amy seemed to have collected herself. "Look, I'm sorry about before. I'm having a sort of bad night. What's your name? Julie?"

"Molly. And we have what I call a situation here. I can't leave you here and I can't let you drive."

Amy opened her mouth, and then closed it. She finally said, "I'm not sure I understand." She stood and swung her leg over the seat.

"I know everyone in town knows everybody's business, but I also don't want you to have an accident." Molly handed Amy her wallet back. "I'm not taking you in. Where do you live?"

"A block down from the Gilbert Garage on fourth."

"Come on. I'll give you a ride home." Molly offered her arm, but Amy ignored it. "How much have you had to drink?"

Amy grinned. "Just one."

What a smart ass. "One what?" Molly reconsidered her decision.

"One twelve pack." Amy started to snicker, then caught herself. "I'm just kidding. A couple beers, I guess. Can I get my gear?"

A couple of beers? Bullshit. "No worries, I'll take it." Molly took the bag off the motorcycle and escorted her to the police car. "I'm sorry, but you have to ride in the back. I won't cuff you or anything."

Amy put her hands out together. "That might be fun."

"We could still head to the station." Molly held the door. "Reckless driving, no helmet, drunk and disorderly..."

"Point taken." Amy quickly took a seat.

As she sat, Molly grabbed her head so it wouldn't hit. "Just a habit." Amy's face fell and dark hair hung in her eyes. Her muscled arms were bare. "Are you cold? I've got a blanket in the trunk."

"No," Amy replied, although she was visibly shaking.

"Have it your way." Molly shut the door.

"At Burger King," Amy slurred.

Molly got into the car, pulling on her seat belt. "It's better to get a ride without going in the meat wagon. And this way you have your bike in one piece; you can come and get it in the morning."

Molly turned back when she heard the yell.

"You're not just leaving my bike there, are you?" Amy was slapping the wire in the window. "Son of a bitch. If it gets stolen, I'm going to be really pissed."

Molly asked, "Are you sure you want to yell at me?"

Amy screamed, "You don't fucking understand. It's an antique. I just finished rebuilding it. What if some jackass knocks it over? It'll be all your goddam fault!"

"I think you need to reconsider that point." Molly flicked off the blue lights.

"You're really an asshole."

Molly pushed the button on her seat belt and got back out of the car. She opened the back door. "Out."

Amy stepped a foot out. "What the hell?"

Molly grabbed her wrist as Amy stood, quickly slapping on the cuffs. "Sit."

Molly shut the rear door a little harder than she needed to. She got back into the front of the car, cranked the engine and drove toward the city jail.

CHAPTER 5

Robin stood in the police station hallway waiting, her posture stiff. "So, there's my little jailbird."

Amy shuffled toward her. "Shut it, already. I had a crappy night."

Robin tipped her head. "Really? Let's see. I got a call at 6 am after partying all night with the cutest little blond and you want me to shut up? Oh, man, I haven't even gotten started yet."

Amy sighed. "I suck, really, thanks a bunch for coming to pick me up."

"What happened? I left you just chilling out. I thought you were coming to the bar; I figured you might ditch me. I was a little worried about you."

"I can take care of myself. And I call bullshit. You were busy getting busy." Amy signed the paperwork the clerk had pushed her direction over the counter.

"All evidence to the contrary, you cannot take care of yourself." Robin laughed. "You know I can't deny it. You're lucky I headed home by four since I gotta work or your ass would still be in a cell."

Molly opened the glass door, passed them both, and walked down the hall.

Amy said, "She's the cop who brought me in. I thought she was nice, and then, bam, here I was." She called out a little louder, "I'll be seeing you around, Miss Officer lady."

When Molly reached her office, she unlocked the door and took a quick look back. She answered, "I hope only for softball," and went inside.

Robin tipped her head. "I don't think you're all that mad. You just watched her the entire length of this hall. She has a nice ass."

"She is an ass if you ask me. Totally."

"I think you doth protest too much. Come on, let's bounce, I need breakfast. I'm starving."

Amy said, "Nah, I have to get to work."

"No, you don't. I called your folks so they wouldn't worry where you were." Robin held the door open.

Amy followed her out. "Great. Thanks for that, buddy, ole pal."

"Any time." Robin laughed. "Besides, you look like shit. You need some coffee."

After Robin stopped the car for the second time so Amy could throw up, they both agreed Amy should just go home to bed and skip the eggs. As they rolled past the Gilbert and Son Garage, both of her parents watched them drive by.

"I think your parents saw us."

"No shit, Sherlock. More fun times ahead." Amy climbed out. "Really, I'm serious now, thanks again for picking me up."

"No problem. See you tonight." Robin backed the car out of the driveway and peeled out as she headed down the street.

Amy had barely unlocked the back door when she heard the phone ringing. *Dammit.* She ripped the phone off the cradle. "What?"

Her mother's voice sounded a little too pleasant. "Everything okay over there?"

Meow sat on the table, looking up as if she wanted to hear the answer as well. Amy rubbed her face. "Yeah. Can you get Dad to take Donny to pick up my bike? It's still at the ball field in the back. I won't be at work until tomorrow." She hung up the phone and hurried into the bathroom, her stomach cramping. She still felt a little drunk even with the hangover, and it was a doozy. Her head felt four sizes too big, like a cartoon caricature you get drawn of you at the amusement park.

A small tap at her back door echoed through the empty house. She dragged herself to the back door and saw her mother at the window. She waved her off and raced back into the bathroom to vomit. She splashed her face with cool water. She crawled up the stairs and flopped onto her bed. The spinning stopped after a while, and she dropped into a fitful sleep.

Amy woke and gauging by the full sun in her room, it was well into the afternoon. Every muscle ached, her stomach was tender from the earlier vomiting, and her head still throbbed. She stood and drifted into the bathroom. She grabbed a toothbrush while she peered in the mirror. Her eyes were bloodshot and her stomach wasn't sure if she should flip up the toilet seat or not. She heard the key and the backdoor open.

She turned to Meow. "It damn sure better be someone who knows the secret hiding place in the yard gnome, because I'm not up to facing a burglar. Why don't you go see who it is?"

Meow stopped licking herself, stared evenly as if she understood and darted down the stairs.

"Amy, are you home?" Rosie called out.

"Yeah Mom, what do you need?" Amy yelled, her head pounding.

"Just checking on you. Donny put the bike on the carport. Your father wants to talk to you later when you feel better."

Amy stopped at the top of the stairs. "I look forward to it."

Rosie put her hand to her mouth. "Oh, my. You look terrible. Self-inflicted, I suppose."

"Possibly." Amy turned. "I'm going back to bed. Make sure Meow doesn't sneak out."

"Okay, alright then," Rosie called out. "Bye."

She took two aspirin and fell back into bed. She woke and remembered her mother's request for her to talk to her dad. Sometimes he was cool, sometimes he was an asshole. She grabbed a beer out of her fridge for a little hair of the dog that bit her. Inspired, she popped in a cassette of Nazareth, *Hair of the Dog*, and turned the volume down. She flipped on the TV and soon was engaged in a racing video game.

She heard the rumble of Robin's sportscar. The back door banged open and Amy didn't even look. She heard the creak of the steps. Robin parked on the lawn chair next to her and grabbed the other remote. Amy reset the game for two. The friends raced each other, occasionally one leaning with the car images on the screen.

"Heard you rode your motorcycle on the softball field," Robin said, her cartoon car taking a turn too fast, flipping into the air, crumpling into a rock wall, then magically reappearing on the track unharmed.

"Mm," Amy grunted. "Yeah. That was kinda stupid."

"Ya think?"

"I met someone new, though. And I think she's a member of the church." Amy tipped the remote as the car careened around a canyon wall on the television screen."

"You mean the cop?" Robin asked.

"Yeah. I think I caught a vibe. She didn't have to be so mean, though."

"This new woman of yours had every right to bust your ass. What the hell, Amy? On the field? You probably rutted it all up." Robin burped. "Seriously, though. You didn't seem that drunk to me. Although you owe me a six-pack."

"I wasn't, really. I just felt like riding. Probably should have stayed on the parking lot, though," Amy said.

"Ya think?" A long silence fell between them as the stereo quieted, the TV echoed the sound of race cars revving and screeching brakes as they continued to play. "You puked a lot for someone that wasn't that drunk. And you shouldn't have been riding your motorcycle on the field. You're an idiot."

"Alright, alright, I was tanked. But I have a bone to pick with you. It's okay for you to speed around town all the time, sometimes with an open beer in your hand, but I get a rash of shit about one little mistake? Fuckin' A." Amy remembered her beer beside her, sipped from the bottle, and sat it back down.

"Totally not the same thing. I'm in my car. You were on

a motorcycle." Robin burped again. "Besides, I have an under-standing with the police in this town. I don't get stopped, they get free breakfast at Denny's any time I'm working." She referred to the place she worked a short grill.

Amy considered this for a minute. Failing to think of any smart-ass retort, she tossed down the remote, and reluctantly drained her beer. Her stomach was starting to protest. She leaped up and made it to the bathroom just in time. Robin fol-lowed her.

"You're a pathetic lightweight. Bang twice if you need any-thing; I'm headed downstairs." Robin threw Amy a washcloth.

Amy wet the rag and wiped her face. She laid on the floor and put the cloth on her forehead. Sometime in the dark of night, she woke on the cool tile floor and headed to bed.

The next morning Amy didn't feel much better. While she was getting dressed, Amy could hear Robin in the kitchen, the smell of food made her mouth fill with spit.

"Do you have to do that?" Amy eased her way past the stove.

"What? Cook? It's my life." Robin stirred one of three steam-ing pots.

"I think I'm gonna walk to work. I need some fresh air."

"If you're going to repeat tonight, I need more notice. I'm working the late shift." Robin grinned.

"No chance. See ya." Amy closed the screen door and took a deep breath. The sweet scent of lilac greeted her. The purple and white flowered bushes where in full bloom. She followed the ce-ment sidewalk down the street and crossed kitty-corner to the Gilbert garage.

Amy stopped at the back of the shop. The awning covered a giant pile of parts and old barrels. She rummaged around and found her stash of cigarettes. She put one in her mouth and then decided against it.

"Here, have one of mine." Donny, her brother-in-law, sud-denly appeared at her side.

Amy took the cigarette that he lit for her. "Thanks. Mine are probably stale as hell." Amy ran a hand through her hair. She pulled in half a drag and blew it out. She shifted her weight back and forth. "I don't think I've had a cigarette in six months."

"I hate quitters." Donny laughed. "These menthols are better than the reds anyway."

"I could smoke Newport like the teenagers." She laughed too. "I guess I can quit again."

He dropped his cigarette butt into a pop can. "The bike is running sweet, Aimster. I'm thinking it's time for another kickass paint job. Maybe pearl white for a base this time?"

Donny was kind of a tool, but he was sweet to her sister Olivia, and he really was a master painter. Amy ran her hand across her head again, the cigarette pointed upward like a magic wand. "Most definitely. You're the man, for sure. I was thinking maybe you could do a little art for me."

He grinned. "Anything I want?"

Olivia walked up behind them. "As long as it doesn't involve genitals. I know how you think, Don."

"Male or female? It'd be pretty funny either way," Donny said. "Riding around town on a giant boner."

Olivia smacked his arm. "See, that's exactly what I mean."

"Speaking of stupid dick things, Mom said to tell you that Dad put in for Elk permits for you and him next season." Amy took another puff.

Olivia said, "Hey, hunting isn't stupid. I haven't had to buy beef in years."

Amy made a face. "I'd rather go to the store."

"Your dad is wasting his time. We won't ever win that lottery," Donny scoffed.

Olivia said, "He just wants you two to hang out together."

Don said, "I haven't seen an elk in the lower peninsula since I was a boy. And the U.P. in the winter? Forget it."

"Don't shoot the messenger." Amy shrugged. "I'm sure it's better for the Elk if you don't. You're a crack shot."

"Thanks, and you're right." He asked, "You good with a paint job?"

"Of course, thanks," Amy said.

"I'm gonna go see if I have some of the white in the overrun cupboard." Donny picked up the pop can and flicked it toward a trash barrel and went back inside.

"Hang on." Olivia touched Amy's arm. "Have you talked to Dad yet? Tina says he almost shit a brick talking about you getting arrested. And Mom seems a little wired, you know, probably about the police station thing and all."

Amy rocked on her heels. Pulling a last drag, she dropped the butt, grinding it out with a toe. "I'm an adult. I can do whatever I want."

"Only people who are acting childish announce that they are an adult." Olivia folded her arms across her chest.

"You're right. I passed the limit." Amy sighed. "I'm not really in the mood for a fight but I might as well get it over with. Is he here?"

"Yeah, but I don't think now is the best time." Olivia took Amy's hand. "Look, I know it's been hard with Deb and all."

Amy shrugged, her voice caught in her throat.

"We've all been burned by someone we loved. And we've all done something mega stupid. It's going to be okay." She gave Amy a squeeze on her arm. "You aren't looking so hot. You should get something to eat and maybe go see Dad tonight after work. Give him some time to think."

CHAPTER 6

Molly opened one eye to look at the alarm clock. It had been a long night. Twice she woke up in a full sweat, her heart pounding. The dream was so real, she could almost feel the blood sopping off of her hand. Each time she awakened, she got up and washed her face with cool water. It had been almost two months, but so far, the dreams hadn't stopped. Naturally, once she finally was sound asleep, the alarm started to chirp on the bedside table. Molly peeled both her eyes open. She'd been working at the Diamond Lake Police Department for almost a month, and she still couldn't get used to an early morning. She pushed back the blanket, and goosebumps raised on her bare skin. Standing upright, she wiggled her toes in the lush carpet. This apartment wasn't the Ritz, but it was more comfortable than her last place.

She trod into the master bath, turned on the shower, and started to brush her teeth at the sink. A quick hop on the scale showed she weighed exactly the same as she did the day she graduated from the Police Academy. Looking at her image in the mirror, maybe she could use a few pounds.

She pushed back the curtain and stepped into the shower. The hot water soaked her hair as she studied the scarlet scar on her bicep. She started scrubbing with the shampoo, the jagged line twitching as she moved.

It started as a typical traffic stop, although there really isn't any such thing. The navy-blue Lincoln had gone through a red light, and it had a tail light out. She flipped on the lights, and the car eased to the side of the road. She called in the tag, asking for backup, and it came back a felony warrant on the owner of the car. She stared at the car for a moment trying to remember if she had seen the brake lights flick as the car went into park. No, he was going to run. There was some movement in the car, and it seemed that it was taking a long time for that other police car to arrive.

She opened her car door, and stepped out, her hand on her baton. She approached the car in the dark, avoiding the bright path of her headlights to hide her approach. She peered in the backseat of the driver's side, stopping just a bit shy of the door.

The driver lowered the window part way. "What's up, sweetheart?"

She said, "That traffic light back there was red. I need your license and registration." The driver shifted as if to pull a wallet from a back pocket. She saw the Glock the same time as it fired. She felt the burn on her arm but still drew her weapon. The driver jammed the gas and the car lurched forward. She heard the sirens of the second car, and then she dropped to the ground.

The hot water ran out, and the chilly water brought her back to the shower. She stepped out, dried herself off and studied the rows of black shoes and boots in her closet. Above them hung six pairs of navy pants, and maybe two dozen navy shirts, some long sleeve but most short sleeve. Just her luck this department wore black uniforms. She picked up a shirt from the tiny section of civilian clothes that hung at the far side. Molly might not control what would happen at work, but her castle was her domain.

She went down the stairs to the parking lot and headed to her car, a shiny red Mustang. It was her first new car, and it was her baby. She eased into the leather seat and flicked a cassette into the tape deck. With a satisfying roar, the engine rumbled to life under the hood. She took the long way to the station, swinging around the park at the river. The weather was perfect for a long hike, but today it didn't look good to get outside at all. At the station, she parked in her spot, and then went in to change. When she first arrived in town, she decided that she could just change into her uniform in her office. If she stayed on permanently, that would be the time to get a women's locker room built. Right now, it was just an inconvenience. She tucked in her shirt, blousing it at the bottom. Quick check in the mirror and she sat at her desk.

A cardboard package sat on the corner. She picked it up and looked for a return address...no shipping label. She took out scissors and slit the tape. Easing the flap open the edges of a wooden frame appeared. She pulled it out and discovered a framed and mounted copy of the newspaper article announcing her arrival.

> **Interim Chief Hired** *A veteran of the Detroit Police Department is the Diamond Lake top cop. An employment agreement for Molly Gorman was unanimously approved Thursday during a special meeting attended by five of seven members of the Diamond Lake Village Council, Yancy Wilson said Friday. With the disappearance of Chief Barry Tristan, the Council felt that leadership was needed until the situation was resolved.*
>
> *Gorman was chosen from a field of 28 applicants that was whittled down to seven finalists.*
>
> *"She was everybody's first preference," Wilson said of the search committee that helped in choosing Diamond Lake's next Police Chief. "She just wowed everybody at the interviews and she's just going to be excellent here."*
>
> *Previously a Sergeant with the Detroit Police Department, Gorman earned a Business Administration Degree from Eastern Michigan University.*
>
> *Mayor Cooper said, "Retention hasn't been an issue here in Diamond Lake and it is unusual for us to have to fill the chief position. Many residents may recall that her grandfather held the same position back in the day."*

The picture surrounded by the article was from the police academy, total baby face. She looked like she was about fifteen. She turned it over, wondering who had sent it. Her grandmother?

Her phone rang. "Chief Gorman." It still sounded odd to her ear.

"This is Uncle Yancy," a tight baritone rang out. "Did you see the package I left you?" He was her mother's sister's husband. A little on the handsy side but overall harmless enough.

"Yeah, thanks." She turned the picture over to see if the frame had a fastener attached or not.

"Won't be long and you'll have a lot more than that one if you know what I mean. I don't want to hold you up, but maybe we can go golfing next week?"

"Sure, that would be great. Thanks again, bye."

Molly picked through her phone messages. The sergeant left a note that asked her to stop in. Charley couldn't just walk into my office? Power play. She blew out a breath and went down the hall.

Molly shut the door behind her. The man was already dripping sweat onto the desk. His menthol cigarette butts piled into the ashtray. Décor wouldn't be the right word for the blonde, nicotine-stained paneling, and fluorescent lights. A Chinese take-out calendar was on one wall, an area promotional poster on the same side. A window faced the parking lot. File cabinets lined the other wall. Two children's faces smiled up from a photo at the corner of the side table, next to a file basket and a cup with pencils and pens.

"What's up, Charley?"

"What's up? Jesus. Total train wreck for us in the newspaper." Charley lit a cigarette. "There's a couple of articles about our department that you need to be aware of before the hundred phone calls start. First, the Lansing paper. Evidently, they have just realized that our chief has been missing for almost three months. They want to know what we are doing about it."

"We aren't doing anything-it's at the county sheriff's office."

Molly leaned back. "And."

He took a long drag from his cigarette. "I don't know if you know that he was out hunting wild turkey and went missing. Probably drank too much, tripped and shot himself. Some hunter will find him next fall during deer season. Poor guy. Barry's been the police chief around here for so long, people can't remember who had the job before him."

Molly nodded. The point was rhetorical. He knew damn well it had been her grandfather, but she didn't feel pressed to mention that. "Without a body, the investigation is stagnant. Shouldn't be much for people to talk about."

Charley used the cigarette as an emphasis. "And we gotta keep it that way. People get nervous and start chatting, it'll be my ass first, I can tell you that." He stubbed out his cigarette, causing a small avalanche in the ashtray.

Molly considered the huge man in front of her, restless, and harried. His mustache poked forward like porcupine quills as he pursed his lips. He leaned across the desk. She leaned part way as well. "Why would they go after you?"

He whispered, "They pulled in the sheriff, didn't they? That's a vote of no confidence, right there, I'm telling you."

Molly stopped herself from arguing the point. He seemed a decent guy, even if he was a little paranoid. "So, what's the second article?"

"Oh, the local rag printed all the crime statistics, and we have twice the number of burglaries in our town than any other in the county. They want to know what we are doing about it." He lit another cigarette.

"And what are you doing about it?" Molly deflected the question back. She was the chief now, not a beat cop.

"The usual crap. Setting up a meeting for the neighborhood watch, and I thought we might do one of those engraving days for people's valuables. You know, where a truck comes into the Kroger's lot and marks numbers on stuff like TV's and tape players."

Molly put her fingers on the edge of the desk. "Make sure to notify the media ahead of both events. And we both know the engraving bullshit doesn't work, but it does get people thinking about maybe locking their front doors for a change."

He shrugged. "From what I've seen, all of the local towns are over the national average. Not just us. There's that."

"Not too comforting to the guy who's TV just got ripped off." Molly knew she'd made her point as his eyes narrowed.

He deflected. "How's it going with the guys?"

Molly raised an eyebrow. "Fine."

He said, "They didn't like you saying that they couldn't wear those polo shirts anymore."

"We don't work at a golf course."

"No, we do not." Charley nodded. "I want you to know I got your back. Dougie can be a bit of a tool. Everyone knows he wants my job. Thinks he's in charge. Wouldn't want him hazing the new guy, so to speak."

"How thoughtful of you." Molly studied Charley's face.

"We've all worked together for a long time, and it might be difficult to fit in." He paused staring into her eyes. "Because we're men."

"I have nothing to prove to anyone. Look, I was top shooter in my class, and I spent five years chasing trouble in the worst neighborhood in Detroit. I think I can handle a few good old boys who are intimidated by a little estrogen." Molly crossed her arms. *I should have made him come to my office.*

Charley leaned a little closer. "I have no doubt. But just keep in mind, as an outsider, you might not ever fit in."

"You do remember that I'm your boss, right?" Molly asked.

"Of course, that's why I'm looking out for you." He leaned back in his chair.

Alpha male bullshit. Molly gave him a steely smile. "How about you look out for the people we're supposed to protect."

She stood and walked down the long hall toward the drink machines, and passed the door to the Mayor's office. His door was open, so she stuck her head in. "Hey, Eddie. My uncle says to ask you about golf next weekend?"

He waved his hand downward in no. "Yancy took me for fifty bucks the last time. He bets on every hole." Eddie laughed.

Molly grinned. "I got him for thirty. He can't make the shot out of the sand, but he always thinks he will."

"Excellent observation. Thanks." He considered her with a quizzical look. "I better be watching or you'll have my job before I know it."

Molly noticed a flash of sincerity, and then it was gone from his face. "Not me, boss. I'm just a cop."

He smiled. "Most of us old dogs remember when your grandad was the chief. He'd be proud of you."

"I appreciate that, sir," she said.

"Your last name means something around here. Don't forget that. Keep sharp out there."

She knocked twice on the door frame for luck. "Always."

She took the stairs down to the basement file room. The lights flickered as they warmed, casting a yellow tinge to everything in the room. Between racks and racks loaded with boxes, a previously empty file cabinet in the back now held the files for all the unsolved burglaries for the last year. She opened a notebook and began jotting notes on methods, general items stolen and the street address. When her eyes started to get dry, she turned the next file backward to find the spot again. She slid the notebook into her pocket and headed upstairs.

In the lobby, Doug was speaking to a lady wearing what might be considered a Halloween gypsy costume with a calico skirt, white blouse, a cluster of bracelets on each arm, and probably a half dozen chains around her neck. The only thing missing was a crystal ball.

Doug turned to Molly with a wily smile. "This is our Chief, and I bet she can help you out with this sensitive issue."

"Let's go to my office," Molly directed as she led the woman down the hall.

Once seated, the woman looked less mystical and more bat shit crazy. She brushed her long hair back from her face. "I am Lady McKenzie, and I have a predicament. You see, I have an object that is quite valuable and I need to have the police escort me to the bank so I can put it in a lockbox, you know, those little vaults you can rent?"

Molly bit at the inside of her lip. "Generally, we don't do security services. May I ask what this object might be?"

The woman craned her neck around, and then whispered, "I have a very, very valuable ring."

"Why not get it appraised and insure it?" Molly suggested.

"That's just the problem. The jeweler over on Second Street couldn't really determine a value." She peered around the room again. "It was created by the Maharishi Mahesh Yogi himself. It is virtually priceless."

"The transcendental guy? I didn't know he was a jeweler," Molly noted, quite pleased with herself that she knew who he was.

"Oh no, it was a miracle. He does them often, you know, miracles. He took a rose petal, and clenched it in his hand, and formed the perfect stone. And now that stone is the stone that is in the ring. Amazing, right?" She nodded like a bobble doll.

"That is quite amazing." Molly stood up, signaling the end of their meeting. "Ma'am, just be sure to leave a message up front letting us know the time and date you are transferring the item. I will be sure to put the entire department on full alert."

Lady McKenzie stood and grasped both of Molly's hands. "I knew that a woman would understand. Oh, wait. I am getting something. You have met your soulmate. It will be a long, wonderful life together. I'm so happy for you."

"Uh. I don't really..." Molly pulled her hands back. "Thank you?"

"And thank you, I am so relieved." With a small curtsy, the woman scurried from her office.

Molly sat down and scooted her chair in. She heard the laughter approaching from the hallway.

Doug and Jeff were walking by, and Doug said, "then I told her the new police chief would take care of it." The men roared.

Either Lady McKenzie was a total wackadoo or they were

playing a joke on her. Or both. It was like working in a damn fraternity house.

Her phone rang. "Is this the Chief? I'm calling from the Currier..." And so, her day went from the frying pan to the fire.

CHAPTER 7

Through the front living room window, Amy could see her dad sitting in his La-Z-Boy recliner. She took a deep breath and steeled herself for the confrontation. Her mom was not in sight, so maybe this wouldn't be so bad. She tapped on the door and walked in. The *Jeopardy* theme song was playing in the background.

"Hi, I should have come at a different time." Amy stood, debating whether to sit down or not.

"It's fine. What is the capital of North Dakota?" He didn't look away from the TV screen.

Amy knew better than to interrupt. Uptight looking people in suits were being challenged by Alex Trebek. A commercial came on.

"Hey, boozer. Nice show for the whole town the other night. My daughter riding around in the back of a police car." Frank finally turned to face her.

"I'm not sure who would notice…."

"Not really my point." He gazed at her evenly.

Amy still stood. Deflection seemed the best defense.

"Is that your new trophy?" Amy walked near the mantle where a stuffed ruffed grouse was frozen forever in an agitated state, his tail splayed out. He stood on a little log with fake grass around his feet.

"Yeah, me and Donny went and we made trophies out of 'em.

Can't really eat them."

"Then why shoot them?" Amy didn't like hunting, and in particular her father's hunting. It disrupted the shop and the meat, if he had it processed, did time in the freezer until it was frost burned and thrown out.

"Don't start it. I don't want to argue with you. I really don't." The theme song came on the TV, and he looked Amy in the face. "The thing about the cops."

"Dad," Amy started.

"Stop. Listen to me. Is this drinking thing becoming a thing? You know, because maybe we can help you out. Your Uncle Joey goes to that Triple-A thing at the church." Frank stared in her eyes.

"You mean AA? Nah. It's nothing like that, I'm sorry if I embarrassed you." She tried to sound sincere.

He seemed to be considering his next words. "Forget about it. Shit happens, you know? But your mom is a little freaked out about it. Go see your mother. She's in Michaels room."

Dammit. She had almost made it scot free. If her mother was in Michael's old room that meant a long drawn out discussion. "Thanks." She kissed his cheek.

He cleared his throat. Amy hugged his neck as he shouted, "What is the Mississippi River?"

She sucked in a breath and headed down the hall. The door was open, so she stepped into the dim space, her mother sitting on a chair at his desk. Amy had seen that brooding look on her face and it wasn't a good omen. Nothing had changed since the night that he had died. The room was a shrine to his life, just in case anyone should forget that he had existed. Frank offered many times to change it to a sewing room but Rose wouldn't hear of it.

"You okay?" Amy sat on the bed. Michael's many music posters covered every inch of the room, and his prized Farrah Fawcett image smiled down at them, her blond hair billowing around her face. On the shelves, trophies and ribbons stood tribute to his athletic skills.

"No. I am not. After what happened, how could you possibly drink and drive that blasted motorcycle?"

"I wasn't driving it." Amy stretched the truth to ease her mother's worries. "I was just in a public park after hours. I got a little mouthy. Everything is all right."

"You know that's crap, Amy. I saw you yesterday morning. You were still drunk. And you were hauled off in a police car. Like some common criminal. Your brother would never have done anything like that." Rosie sprouted tears.

Amy sighed. It didn't take long to become about Michael. He was the golden boy. The Adonis. The Son. He was supposed to co-own the garage with their father. And then it was all gone. He had died the night of his high school graduation. Her parents never quite recovered. "Mom, it's not like that."

Rosie turned in the chair. "It is just like that. You don't think. And smarting off to the police was probably just the start. It'll be in the paper soon for everyone to see. Michael was always responsible. He would not endanger people like that. You know he would never drive drunk."

He died before it was even legal for him to drink. There was no reason to throw salt in the wound. She clenched her fists, but Amy kept her voice even. "It won't happen again. I was just upset. About Deb, splitting up and all."

"You could try and talk to me you know. I am still your mother, even if I don't understand this phase at all. What is it again you want us to say? Lesbian? Gay?" Rosie said, her voice rising louder.

"It's not a phase, I told you a million times," Amy protested.

Rosie said, "I wonder what Michael would have thought about a homosexual sister."

"He wouldn't care. But now you're stuck with me? I am right here. I can hear you. You can see me. Michael is gone." Amy tried to keep her tone respectful but it was still louder than she intended.

Her mother just couldn't seem to quite contain herself. She reached out and picked up the picture of his high school sweetheart, in the corner the graduation year '76 was marked in gold. "I might have been a grandmother you know. Another Gilbert. And now…"

Amy exploded, "Dammit, Michael is dead. He was not fucking perfect. He got drunk and he drowned in that fucking lake. No one pinched his nose and made him drink. I can't help it his friends thought he was fooling around and he god-damned drowned."

She stormed out of the room, slamming the door behind her. "Son of a bitch. I can't talk to her when she gets like that."

She stood in front of her father's TV. "She's damn impossible."

"You kiss your mother with that mouth?" he replied.

"For Christ's sake. I'm leaving."

She trudged all the way to Robin's house, grabbed the keys, a pint of Jack Daniels from the cupboard and let the door slam behind her. She got into her Jeep before the tears came. She cranked the engine, slammed the gear shifter into first and lurched out of the driveway. Five minutes into her drive, she turned onto the highway, radio blasting. *Fuck you, Michael. How could you leave me?* He had been the only one who could run interference between her and Rose. Ten years later and they still couldn't talk to each other. More than that. She couldn't compete with his memory. He would always be perfect. And she would always be…not.

She swung into the state park and drove down to the boat ramp. She parked right at the edge of the water. Opening the bottle, she took a swig, grimacing just a bit at the sharp taste without her usual sweet mixers. Staring out at the lake, her memories swirled. The water reflected back sparkling white as the surface chopped. The air today was cool for this late in spring, but still hot in the car. She stood and took the soft top off the Jeep. She sat back down, pulled a long drink and sat back. The light hit her right in the eyes, so she fished around in the glovebox and found her sunglasses. She leaned back and took another swallow. She imagined Michael and his friends, the large bonfire lighting up the night sky, the alcohol flowing.

Probably lots of laughter.

Until there was none.

That night she had been in bed when her father woke her with the news that Michael had an accident and she had to come now. A few years older than her brother, she thought she was too cool to party with the kids at the lake. Her dad drove the truck as fast as he could, her mother crying. Her mom kept rolling her beads, and Amy already somehow knew the truth. When the truck slowed, the lights of the firetrucks and police cars flicked through the dark. An ambulance stood ready although it wouldn't be needed. The black word CORONER on the white station wagon blinked like a neon sign as the red lights skimmed past. Images popped in her mind like photographs. The divers bringing the boat from the trailer, preparing to search to find his body. The clusters of teenagers, draped in towels as they huddled in the dark. The stars in the moonless night.

The rest of the scene played over and over in her mind, like a record player stuck in a groove. The silence near dawn as the divers surfaced, pulling a body into the boat. Michael. Her father clutching her mother as she collapsed. The scream in her ears that she knew came from her own throat. The arms holding her back as she tried to run into the water.

And now, that water kept the secrets of that night in its murky depths, a deceptive pleasant blue on the surface. Oh, sure, other people had drowned in the lake, a fisherman with an upturned boat, that sort of thing. Shocking, yes, surprising, not really. It was a pretty big lake. Amy pinched her nose at the bridge as her hangover headache remained. Getting upset made it worse. She wished she had aspirin in her glovebox. *Michael, how could you drown? You were a champion swimmer. Region fucking champion.* Another wave of emotion swept over her, and she shut her eyes as the tears slid out. A soft breeze brushed her arms. Exhausted from the argument, and the booze, she drifted to sleep.

A tap on her window woke her with a start. A police officer stood at the side of her car. Amy yanked off her sunglasses and rubbed her eyes. It was Molly staring at her through the glass. *Now what? Is it illegal to sleep in the park? Hells Bells. Maybe it is.* She rolled down the window. "Can I help you, officer?"

"Uh, no, I was just checking. On you." Molly peered over her sunglasses. "You good?"

The moon was hanging low in the sky. Amy rubbed her face and it stung. Her cheeks still had dried tears. She must look like a wreck. "Yeah. I must have fallen asleep."

"I gathered that." Molly shifted her weight back and forth. "You might need some Noxzema. Or if you have an Aloe Vera plant, my grandma uses that on sunburns."

"I don't get sunburned, I have pretty dark skin..." Amy looked in the rear-view mirror. She looked like a reverse raccoon. "Son of a bitch. I have a sunburn!"

"Yeah. A cool shower might help. Anyway, you cut the leaves and smear the juice on the burn. Aloe Vera."

"Right. The plant." Amy still stared in the mirror.

Molly took off her glasses, sticking an arm into her shirt pocket. "Alrighty then, the park closes at dark. You aren't planning on staying?"

Amy shook her head. "Just resting."

"Good. I don't want a repeat of the softball park incident." She didn't smile.

Amy considered the woman standing there. She has pretty eyes. Surely Molly was kidding. She always had a ponytail at softball games, she was cute, she seemed quiet, kind of distant, but not unfriendly. And here in her police uniform, she presented as all business. *Damn, confidence is sexy.*

"No, ma'am. See you at the field some time?"

There was just a hint of a twinkle in her eye. "Count on it." Molly turned and was gone.

Is that good or bad?

CHAPTER 8

The city municipal offices were stark. The strong scent of pine cleaner mixed with floor wax and a hint of tobacco smoke permeated the space. Molly walked through the narrow corridor, the walls covered with dark cheap paneling, which was starting to peel at the bottom. The third door on the left said her uncle's name YANCY WILSON in white letters on a black sign. The door was open, but she tapped on the frame anyway.

"Uncle Yancy, sorry to just drop in on you."

A middle-aged man with a cheap suit and slicked back hair popped up from behind his desk. He reached out and grabbed her shoulders, kissing her on the cheek. "No problem. Come in, come in. My calendar is a total mess today, but I am always glad for you to stop by. Family sticks together. What can I do for you?"

"I don't want to take much of your time. I just wondered about a place in town. Gilbert and Sons."

"Oh, my niece the big city policewoman trying to find crime under every rock?" His laugh filled the small office and bounced out into the hall. He stood and shut the door. "What about it?"

Molly fidgeted. "Just wondered if you knew any history of the place, you know, generally."

Yancy smacked a cigarette out of the box and stuffed it in his mouth. "Won't be long and I won't even be able to smoke in my own office." He flicked a disposable lighter twice to get it to light. He offered her the pack and she shook her head. "You don't mind, do you?"

"Nah, my folks still smoke." Molly slid back away from the desk into the chair. "It's been a nice change working here. I appreciate you helping me out."

"My pleasure and relief. I know I can trust family. If you know what I mean. And your Grandma was on my ass to get you out of the Cass District. You could have been killed. Really. I'm not kidding."

Molly nodded. She was ready to transfer out of Detroit. Not so much for her own skin, although that was a factor. Her life was only her job, and the constant calls and the intense pressure were wearing her out. She went to work; went out afterward with the guys; stayed up too late playing pool; slept, mostly alone; and repeated until the days were all faded together. Not that Diamond Lake didn't have its share of problems, just not so many. She didn't go out with the guys here since she was their supervisor, so she had more free time. She just wasn't always sure what to do with it yet.

Yancy took a long drag on the cigarette, then set it in the ashtray. "You getting to know some folks?"

"Oh sure, I joined a softball team. The coach owns a flower shop. I met her on a false intruder alarm." Molly looked over the various town related promotional items on his shelves. "It's going good. Do you have any extra maps of the area in here?" She squeaked a ball stamped *Diamond Lake: Welcome to a slice of heaven* on it.

"Sure, top shelf. Take all you want."

She stood and took only one, folded it carefully and tucked it in her chest pocket as she sat back down. Yancy stared at Molly for a moment. She waited, hoping silence would remind him of her question.

"Gilbert and Son, just the one boy, was a gas station back in the day. The old man died a while back. He was Italian. Gilberta. He didn't fool anyone. I won't say he was affiliated with the mafia, but there were a lot of damn black Cadillacs at his funeral. If you know what I mean."

Molly considered this information. Her family was as WASP as you could get, so she wasn't that surprised her uncle thought all Italians were in the mob.

He said, "Now it's just the son and his daughters that work the place. Nice people. But stay away from his oldest daughter or people will talk. She likes the ladies if you know what I mean."

Interesting. Molly could feel the warmth creep up her neck and hoped that Uncle Yancy didn't notice. He pulled on his cigarette and stubbed it out. "And it was really sad about their boy. He drowned out at the lake about ten years ago. Top swimmer too. Real weird."

"That is sad," Molly said, unable to think of anything to ask that wouldn't sound prying.

Uncle Yancy paused. "If you need your car fixed, they aren't as expensive as the big dealership on the main highway. I would avoid them like the plague." He grinned at Molly. "I have a meeting in a few minutes, I'll make sure the mayor remembers that you're my niece. Always good to have a few connections."

She managed to duck out of another kiss. "Thanks, Uncle Yancy. Tell Aunt Anita I said hello if you know what I mean." She smiled at copying his catchphrase, even if he didn't seem to notice.

She slipped out the door and headed down the hall past the secretary painting her nails. Her belt chirped, she peered at the numeric message on the pager and hurried out the door. Her pager beeped again, this time flashing a number for all clear.

She strode to her office with purpose, shut the door, then relaxed at her desk. She picked up a pen and started to doodle on a note card. So, Miss Gilbert likes the ladies. She was yelling about some woman in the park. Her ex? Was there more to her "friend" that picked her up from the police station? The friend with the yellow Corvette, which stuck out like a sore thumb in a small town. Her pager went off again. She headed to the receptionist in the lobby.

Molly asked, "What can I do for you?"

She looked up from her nail polish. "You had a phone call. Here's the note."

"Is it urgent?"

"They didn't say. I just write down the message."

"Thanks for that, and maybe just forward it to my voicemail. I was right in my office." Molly gave a tight smile. "I appreciate your efficiency."

The woman smiled. "Thank you. Most people around here don't realize how much I do."

Molly wandered until she realized she was past her office. The women on Nancy's team are all couples. *Do they even know I'm gay? I think so.* She stopped walking. *Where was I headed? Dammit, focus. You're in charge.* She stopped to get a pop. There was something about Amy, damn she was reckless, but underneath she seemed, what, vulnerable. Someone needs to protect her from herself, that's for sure. *A real project, that one.*

***

Amy grabbed the keys for her first job of the morning and went in search of the vehicle. Spotting the station wagon, she opened the door. The smell of an old milk bottle hit her nose. Papers had been stuffed into a McDonald's bag, but the car was filled with assorted toys, plastic sippy cups, and two car seats. She slid the paper floor mat in and flicked the plastic seat cover over the upholstery. Instead of protecting the car, they protected Amy. She immediately felt sorry for the car. She cranked it up and listened to the knocks. She eased it into the shop.

Popping the hood, she pulled the dipstick, wiped it, and slid it back in to read the oil. Barely a bit on the end of the stick. She pulled down the oil hose and filled the engine. With a hopeful turn of the key, the rattles of a dry engine disappeared as the oil worked its magic.

She leaned over the counter to the office. "Hi Mom, can you call Mrs. Taylor and tell her it was low on oil. Sell her an oil change, and a tire rotate. Have Tina change it would you?"

"She's got class this morning. Too good to do an oil change?" Her mother peered at her over her glasses. "Do you have a sunburn?"

"Just a little on my cheeks, so the oil change?" Amy tapped the counter impatiently.

"I remember when you did any job that came in," her mom scolded her.

"I didn't start the hour thing, Dad did. I can't turn enough time changing oil." Amy laid the paper on the desk, marking .5 for a half hour of diagnosis. "I'll do it but sell her fast. It's tying up my stall."

"I already wrote it for a hundred, so just do it already." A box of donuts sat on the corner of the desk. Amy reached for one, and her mother slapped her hand. "Those are for some people coming to look at the shop."

"Fine. Give me the next job."

Amy had just finished a tune-up and was ready to change the serpentine engine belt when she heard her father behind her. She turned to face two men in suits.

"Hi, nice to meet you." She wiped her hands on her rag and then reached out. The first man smiled and shook her hand. His manicured hands were so soft, she was sure he had never actually worked a day in his life. The second man didn't seem inclined to offer his hand. She ignored him. "Sorry, I need to get back to work." She turned back toward the car. Soon the step by step process became meditative.

Finishing up the job, Amy carried the work order to her mother in the office.

"Are those two douchebags gone?" Amy asked.

"Language. And yes. They own a string of garages across the county. They left about ten minutes ago. You need to remember customers might hear you and watch that filthy mouth of yours." Rose stacked some papers on the desk.

Amy fished a peanut butter and jelly sandwich out of a paper bag on the counter, stuffed a bite into her mouth and began listing the completed repairs on the form. Amy popped open a

Munchos and a Sprite. Chugging half the can, she almost shut her mouth when she burped.

Her mother raised an eyebrow. "You'd think you were raised in a barn."

Amy said, "Nope, a garage."

She flicked the work order into the "finished" box. She plucked the next work order from the stack. She tucked the pen behind an ear and stuffed the rest of the sandwich into her mouth.

Rose blinked her eyes several times. "Really? Did you actually chew any of that? And I almost forgot. Your father wants to see you when you can spare some time."

Her mouth cemented shut with peanut butter, she nodded. Amy started toward the rear parking lot but spotted him in the parts room. *Might as well get it over with.* "Hi Pops, what's up?"

"Hi, Pops? What the hell is wrong with you Amy? I have never been so embarrassed in my life."

Amy raised her hands. "Hey, what did I do?"

"I was busy telling them all about our high-tech garage, even though it's small. And as I went to show them the new paint booth, I opened the door and guess what?"

"What?" Amy put her hands on her hips.

"The entire floor is covered with your stupid motorcycle parts! I'm trying to run a successful garage here, Amy. I can't sell it if it looks like all we do is bullshit like your motorcycle."

"Bullshit like those few small parts covered the whole floor? What good is having a paint shop if I can't use it?" She set her jaw forward.

"Conveniently left in the booth the morning I have buyers coming through. I think you're trying to sabotage me!" He yelled, his neck veins bulging.

Amy shouted, "Dammit, I didn't even know you had a meeting. You don't tell me shit."

He yelled back, "Why would I? You have no interest in anything but your money and getting the hell out of here!"

"Why would I have any interest in Gilbert and SON? Damn

it, Dad, Michael has been dead ten years. Change the goddamn sign."

Amy kicked the toolbox as she went by, muttering under her breath. "Fuck this whole place." She marched into the paint shop, and all of her bike parts were neatly arranged on a bench. "Thanks, Sis, I owe you."

"No, I'm just sorry I didn't see them before Dad. They look fricking hot. After you put 'em on the bike, I'll pinstripe it if you want."

Amy nodded. "That would be awesome, I'm headed out. I need a mental health day."

Her sister tossed her a look. "You know he loves us, right? Go on, take tomorrow off. But today, why don't you work here with us; we can have a good afternoon."

"Nah, I think I'll just take them with."

Back at Robin's, she decided to work under the carport. Amy carried the parts and carefully laid them next to her motor-cycle. She went into the storage shed, brought out a painting tarp and a five-gallon bucket which she flipped upside down to sit on. She pulled the tool bag out of the side saddle bag and started to reinstall the pieces. The sun warmed her back as she crouched while she worked. A soft breeze rustled the leaves of the giant oak tree. Squirrels played tag, running from branch to branch, shaking the branches, and chattering at each other. Once finished with the install, she took out a clean rag and started to clean and polish the chrome. She started to whistle to a made-up song.

Amy placed the tools precisely in each slot and put the bag back on the bike. She smiled as she swung a leg over the bike and settled on the seat. She kicked the engine to life, nudged in the crank and let her feet leave the ground as she accelerated. She rested her feet on the pegs and rode around the town, the sultry afternoon air filling her lungs as the sun slid lower in the sky. She squeezed the brake at a red light and noticed Deb in a pickup truck coming from the opposite direction.

Amy would have flipped her off if she hadn't needed both

hands to clutch and accelerate on the green light. Her sudden anger caught in her throat and turned into chest pain, taking her breath. *Is that why they call it a heartache*? She squinted into the sun as a stray tear slid down her cheek.

CHAPTER 9

Amy stood looking at her jackets in the closet and was trying to decide between denim or leather. She jumped when she noticed Robin standing in her bedroom. "Do you even know how to knock? What if I was, uh, indisposed?"

Robin shrugged. "Not anything I haven't seen, bestie. You want to go to the Lounge tonight?"

"Nah, I promised Stacy I'd go to the potluck with her." Amy considered saying more. She picked up the denim coat.

Robin arched an eyebrow. "Stacy, first base? She's single?"

"Eh, sort of. Her girlfriend moved to Toledo, so we're just hanging out." Amy picked at a loose thread. She repeated to herself, "Just hanging out."

"If I never go again it will be too soon. Bunch of old women talking about the old days. Boring." Robin stretched to her full height. "I'd rather go dance and mingle."

"Mingle. Is that what you call a one-night stand now?" Amy laughed. "You're lucky you haven't caught anything."

"And just what is 'hanging out' going to lead to?" Robin grinned. "Besides, lesbians don't catch stuff, we're the chosen people. Remember?"

The 'moral majority' is neither." Amy sighed. "But you can still get things."

"Amy, give it up. I'm not using any fucking Saran wrap on my crotch, or anyone else's." Robin shrugged. "Condoms for women, what the hell."

Amy jabbed her in the shoulder. "If you can't be good be careful."

"Oh, trust me, I'm good." Robin blew on her fingernails and rubbed them on her shirt.

"And modest. Get out of here, slut puppy." Amy pushed Robin out and shut the door behind her.

Amy was right on time to pick up Stacy, and they drove in awkward silence to the address on the flyer for the potluck. The local lesbian bookstore was the official hostess, but every month the ad hoc group met at someone's home to eat and converse. Robin was right. Many of the women were older, but Amy thought they were fun to talk with, and she wasn't in the place to pass up a good meal. She tried to be careful, but money slipped out of her hand as fast as she got it.

The neighborhood was one of the developments centered around a local elementary school and shadowed by the local auto plant. Built in the 1950s, the modest ranch houses all featured the same style brick façade and white siding. A few had larger porches, and maybe a breezeway to the garage. Spotting the address and the many surrounding vehicles, Amy pulled up at the curb several houses down.

Stacy shut the Jeep door. "Are you sure we don't have to bring anything?"

Amy nodded. "There'll be enough food for 100 people. They always have a jar for donations, more if you can, less if you can't. I just toss some money in."

"Cool beans," Stacy said. A sizzling hot smile crossed her face. She winked at Amy.

Amy winked back.

A really tall woman opened the door just as they approached. "Welcome, I'm Marilyn, come on in. Julie is the hostess, she's the one in the purple ball cap. Let her know if you need anything. Grab a plate. Drinks are in the cooler, and there's some tea on the counter. Most everyone is on the deck in the backyard. Come join us."

"Thanks, we will. We know Julie. She plays ball with us sometimes," Stacy said.

"Cool. You should have seen her back in the day. Couldn't strike her out. She threw a ninety mile an hour fast pitch." Marilyn headed out the French doors at the back of the large dining room.

Stacy and Amy grinned at each other.

Amy whispered, "I bet Julie could still rip the seams off the ball if she wanted to."

"Especially if it meant she didn't have to run the bases," Stacy said with a smile.

The kitchen still wore the oranges and browns of the seventies; the golden Formica countertop was covered in hot plates, crock pots, and assorted trays and pans. A side table was buried in desserts. A large cooler was labeled "pop only."

"The only thing missing at these things is a nice cocktail. A lot of the women are in AA and there's no alcohol allowed," Amy whispered.

Stacy leaned in. "Does just the presence of alcohol tempt them, or do they dislike the foolishness of drunk people?"

"Maybe both," Amy said piling a mystery casserole onto a paper plate.

"It's fine by me. I can take it or leave it." Stacy stuck a pop can under her arm to open the back door.

Amy opened the back door and waved to Gail, their softball coach. Women sat all around the deck, some in lawn chairs, some at a round table with a tilted umbrella. Citronella candles burned in yellow glass globes, the sticky sweet scent floating around the yard. Stacy touched her back to pass, and Amy turned.

Deb was standing in the backyard. Her hand was on the shoulder of some woman Amy hadn't seen before. As she spoke, she held her arms out like she was carrying a stack of wood. She waved her hands enthusiastically like her story needed the pantomime.

Stacy hissed. "Look at those hands. She could be an NFL receiver with those things."

"Uh huh," Amy grunted.

"And she's not half as pretty as you are," Stacy said, sliding into a seat next to Coach Gail.

Deb rested against the woman, gently touching her arm and the woman kissed her. Amy tasted the jealousy followed by a wave of grief. She stabbed at the plate with a fork and then set it aside.

Amy asked, "Stacy, I hate to ditch you, but I am suddenly not feeling so well. Coach, can you drive her home?"

"Sure, I can show her my new Blazer. It has four-wheel drive," Gail said with pride.

Stacy whispered, "No worries. I saw Deb. She's making me sick, too. Just go on. See you at practice."

Amy checked her pocket for her keys and headed out the door. As she started the car, she popped in the worn cassette of AC/DC.

Singing along "Have a drink on me," she decided that it was pretty good advice. She pulled out of the neighborhood and went left to head out of town. She thought about how to deal with her ex. Deb was going to be around, and probably with plenty of girlfriends. It couldn't keep setting her off; Deb didn't seem to give a shit. Her eyes watered and she slammed her steering wheel. A tear threatened to fall. She never was one to hang out with her ex's and was perplexed by those who seemed to collect them like shot glasses or key chain fobs. Coach said that women who hang out with an ex either were still in love with them or never in love with them in the first place. It seemed cynical, but maybe she was right.

Amy pulled into the 7-11 and picked up a pony because it had a screw top and a bag of Fritos since she hadn't eaten at the potluck. Even though the large bottles were usually crap beer, she didn't want an open beverage spilling in her car. Leaving it in the paper bag, she considered it a moment before cracking the lid open.

The familiar flavor and the coldness brought a sense of relief. Robin would be at the bar, but Amy didn't feel like a crowd. She ripped open the plastic baggie and popped some chips in her mouth. She took another long pull from the bottle. She put the screw cap back on and headed out toward the lake.

She twisted off the cap with one hand, and after a quick look around, tipped the bottle back. She slid the bottle back down, sighing. As she pulled onto the two-lane road, she realized it had gotten dark and pulled on her lights. She switched the cassette to Molly Hatchet. After the final drink, she tossed the bottle into the back seat. With the music going, and speed of the Jeep, air blowing in around the soft top, she relaxed.

A dreaded blue flashed in her rear-view mirror. *Shit. Not again.* She eased the Jeep over and reached into her glovebox for the paperwork. After several minutes, the officer exited the car. *Of course, it was Molly.* Amy exhaled. County sheriff and state troopers patrolled this road, maybe. But there were only, what, like six cops in town. And yet here she was, the same cop again. She blindly grabbed for the bottle and shoved it under a coat. With a huff, she grabbed the crank and rolled down her window.

CHAPTER 10

Molly sat in her cruiser watching the headlights dip as people spotted her, slammed their brakes, and thought she hadn't noticed they'd been speeding. She wanted to slow them down, not give out tickets all night. *How am I going to find the single women in this rural area, besides the bar?* As an interim police chief, she couldn't exactly go wandering in unnoticed. That's about when the Jeep passed. She was sure it was Amy. And Amy had crossed her mind often in the last few days. Not like obsessed, but curious. And maybe a little infatuated. Amy was certainly reckless, even careless. Something about Amy intrigued her. Maybe because she felt compelled to protect her? To defend her? Whatever the impetus, they seemed to cross paths a lot.

Molly looked down at the woman in the car. *Amy has the darkest brown eyes I have ever seen.* The radio was blasting "Flirting with Disaster" which summed up Molly's mixed feelings exactly. This woman is either very unlucky or very lucky.

"Good evening, going a little quick tonight. Where are you headed?" Molly asked.

Amy handed her the paperwork. "Nowhere particularly. I guess I was daydreaming a little and not paying enough attention."

Molly watched Amy's hand movements. She appreciated her honesty. "You were moving pretty fast for someone with no destination."

She took the paperwork. "I'll be right back." She trudged back to the police car. She'd planned on running the tags, and then letting her go. She wasn't speeding that much. There was the distinct smell of beer in the cab. *Shit. Why can't people just be sensible?* Molly tapped her foot as she waited for the dispatch to answer.

Finally, the all-clear came, and she did a quick check in the mirror before she walked back over. *There have to be more single lesbians in this town. This woman is going to think I'm stalking her.* Approaching the window, she couldn't hear the music any longer. "Here you go. Have you been drinking?" Molly thought about her Dad. It was a miracle he never hurt anyone or himself.

"Yes, I have, but just one beer. I didn't eat dinner, so it may have gone to my head a little." Amy rushed the words out, now seeming more nervous than angry.

Dammit. Here we go again. "I hope not one keg," Molly said. Amy didn't seem in a joking mood. "And how long ago was that?" Molly exhaled. She saw a repeat of the park situation.

Amy sheepishly said, "Maybe a half hour."

Molly tipped her head and rubbed her chin. No problem. "Tell me, why is it every time we talk you've been drinking?"

"Uh, bad luck?" Amy weakly smiled.

"Your luck is that you didn't have a wreck. You might think about attending an AA meeting or something. If you keep drinking and driving, I will stop you again, and I promise I'll drag you in for a DUI."

Amy actually looked shocked. "It was just one beer, jeesh."

"You're giving me crap?"

"Right. Sorry." Amy started tapping her leg as she was talking and seemed to catch herself and stopped.

Molly cleared her throat. "You do know I should have thrown the book at you, right? Public drunkenness is one thing, but driving under the influence is not funny."

Amy had the sense to stay quiet.

"Not to mention you could wreck your car, hurting yourself,

or worse someone else."

Amy still stared out but said, "Why do you care?"

"Because I think you're better than that," Molly said. "And I think you're cute."

Amy turned her head toward Molly. "You are a charmer. Is that appropriate behavior for a police officer, Chief Gorman?"

"If I was doing what was appropriate, I'd be taking you to jail," Molly answered.

"Touché," Amy said.

"You keep drinking and driving, I'm sure I'll have another chance to haul you in." Molly put her hands on her hips. "Have a good night."

"Thanks for everything," Amy said. She popped the clutch and put the car into gear and drove off.

Molly watched her departure. *Please don't make me regret this, Amy.*

***

Amy grinned when she saw Robin's car still in the driveway. She needed a drink and some loud music. Not the Lounge tonight, though. She already had enough drama without running into Deb.

She freshened up in the bathroom where Meow was busy chewing the corner of her bathmat. "You won't believe it. Molly, she's a cop, she's making a mountain out of a molehill. She thinks I drink too much. I just like to drink. It's legal."

Meow stopped chewing and let out a weird chuff.

Amy looked down and said, "I do not have a problem. My only problem is Molly. She needs to get off my ass. She has a nice ass. And she thinks I'm cute. Huh. What about that!"

"Who thinks you're cute?" Robin said as she walked in.

Amy asked, "Can I use my raincheck on the nachos?"

"Sure, roomie. How about the new place out on River Road? They have six jumbo TV screens and free popcorn."

"Sounds good," Amy put her brush down. "By the way, you look really hot tonight. Is that a new shirt? It's almost a shame to waste it on a bunch of horny redneck boys."

"You never answered my question."

"I guess I didn't," Amy said. "We're taking your car, right?" She hung her keys up by the back door.

"Naturally. I'm not riding in that piece of shit you drive."

Amy said, "I love my Jeep."

"That thing is a money pit; you need a new car." Robin opened the door and hit the electric locks. "Look at this key. It has a computer chip in it so it won't start without it. Fucking amazing, right?"

Robin revved the engine and they blasted to the bar. They could hear the music from the outside as they approached the building. They worked their way through the tables to an open booth where they could watch the Tigers win on one screen and the Cubbies lose on another.

"Hey, ladies, you look like a lot of fun. You just have to have some Mello Jell-o to start off the night." The waitress must be used to flirting for tips. She slid two menus onto the table. "It's Jell-o shots with vodka. So much fun."

Robin smiled. "Sounds great. You want a burger too, Amy?" She nodded. "Two with fries and cokes."

In addition to the burgers, they destroyed a huge plate of macho nachos Robin won in a beer pong contest. Amy won a round of darts against some barely legal young men and took them for twenty bucks.

Once again, the waitress flitted to their table. "How about Sex on the Beach?"

Robin grinned. "All three of us?"

The waitress winked. "Maybe if I wasn't so tired. It's our featured cocktail."

Amy, suspicious it would smell like Coppertone, asked, "What the hell is in a Sex on the Beach?"

The waitress laughed. "Don't worry. Unlike the real thing, you won't get sand places you don't want it. It's vodka with peach liquor and a fruit juice mixer. Yummy."

After two rounds of the tropical cocktail, they finally called it a night. On the way home from the sports bar, Robin drove like a grandma.

Amy glanced at her watch. "I thought this thing had the V8."

Robin eased the car to a stop. "Yeah. It does. So?"

"You only had like three drinks all night, and now you're driving like there's a dozen eggs sitting on the dashboard. What gives?"

"Nothing." Robin slowly accelerated. "Did you know that it's not considered a full stop unless the hood of your car rises?"

"You got a ticket!" Amy roared with laughter.

"It's not funny." Robin glanced over, and then back to the front. "I may have made a slight error in judging distance."

Amy said, "What the fuck are you talking about? Did you get a ticket or not?"

Robin pulled a pack of cigarettes from the console and smacked the bottom. She pulled the cellophane tag and peeled the paper. After she popped the car cigarette lighter in, she asked, "You don't mind, do you?"

"Yes. But it's your car." Amy rolled her window down about an inch.

"I swear, nothing is worse than an ex-smoker." Robin stuck a cigarette in her mouth, closing her eyes as she lit the end and pulled in a long breath. She blew out and sighed. "God I've missed that." She took one more hit, then tapped the ashes out the window. "I got stopped by your new friend, the lady police chief. She didn't respect the understanding I have with the other cops. Let's just say it didn't go too well."

"Molly," Amy said.

"What?"

"Her name's Molly. She stopped me on my way home from the potluck and let me go."

"Really? Damn. She likes you." Robin sucked her cigarette again and blew out the side of her mouth toward the window. "She must've been ragging when she stopped me."

"Robin, really." Amy scolded her friend. "If you don't want men saying shit like that about women, we can't either."

"Fine, that hormonal little bitch gave me three fucking tickets. Three!"

Amy felt the smile creep on her face and tried to pull it back. "Really?"

"I thought she was going to hit my tail light with her stick thing and give me another one for that too." Robin sucked a long pull off her cigarette.

That didn't seem quite like the same Molly that Amy had seen, what like three times now. *Is that weird?* "So, what did you say? I mean, to her, to piss her off like that."

Robin shrugged, took a last hit off her cigarette and flicked it out the window.

"That's littering." Amy crossed her arms. "You must have said something."

A smirk crossed Robin's face. "Yeah. Maybe."

Amy waited patiently. Robin might be a little embarrassed about the tickets, but she wouldn't be able to resist bragging on her own story if she thought it was clever. Amy nudged her. "Come on, you know you'll tell me sooner or later."

Robin said, "She is kind of hot, don't you think?"

"I guess." *Does it show much that I think she's very hot?* Amy hoped her voice seemed nonchalant.

"So, I asked her if she ever wore her uniform on dates, and then I told her that she didn't need to bring those lights into the bedroom because I wouldn't stop no matter what." Robin chuckled.

"You didn't!" Amy said.

"And then I asked where she kept the key to her handcuffs." Robin snickered. Then she started to belly laugh. "That's when she asked for my license and went back to her car."

"You're an idiot you know. She was just doing her job."

Robin tilted her head and squinted. "You do like her."

Remembering the AA comment, Amy scoffed, "As if. You know you can't treat cops like that. Not if you're trying to talk your way out of trouble."

Robin nodded. "Yep, Damn Skippy! She gave me a field sobriety test."

Amy started to snicker again.

Robin added, "And it was seven in the morning. I was late to work."

"Serves you right."

Robin slowed the car and eased around the corner. "And I never did find out about the key."

"You're a lunatic." Amy grabbed her seat belt strap as Robin reverted to her old self and peeled out on the street, rubber smoke filling the air. Robin might be reckless, but she was right. Amy did like Molly, more than just a little.

CHAPTER 11

In the morning, when she headed downstairs, Amy discovered that Robin wasn't home. Amy stowed her leather jacket in the saddle bag before kicking the bike to life. She pulled up at the condo where Robin's latest love interest lived, hoping to catch her for breakfast, but her sports car was not in the parking lot. The engine whined as she swerved out onto the interstate, the cars looming like obstacles on a dirt bike path. She leaned back and forth to pass them like they were standing still. She twisted the throttle to urge the engine faster. The only good thing about her helmet was that people couldn't see her goofy smile behind the fiberglass protection.

She stopped at a truck stop greasy spoon. Amy crept to a corner seat; she hated to eat alone, especially without a book to look engrossed. She worried that she looked lonely and pathetic. Alone was not the same as lonely, but the truth was she was both. And a tad pathetic.

The waitress refilled her coffee cup and smiled. "Whoever broke your heart ain't thinking about you, so you should stop thinking about him."

Amy considered correcting her but decided the other patrons might not be as understanding as she hoped. "It's that obvious?"

"Darling, no one stops here in the middle of BFE to eat if they aren't running from something. You look like a broken heart with legs."

Amy paid the five dollars for her meal and left a twenty-dollar tip.

Back on the road, she wondered where exactly she was. Although fairly rural, there was still a divided highway. Amy shifted the bike fast and cranked the handle until she could barely hang on to the bike. She ducked behind her windshield, still feeling the wind buffet her head around. She looked at the speedometer that was pegged at 110 mph. That's the funny thing about a motorcycle. The faster you go, the more stable the ride. Somewhere along the speeding road, her pain reduced into fear. *What if I wrecked out here in the middle of nowhere and no one knew who I was? That is stupid; my wallet has my ID. What if I wreck and no one cared? Do I even care? Yes.* She slowed the bike some, releasing the throttle rather than braking. At legal speeds, the wind allowed her a more comfortable ride. After regaining a more upright position, she passed a state trooper. She laughed out loud. Finally, she could pass a cop and not get stopped.

Molly crossed her mind. She did seem to run into her a lot. Despite the incident at the park, which honestly was sort of my fault, she seems nice. Molly intimidated her, maybe because of the whole police chief thing and Amy didn't make good observations. *How can I use my gaydar if I'm not paying attention?* She couldn't even remember what color Molly's eyes were. That was stupid. Eyes told you everything you needed to know about someone. She made a note to herself to make sure she looked closer next time. Next time?

At the first exit across the state line, Amy slowed. She pulled over and tugged off her helmet. She clipped it onto her backrest. Her father would be furious if he knew, but it was legal and she was thirty damn years old. She pulled out onto the highway and enjoyed the air rushing around her face. *This is great! I hate wearing a helmet. Maybe I should ditch my full-face helmet? Maybe not, then I'd have to quit grinning when I ride.* She followed the turn in the road, leaning to steer the bike.

Bam! Amy found her perma-grin interrupted. Something hit her in the face! She slammed the brakes and moved to the shoulder of the road. Based on the bug guts, a beetle had struck her right in the forehead, breaking her sunglasses in half and they dangled on her ears. *What the hell*? Continuing to curse she pulled the bike over further from the highway. She flicked the remnants of her glasses on the ground in a fit of anger. *Yes, I am littering.* In her side mirror, she studied the bug guts and a rising red welt on her forehead. She decided to go ahead and put her helmet back on. While she was stopped, she pulled out her leather jacket, glad for its warmth. She turned north and was surprised it took six hours to get to Diamond Lake; she hadn't bothered to look at a map before she left home that morning.

Relaxed and calm after her motorcycle therapy, she glided past the 'Diamond Lake city limits' sign. All the sidewalks rolled up at six, so she didn't expect to see much going on. At the Dairy Queen, two parents were surrounded by some kids racing around. No doubt sugared up. Sex was a lot more fun not worrying about getting pregnant, but kids aren't that bad. Especially if they were somebody else's. *Maybe Olivia and Donny would have a baby? I'd be a terrific aunt.*

She slowed by the Lounge and spotted Robin's car. And Deb's. She pulled onto the sidewalk and parked her bike. Stretching as she dismounted, she steeled her nerves. She paid the bouncer at the door and got a little annoyed that he didn't ask for her ID.

Amy spotted Robin at a table right by the dance floor, there were already several empty beer bottles. Amy slid into the bench next to her so she could hear over the pounding bass.

"No company yet?" Amy teased.

"Nah, I've just been relaxing. Glad you stopped by. It's good for you to get out. Mingle where they're single."

Amy swiped at her hair, a little worse for the helmet, but the bandana look wasn't her thing. She waved at the bar, and the bartender nodded. "Needed some air. Missed you for breakfast."

"Didn't sleep at her place. She's getting a little clingy."

Amy stared at Robin. She knew better than to ask.

Robin smacked the table. "It would do you some good to get a little action. Look, Stacy is here. Seal the deal, my friend." She waved her arm and Stacy nodded back. Stacy moved through the crowd and sat across from them.

Robin slid from the bench. "I see someone I need to say hi to; don't give up my table."

Amy watched Robin slide up next to a tall blonde woman, speaking into her ear, touching her arm as she spoke. Robin was a huge flirt. Maybe she should watch Robin for some tips.

Stacy moved next to her on the bench seat. "I'm sorry, I can't hear you talk over the music. I usually sit in the back."

Amy said, "I'm just glad to see a friendly face."

"Yeah, I saw Deb. If she walks by, I'll trip her."

Amy smiled. "No need, although I won't stop you."

They both laughed. Amy felt Stacy's knee press against hers under the table. Stacy asked, "You going to be at practice tomorrow? There's a concert later at the Blind Pig if you want to go with me."

"What the hell kind of name is the Blind Pig?" Amy asked.

"I think it's from the saying that even a blind pig gets lucky and finds a mushroom once in a while." Stacy shrugged. "Anyway, it's a trio from Ann Arbor. Julie mentioned them."

Amy slid her hand onto her lap, twisting just a little bit toward Stacy. It was an unconscious movement, but she recognized herself doing it. "You're right. Even a blind pig finds a mushroom once in a while."

Robin slapped the table. "What did I miss?"

Amy answered, "We're talking about going to the Blind Pig for a concert after practice tomorrow. You good?"

"As much as I hate to say it, I am not much for the granola eaters." Robin tipped her head toward a woman in a colorful skirt and tie-dye shirt twirling by herself on the dance floor.

Stacy winked. "Didn't realize you were picky."

Amy waited for her friend's response; she slid her hand over, lightly touching Stacy's leg. Stacy responded by placing her hand on top. *This is easier than I remembered.*

"So funny I forgot to laugh." Robin looked toward the bar. "Is Tony ever going to send the new girl over here or do I have to go up to the bar myself?"

Amy offered, "I'll go. Three Buds?"

When Amy returned carrying the bottles in a cluster, she held them out as Stacy and Robin each took one. Sitting down, she held out her bottle. "Cheers to good friends."

Robin clanked back and then stood up, holding her bottle high. "Here's to the women we love, and here's to the women who love us, and if the women we love aren't the women who love us, fuck them all, and here's to us!"

Amy watched as Stacy laughed, tossing her head back. She was quite pretty. Amy dropped her hand onto her leg, fully pressing against Stacy.

Stacy tipped her beer. "Is tomorrow night a go? I don't think we need to get too fancy. But I'll want to change."

Amy smiled. "Absolutely, I owe you for abandoning you at the potluck."

Stacy picked up Amy's hand, slowly clasping them together. "You don't owe me, I'm just hoping you'd want to hang out some."

Amy intertwined her fingers with Stacy's. "Yeah, we should definitely hang out some."

Robin tapped the table. "How about letting me use the restroom before you two ditch me?"

Amy looked up startled. *Was it that obvious?* She felt her mouth go dry and her stomach lurch in distress.

CHAPTER 12

Amy drove her motorcycle home with Stacy following behind in her little Datsun. It was hard for Amy to not judge people for what they drove. Even if it wasn't important to everyone, it was important to her. There just was something different between people who drove an old beater, or a piece of shit like a Datsun, and those who drove a muscle car, or at least not some grandma car if you weren't a grandma. Careful to stay at the speed limit, the bike was still a cold ride in the dark. She pulled under the carport and smiled as Stacy parked her car.

Amy almost dropped her keys unlocking the back door. *You can do this.* They headed up the stairs to the extra room, now a sort of den. "I just moved in and haven't unpacked much yet."

"You and Robin?" Stacy asked.

"Nah, she's my best bud. She moved to Diamond Lake during middle school. We hit it off right away. She's from the U.P. ya know."

"You don't say. Eh?" Stacy said, in a full Yooper accent. "I'd have thought she'd have made a move on you by now."

"It'd be like kissing my sister," Amy said. "You want a beer or something?"

"Something." Stacy grabbed an unhappy Meow off a large cardboard box. "Oh, a kitty! Hewwooo little kitty." Meow hissed. "Grumpy cat?"

Amy shrugged. "Meow has her moments. I guess today is not the day."

Stacy set the striped feline down and turned toward Amy. "I guess she can tell I'm more of a dog person, you know because dogs are always friendly. Like me." Stacy leaned forward and lightly touched her lips to Amy's mouth.

Amy gently kissed her back. *Shit. What underwear do I have on?* She reached out and pulled Stacy closer, their kisses slow, exploratory, like teenagers at a high school dance in the gym, lights low with the scent of floor wax and sweat. Awkward, nervous, excited.

"Will you stay?" Amy took Stacy's hand and led her to the back bedroom, shutting the door before Meow could join them.

"Cat," Amy said as if she needed to explain. Meow found human interactions on beds to be irresistible, pouncing at the most inopportune times if allowed in the room. Deb swore she had scars on her arm. *Dammit, woman, get out of my head.*

Stacy reached for Amy, stroking her back as they snuggled in. Amy tried to push images of Deb from her mind, forcing herself to look at the woman before her. Stacy was slight, her black hair straight and even. And she wasn't wearing a bra. Amy slid her hands from Stacy's back around her sides, touching lightly.

Stacy grabbed her wrist. "No, that tickles."

Amy increased pressure, sliding her hand around the front of her shirt. *Now what? Gentle or not?* She slid herself back and tugged at Stacy's shirt. Stacy stood and pulled off her shirt and dropped her pants. Amy felt a wave of nerves as she began to unbutton her own shirt, feeling the clamminess of her hands.

Stacy reached out. "Let me." After each button, Stacy kissed her. She tasted like mint candy and beer. And her mouth was dry. Stacy was nervous too. Amy shuddered as her shirt dropped and Stacy unhooked her bra with one fast flick. Stacy's hands cupped her breasts tenderly. Suddenly Stacy dropped to her knees and pushed Amy back onto the bed.

With a clumsy motion, Amy shifted her hips as Stacy unbuttoned her jeans. *With Deb it was like a choreographed dance, leading gracefully to a screaming orgasm. This is a hot mess.* Her belly tightened each time Stacy brushed against her, the cool night air caressing her legs as the pants fell to the floor. The feel of Stacy's body against her brought a hot rush between her legs, her body knowing what to do even if Amy wasn't aware of it. Kissing her harder, Stacy was moving her body against her, Amy lifting up to meet her, clutching her back. Amy's head was swimming, unaware of the room, the time, the only thing that mattered was the scent of Stacy's perfume, and the sensual urges between them.

Just as Amy ran her fingers across Stacy's damp underwear, Stacy sat up. "I can't."

Amy focused and looked her in the eye. "Um, what?"

"I know this is a little late to say this, but I can't. Not tonight. All I can think of is Vicky." Stacy looked down, a dark expression on her face.

Amy propped up on one elbow. *What the hell?* Her brain finally caught up with what her ears heard. "It's okay, we can stop." *If we must.* "If you're not comfortable, it's cool." *It is so not cool.*

"I'm really sorry, I just don't know where I stand, and since Vicky moved, she still seems to think we can make it work. I'm not so sure, but I still can't, you know." Stacy looked at her with puppy eyes.

Amy exhaled. "It's okay, really. You can stay, still. If you want. Do you need something to drink or anything?" *What the fuck is wrong with you?* In just a few more minutes Amy would have been really unhappy to stop. She wasn't that happy now.

"Look, you are really nice and all, my head is just kind of fucked up right now." Stacy started pulling her pants back on. "Maybe when Vicky is here, we can all hang out. You know, the three of us. We do that sometimes."

Amy blinked. A three-way? That would be a hard no. "Yeah, maybe." She stood and got her robe from the closet while Stacy got dressed. "Hey, I understand about Vicky. I didn't know. I won't say anything."

"It's cool, we have an understanding. I'm telling you she'd

really like you, too." Stacy clutched her hands together.

"This doesn't have to be weird." Amy listened to herself but didn't believe it either. This was going to be really weird. How the hell does Robin do this like it just doesn't matter? She walked Stacy to the back door. "I did have fun with you tonight, but maybe tomorrow night isn't such a good idea."

Stacy paused at the door. "I guess not." She looked solemn. "I am sorry."

Amy shut the door and headed back to bed. Meow, indignant, flicked her tail as she walked past the bedroom door. "Hey, at least I tried. Today is not the day." She flipped the blanket over herself and slid her hand between her legs. She grimaced when Meow clawed her arm. *Damn cat.*

CHAPTER 13

The sun hadn't risen yet when Molly pulled into the parking lot at the police station. A hundred interruptions, necessary but irregular, distracted her focus all day so she came in early to do some brainstorming. She laid out the city map from uncle Yancy and marked the location of burglaries. No commonality at all. She opened the file cabinet and eased the thick folder out of the drawer. She slid in the papers from her top center drawer and began comparing the list. She startled when Charley was in the doorway.

"You're here kind of early," Molly said.

"I could say the same." Charley rubbed his ear absently. "Just between you and me and the file cabinet, you need to be a little less intense when you do traffic stops. You scared the shit out of my mother-in-law coming up with your hand on your gun."

Molly remembered the lady practically shrieking. "I guess everyone else in town knows that a particular navy-blue Lincoln belongs to your family. Tell your mother-in-law to stop putting on lipstick while driving." For just a moment, she saw the car in her mind, the sound of a gun firing. She forced herself to look at his face. "More officers get killed during traffic stops than in any other scenario."

"We don't need some gung-ho Gorman riling folks up, terrifying little old ladies, that's all." He scratched his ear. "Things get around in a small town. Your family is from here, but you're not.

That's all. Wouldn't want to have any issues with the public."

"I get along with pretty much everyone. I like to keep my head down."

"Good thing or that bullet might have caught your head instead of your shoulder." Charley seemed relaxed.

"Yeah, there's that." She watched his vision flick to the cabinet behind her, and she suspected he'd be in the drawer within the hour. She had a code for putting the notes in plain sight. Each looked like a receipt for a gas purchase, with the time and date matching the suspicious residential break-ins. Anyone reading the list would assume it was for a budget or maybe tracking mileage.

"We good?" Molly asked.

"Yes, I believe so. Just try to refrain from pulling your gun on jaywalkers," he said.

"Hilarious, Chuck." Molly stacked the paperwork, flicked off the lights and headed out the front office. She inventoried the information the sergeant told her; she suspected he vastly underestimated her. He didn't like her being related to the former chief, which was too bad for him. Gung-ho Gorman... that would be a good thing. Maybe the warning about her reputation, followed by the reference to her being shot upset her the most. That was a threat. Thinly veiled. She'd need to talk to her uncle.

She stopped in the break room and slid some coins into the drink machine, listening to the clunks as the Coke dropped through the mechanics inside. Doug walked in behind her just as she popped the snap top open. "Hi Doug, pretty quiet out there?"

"Yep. Spring dance tonight at the high school. Glad I didn't draw traffic." Doug scanned over the schedule. "Not sure why we need a big chart for just the six of us."

"I'd rather it just be in the computer myself. But it helps everyone know where everyone is, or is not." Molly tried to read his expression. Blank. She peered into the snack machine, having decided against the Cheetos.

"Yeah, Charley and his great ideas." Doug tapped the calendar. "Maybe we should be glad it's not color coded."

Molly looked around the room. "That was going to be my next suggestion."

They both laughed. Jeff stuck his head into the room. "There you two are. Wreck on the 51st highway. It's a bad one."

The fire trucks were just ahead of them as they traveled down the shoulder of the road. *Why couldn't people just get out of the way?* The radio crackled, and the dispatch voice rang out, "Coroner notified. Copy."

In the city, people couldn't drive that fast, and most wrecks were limited to vehicle damage and bumps and bruises. These back-country highways with fast drivers and twisting corners led to a grisly mix.

Charley already had flares placed around the scene, and yellow tape fluttered. Two fire trucks were surrounded by hoses, and two ambulances were parked near the perimeter of the area. A rescue squad truck sat closer to two small cars that looked like they'd been crushed at a junkyard. A full-sized pickup was flattened in front, smoke rising from the front end. A sheet was already over the windshield. Probably not wearing a seat belt. Molly walked toward the cars. One driver was still in the car, glass around the ground, another body slumped in the passenger seat, and blood spattered on the side window.

The other car seemed to have the only survivor. Molly leaned into the side window, speaking to the occupant. "Just hang on. We'll get you out."

The coroner walked up to her and spoke quietly. "I'm done with the scene. Three are cleared for transport by the mortuary."

Molly nodded.

A burley fireman brought up the case with the hinged "Jaws of Life" and sat it on the ground. He popped the lid open and methodically arranged the parts. In a smooth motion, he pulled it out.

"Clear?" he shouted.

Molly and Charley both said yes. He slammed the point into the door jam, the pneumatic line jerked and they watched as the metallic cage twisted open. What would have been nearly impossible with axes and sweat was accomplished in virtually minutes. It was a wonder to see. Two paramedics stood ready for access to the victim. Once the metallic screeching stopped, Molly stepped back as they put a foam collar on the patient and eased her onto the gurney. A fireman went to the other car with another sheet. Molly tried to block the scene overall and focus just on the detective work at hand.

Molly opened her notebook and began making notations as she inspected the car. Charley pulled a tape and they stretched the measurements between each vehicle and assorted debris. Doug was stuck on the road directing traffic. They needed to get the vehicles out of the highway to clear traffic and speed up the onlookers, or as they called them, the rubberneckers.

Finally, the officers had captured all of the necessary scene details. A hearse pulled up and the crew began to remove the bodies. A red and blue tow truck maneuvered to collect what was left of the vehicles.

Charley gave his notes to Molly in her car and headed back to his own. After the road had been swept up, they moved their cars and opened the lanes of traffic.

Sweat beaded on her forehead and trickled down her lower back. She frowned when it went right down the crack of her ass. The dark uniform might be sharp looking, but it was hot as hell in the full sun on a highway in summer. The air conditioner was already on high. She closed her eyes and pinched her nose. The sun had started to lower slightly, causing a blinding light over the road traveling west. Molly squinted and then put on her darker sunglasses.

When she walked into the police station, Jeff stared at Molly a moment. "With those glasses on, you actually look pretty tough."

Molly slid them up onto the top of her head. *Don't let him get to you. He will smell any weakness.* "See you tomorrow." She kept her gaze directly at him.

Jeff swallowed and nodded.

Once in her office, Molly collapsed at her desk. She picked up the phone and dialed.

"Hi, Grandma. Just checking in."

"Well, hello Molly!"

"How about I pick you up and we have dinner out tomorrow, my treat."

"Oh gosh. You come on and I'll fix a nice meal here."

Molly smiled. "No, don't do that. I'll be there about five."

"That would be very nice. See you tomorrow, honey."

"Okay, have a good night." She dropped the phone into the cradle. She decided to take the evening loop around town. She really didn't feel like fixing dinner, so she stopped at a chicken stand and noticed Amy's Jeep when she pulled in. She drove to the drive-thru and saw Amy walk by as she waited for her order. Her heart started to pound in her chest. She would wave if Amy looked over. The teenager startled her when she handed out her drink and a paper bag. When she turned and sat it down, Amy was looking her direction. Amy waved at her.

Molly pulled over closer.

"Starting to wonder if you're stalking me." Amy put her hands on her hips and smiled.

"Just a small town." Molly felt her mouth go dry. "I guess everyone wants chicken tonight.

Amy tipped her head. "Or don't want to cook." She got into her car.

"Right." Molly tried to come up with a segue that didn't involve a cheesy line. *What is wrong with me? Come on, you can't just let her go.* Molly tossed a Hail Mary. "You work at the shop at Fourth, right? Gilbert and Son?"

Amy nodded.

Molly asked, "Do I need an appointment? My car is making a funny sound." *What the hell? Funny sound?* At least she could see Amy, even if it wasn't a real date, and then plan something from there.

Amy stared at the cruiser. "Uh, yes. I mean, no, you don't need an appointment, but yes you can bring it by. Maybe at 11 sometime? I take the early lunch and we can take a ride and see if we can figure out what's going on with your car." Amy was tapping on her steering wheel. She seemed to catch herself and stopped. And then she smiled again.

Molly felt her stomach flip. That smile could melt an iceberg. "Okay, then. I'll see you one day. At 11. Drive safe."

All the way back to the station, she wondered what the problem was, usually she was extremely charming. She was losing her touch. Pretty soon Amy would think that she was an axe murderer. And now she had to take in her car on her day off for a problem it didn't have. *Stupid.* Maybe she'd get lucky and the exhaust would fall off or something.

CHAPTER 14

Robin swung the bat and connected a solid hit that flew over the pitching machine. "What do you mean you won't tell me? You left the bar together. Did you sleep with her or not?"

"Well it depends on how you define it, I guess." Amy clutched the chain link fence of the batting cage.

"Keep your fingers out of there, a foul ball could bust back there and break your fingers." Robin swung the bat behind her head, stretching out her shoulders. "On second thought, it might help your grip on the bat."

"Jackass." Amy put her hands in her pockets.

"It's a simple question." Robin rotated her torso and her back cracked so loudly Amy could hear it. "If you think you had sex, you did."

"Either way, I'm not telling you." Amy opened the batting cage door and switched positions with Robin. She popped several quarters into the machine and waited for the light to come on indicating a pitch was coming soon. "I will tell you that her socks match her underwear."

"That's weird because I match mine to my pants." Robin tipped her head. "You did sleep with her."

Amy saw the light change to green and watched for the pitch. "No. I didn't."

Robin smacked her gum. "That's not what she said at practice."

"Interesting. Then why did you ask me?" Amy swung and launched a hit over the third base line.

"Just to give you shit. And Coach is a little pissed you skipped." Robin blew a bubble.

"I didn't skip practice, I had a stomach ache." *I so skipped.* Amy swung, getting a little piece and sending the ball on a wild arch. "I don't know why Stacy said anything in the first place. A lady does not share those things."

Robin shrugged. "Probably because I asked her."

"Dammit." Amy slammed open the screen door, and grabbed Robin around the neck, bending her into a choke hold.

"Okay. I maybe shouldn't have," Robin squeaked out.

Amy let her go. "No duh. I don't know why you're fucking obsessed with my love life."

"I think it's more your lack of a love life. I just wondered if you slept with her. Everyone else seemed curious to know the answer, too." Robin dodged Amy's lunge. "I was just kidding, Amy. Honest. Just make sure you call Coach and get your ass to the game."

"I will, I will." Amy waited for a few beats. "Hey, can I ask you something?"

"Sure."

"Do you ever think about how much we drink?"

"What, like four glasses of water a day?" Robin asked.

"Forget it," Amy said, sliding her bat into her gear bag.

Robin turned to Amy. "You're serious." She pulled off her batting glove. "Well, no, not really. I mean, everybody likes to relax after work, have a few at the bar. We all drink a lot. Why?"

Amy shrugged. "No particular reason. I won't be home for a while."

"You okay?" Robin asked.

"Yeah. Just forget I asked. I'll see you later." Amy walked to her car and tossed her bag into the back. *I think so. Maybe I'm not.*

***

Amy was twisted between the car seat and the instrument panel, replacing a car radio. She tried to reach the fastener, but the screwdriver was just too short. She backed out from under the dash and twisted to stand. She jumped when she turned to get a different screwdriver. Molly was standing there in jean shorts and a polo shirt. She wore her Docksiders sockless, and Amy was very appreciative of the full view of her long, tan legs.

Molly said, "I hope this isn't a bad time."

Amy wiped her hands, forgetting all about the screwdriver. "No, no, this is fine. Let's go take a look at your car."

She followed Molly to a bright red Mustang, clean and freshly waxed. *Nice wheels*. "When do you hear the noise?"

"What noise?" Molly said. "Oh, the noise. That the car makes. Off and on. More off than on."

Amy scowled. "I hope it will do it for us because sometimes these things don't act up when you want them to. How fast are you going when you hear it, or is it when the car is still?"

Molly shook her head. "Let me see. Yes, moving only, and slow speeds."

"You mind if we take a test drive?" Amy asked, opening the car door.

"Of course not." Molly handed her the keys. Just at the moment their hands touched, the keys fell. They both bent to get them, and nearly cracked heads. "Sorry, so clumsy of me."

"It was my fault; shall we go?" Amy felt her stomach sink. *Molly must really think she's a loon.*

They rode in silence as Amy revved the engine, listened as they accelerated, and again as they stopped and then lurched forward again. Amy noticed that Molly was clutching the armrest but seemed relaxed overall. *Confidence is sexy.* Her hair fell around her face as the car jerked. And her eyes twinkled. *Damn, I'd like to have her clutching me.* Remember she's the one who tossed you in jail. Well, it was my fault. *Say something.*

"Do you have time to eat?" Amy asked. Her voice sounded odd, echoing in her ears.

"Yeah, I hate for you to miss your lunch," Molly said.

Molly actually blushed when she answered. Amy was totally enamored. She hoped Molly hadn't noticed her lunchbox on her workbench. She headed toward a little sandwich shop on the river.

CHAPTER 15

Molly pulled out the chair and watched as the feisty mechanic disappeared into the restroom. The diner was supposed to look like a 1950's era burger joint, or maybe it was original and never updated. The floor was black and white checked, and the chairs and benches were covered with red Naugahyde. She flicked the menu open and shut, the speckled Formica table still damp from being wiped off, but still slightly sticky from the last patrons. She sighed and took a deep breath. The ruse of her mystery car problem seemed forgotten. *What makes you tick Amatta Gilberta?*

The waitress sauntered over to the table. "Boss says to comp your lunch. Order what you want."

"No, thanks." Molly fixed a smile on her face. "It's nice and all but it doesn't look right. I sure appreciate it, though."

The waitress sucked her teeth. "K. So what do you want?"

Amy slid into the chair across from Robin. "Hi Gloria, how's Chip? Dodge still running hot?"

"Not so much now that he wrapped it around a tree. He's a dumbass." Gloria snapped her gum. "You want the special?"

Amy didn't look at the menu. "No thanks. I'll just have a chicken salad plate and a Diet Coke."

"Same." Molly touched the menu to slide it toward the waitress. "I guess you know about everyone in town."

"Me? Nah. Just the places to eat and the places to drink."

"Evidently every single place to drink." An uncomfortable silence fell between them. *Nice job.* Molly studied the napkin holder.

"Funny." Amy picked at her fingernail. "I have thought about what you said. About drinking."

"Just something I'm familiar with." Molly blew out a breath. *Just tell her.* "My dad drank enough for all of us. Sometimes being the son of a cop is even harder than being a preacher's kid. Mom used to take us to Al-anon meetings once in a while. It's not for everyone."

Gloria placed the drinks on the table, then flicked out straws.

Molly ripped the paper. *Come on, just ask her a question.* "What's with Gilberta? Italian? Your garage just says Gilbert."

"Yeah. We joke that the sign was priced by the letter, but really Grandpa thought Gilbert sounded more American, you know, for the business. I guess no one bothered to formally change it. The trouble of going to court and all."

Molly nodded. "Gorman was Gurmund and my grandfather changed it. World War 1, I think motivated him to be more English sounding than German." *Pretty sure she doesn't give a shit.*

Amy asked, "Do you want to see a magic trick?" She took Molly's hand. "Besides this."

Molly blushed as she pulled her hand back. She watched as Amy pulled the paper off her straw, folded it carefully, and tipped it with a drop of Coke. The paper expanded up off the table. "Magic tricks are a hobby?"

"Oh no," Amy said. "Just good with my hands." Her face flushed a light pink.

I sure hope so. Molly froze. *At least Amy was embarrassed by the innuendo. Might as well take the bait.* "Do you like working with your hands, you know, fixing things?"

"I have a certain knack. I do like working by myself. Cars I understand. People, not so much."

"I bet you understand people better than you think." Before Molly could say anything else, Gloria appeared with the food. She plopped a bottle of ketchup on the table.

"How did you end up a cop?" Amy asked, her mouth half full of fries. "I mean here, in particular. Diamond Lake is not very exciting."

Molly tipped her head, considering her answer. Amy was just as direct sober as drunk. Was it engaging or annoying? Amy is darn cute. She eats like a cow. Annoying? "I wanted to be a policewoman because I like helping people out. Got tired of running myself ragged in the worst parts of the city. This chief gig is just short term, for now anyway. I planned to be a chief someday, just didn't realize it'd be this soon."

"It's pretty cool we have a woman police chief." Amy nodded and mellowed. "Your car is wicked."

"I know you'll be shocked to discover that I'm not very mechanical," Molly admitted.

Amy said, "Really? I like figuring out machines and how they work. Fixing them when they break. You kind of do the same thing, just with people. Fixing them. When they break."

"Everyone's a little broken. That's where the strong parts come from." Molly bit her teeth down. *Light, easy.* This isn't a philosophy class.

"Some of us are stronger than others, to begin with," Amy said.

"Most of us are stronger than we think." *I like how Amy's eyes twinkle. Engaging.* Molly shrugged. "I haven't been shot at since I got here. My mother is pretty happy about that."

"Damn. Really?" Amy wiped her hands on a paper napkin and then reached for another. "I guess I just see the cop shows on TV and it seems so fake."

"I can assure you that this is not fake." Molly slid up her sleeve revealing the red angry scar near her bicep.

Amy stared with a mixed look of awe and curiosity. "And I wondered if you were here on some secret undercover sting operation or something," she joked.

"Sorry to disappoint. I'm just keeping myself alive." At that, the sounds in the room seemed to echo. Molly hoped her voice seemed normal. She blinked slowly and took a breath, calming herself.

"I'm glad." Amy sucked up the last of her soda. "That you're here. And that you're alive."

There went that beautiful smile. And instantly Molly was charmed. *I wonder if she's a good kisser. What? Stop. Say anything, try something clever.* "I guess I better get you back to work." *Oh, well done, scintillating conversation there.*

Amy said, "How about you drive and I'll listen. These intermittent things can be a bugaboo."

Molly kept her foot light on the way back to the garage. Amy tapped her hands on her legs the entire way to the garage. Molly pushed up her sunglasses as she went to open the door. Amy's shirt opened at the top, allowing a glimpse of her full chest. The lace was unexpected. Molly felt the hot, red, flush across her face. *Amy is damn hot.*

Molly recovered and handed Amy her business card. "My home number is on the back. Thanks for checking out things. You know, the car, I mean."

"If it starts acting up, bring it by again. Good seeing you." And she was off.

Molly watched her figure retreat. *I used to be good with people.* She let her foot slide heavily on the gas, and the car rumbled to life.

***

Amy floated into the garage, and actually smiled at her mother when she got the keys for the next job.

"What was wrong?" Rosie asked.

"With what?"

"The car you just spent two hours test driving?"

"Nothing. Never acted up at all."

***

Amy huffed as she walked backward across the driveway carrying the wild orange and green flowered armchair. "I could have just gotten a new one."

"Don't be ridiculous. This is perfectly good. Besides, money goes through your wallet like a stone through a goose." Robin pushed the chair, throwing Amy off balance.

"That. Is disgusting." Amy clunked her heel against the step. "And I'm not that bad with money. I'm just generous."

"No. You're wasteful." Robin pushed on the chair as she staggered up the stairs blind. "I know. I carried in your clothes with tags still on them."

Amy ran into the door. "Hold on a sec." She searched behind her for the knob and opened the screen. "Okay. Go."

"You realize I can see you." Robin grunted as she pushed the chair against the door frame. "It's stuck. Shit, that was my hand. Turn your end."

Amy leaned into the furniture, her arms flexing as she tugged at the bottom edge. "It's the same size as the door. We should try the front door."

"Nah, just one more big push," Robin urged. There was a creaking noise as the chair relented and lurched into the house. The friends carried the flowered beast up the stairs, then to the spare room and placed it directly across from the TV. "I told you, easy peasy. Now beer me."

Amy opened the mini fridge and tossed a beer can toward Robin. "How's things with the new lady?"

Robin shrugged. "She's pissed at me. And now it's weird at work."

"Told you. Shouldn't mix work and pleasure." Amy took out a second beer and popped the can open. She stared at the can, then she took a long drink. "Thanks for the chair. Really. It saved me a bunch of dough. And it's comfy."

Robin nodded. "It's butt ugly. But you're welcome. Got any big plans for the weekend?"

"Nah, I don't have uncontrollable, raging, animal urges like you do."

Robin seemed to ignore the comment. "You know what? I have an excellent idea. I challenge you. Let's see who can sleep with Molly first."

Amy blinked. *This is such a bad idea.* "Why?"

"Why not? We're both single, she's single. I challenge you." Robin poked Amy in the arm. "And you have to accept."

"No can do." Amy slouched. "Besides, Molly seems nice."

"Nice? Really? Oh, so now you do like her? That should make it easier." Robin took a drink of her beer.

"I don't do one-night stands. I like relationships," Amy said.

"Just think of it as serial monogamy," Robin said.

Amy crossed her arms.

Robin asked, "What's your problem? You think I'll win and you don't want seconds?"

Amy bounced one foot up and down. "Robin, you and your crazy ideas get me into trouble every time. I don't want to do it."

"How could this possibly get you into trouble?" Robin asked.

"I don't know. It seems a little lame."

"That's because you're chicken. You don't think you can score," Robin said.

"I am not chicken. I just am more of a lady than you are." Amy pulled at the tab on the can until it snapped off. "This seems like a high school stunt. It's so plebeian."

"Ha!" Robin snorted. "You can talk all fancy if you want, but you can't beat me at this game. I am the master."

"Baiter," Amy said.

"Good one," Robin said, childishly amused. "You are so going to lose this bet."

Amy stared at her cat, Meow, who was kneading her way onto the table between them. *Did I accept this challenge?* "So, what're the stakes?"

Robin leaned and pulled out her wallet. She took out a hundred-dollar bill and stuck it on the mini fridge with the magnet from Cedar Point amusement park. "I win, I get it back. You win, you keep it. See, you're not out anything either way."

"I'm so going to win. Big time." Amy opened a new beer.

"I kind of hope you do. This cat is getting hair all over my damn pants. Meow needs her own chair," Robin said to the cat.

Meow blinked slowly as if she agreed.

"Women and felines are just drawn to you, aren't they?" Amy asked.

Robin stood up holding the cat. "It's a gift and a curse." She sat Meow back on the chair.

After Robin left, Amy took the phone number from her wallet and slipped it under the magnet next to the bill. This is such a bad idea. She paced around the living room. *Even if I do sleep with Molly, it might just be because I like her. I don't have to just sail on.* Like Robin does. Use them and lose them. Molly is just like any other woman. Just call her. Amy picked up the phone and tapped in the numbers.

CHAPTER 16

Amy rang the buzzer next to the number Molly had given her. *Three, the number of licks to get to the center of a Tootsie Pop.* The steel door lock clicked and Amy pulled the handle to open the door. The hallway smelled of stale beer, mixed with the scent of onions cooking, and just a hint of wet dog. She climbed the stairs two at a time and spotted the door with a script three on it. She tapped once before the door flew open. Molly stood there in an outfit that crossed fisherman with a Boy Scout. Pockets everywhere. Practical maybe, sexy? Not so much.

Soft music played on a top of the line stereo, and a huge TV took up one entire wall. The gaming system on the coffee table topped the dreams of every adolescent male in town. The curtains were pulled back, showing a view of the park in the distance.

Molly smiled at her. A small wave of guilt started to rise. After all, Molly did try to help me out, and she seems pretty nice. The scent of Molly's perfume sent a wave of arousal through Amy's core. *I am in way over my head.*

"I brought you this," Amy said as she handed Molly a bottle of Welch's grape juice.

"You're funny. Find me okay?" Molly asked, putting the bottle on a side table. "Have a seat."

"Yeah," Amy rubbed her sweating hands on her pant legs as

she sat. "Nice digs. I haven't been inside since these apartments were built. Me and my brother got busted for riding our bikes up the construction ramps and around the framing. Mom had to pick us up at the police station. She was really pissed." She smiled briefly and then pressed her lips together. *Why don't I just bring up all my delinquent crimes? Stupid. Just chill.*

"Brother? Is he the son of Gilbert and Son?"

"Oh, no, that's my Dad. Pops took over after Grandpa got too stiff to tinker around the place." Amy crossed her legs and then uncrossed them. "And I have two sisters. Olivia works with her husband in the body shop, and Tina works up front with me and Dad. She takes classes. Business management I think." *Why don't I know what classes she takes? Idiot.* "Do you have siblings?"

"An older brother. He lives up at Houghton Lake. He's a forestry guy." Molly handed Amy a glass of lemonade. "I have pop if you'd rather."

"This is fine, great really. I like lemonade." At a loss for words, she flashed Molly a smile. *Charm might be failing me, but my grin won't.* Molly smiled back. *Bingo.* She took a sip of the drink and looked for a coaster. A short stack of round discs sat on a side table next to the lamp. She sat the glass down.

"When did you decide to be a mechanic?" Molly asked.

"At our house, it would be more like when did you decide you didn't want to be a mechanic." Amy shrugged. "All of us were in the shop as kids, learning by holding the light or handing over tools. Dad learned the same way, helping Pops soup up engines."

"Soup up?

"Bore out the engine, stuff like that, to make cars go faster. Rebuild suspensions to keep it steady, whatever."

"Like early Nascar?"

Amy nodded. "You could say that and more." She tapped the coaster. "Eastern logo. Did you go there?"

"Yes, go Hurons...you can't go to the police academy until you're 21, so I went to school. Business classes."

"Smart and good looking. Good combination." Amy wished she hadn't said that. Molly blushed and it sounded insincere. She picked up her drink as a long silence developed.

"Do you like cats? My neighbor has one. I thought it might be nice to have one. A cat. I already have the neighbor." Molly sat at the edge of her chair.

Funny or nervous? I like funny. But I'll take nervous. "I honestly like dogs better, but I have a little striped feline ball of attitude. I got her from Nancy and Winnie. She was part of a litter they found behind their shops, you know. At the corner, the building has a dumpster and the kittens were there. She was super quiet all the time so I named her Meow. To sort of teach her to talk. I mean meow. You know." Amy slouched. *Get a grip here.* She sipped her drink to shut herself up.

"That's cute. I thought I'd go to the Humane Society." Molly offered Amy her hand as she stood. "Shall we head out?"

At the car, Molly trotted over to open Amy's door. *So sweet. This is such a bad idea.* Amy got in with a quick smile. The ride to the state park was thankfully short. Molly flashed her badge to the park ranger who waved them in. At the second turn off, almost completely hidden in the brush, was a small sign from the Audubon Society. The dirt road faded into two ruts through the woods, ending at a small gravel field. Molly pulled the car under the shade of a row of pines and cut the engine.

"Have you been back here before?" Molly asked. She pulled out a brown covered field manual and a set of binoculars.

"Actually, this is my first trip. I have to admit I'm not much of a hiker." Amy pulled the door handle and stood.

"Listen." Molly held her hand up. The quiet of the woods and the soft rustle of the pine needles in the breeze gave way to the calls and chirps of assorted avian creatures and the steady buzz of insects. "I don't know many of the calls, but it is something to hear them all at one time. That rat a tat tat tat is a Pileated Woodpecker. I think."

As the sun slid down in the sky, long shadows formed around them. Molly stepped toward the first bulletin board and headed down the trail. Amy trudged behind her, appreciating the view of her companion's rear end and legs. Molly's hair fell free just past her shoulders, the camping shirt of some kind was tucked into cargo shorts, the pockets of which perfectly swayed along as she walked. *Just my luck, she's outdoorsy. Ranger Rickie. Just great.* She caught her toe on a root and stumbled.

The climb was slight, and the trail empty. They couldn't have gone more than twenty minutes when Molly stopped and pulled out her binoculars. The ridge they stood on had a rickety wooden rail next to another bulletin board indicating particular hiking trails to the left and right, and a colored poster with pictures of poisonous plants. Amy peered around at the underbrush, searching for the leaves of three or white berries.

"I wouldn't expect any birds that low. Try up higher, at the edge of the canopy." Molly handed over the binoculars. "Look toward the pond, on the far side."

"I was looking for poison ivy, actually." *Do I look that far out of my element? I am, but I'm not stupid. She didn't seem to mean anything by it, just trying to help?* Amy made an attempt to find birds. All she could see was out of focus greenery. *What possessed me to accept an invitation to bird watch? Total lust. And greed.* She blushed at the lies. And now she was stuck birdwatching. The only birds she knew were cardinals and robins. She couldn't remember the last time she'd even noticed a bird. She adjusted the knob on the top of the binoculars and a tree leaning over the water popped into focus. Two brownish ducks swam evenly across the water, eyes staring off as if disinterested. Some little brown striped bird was standing on a limb. She lowered the glasses and looked at Molly who was flipping from page to page.

"I used to come out here with my grandmother when I was a kid. She knows all the birds both by call and by sight." Molly studied a page. "I think that's a Carolina wren on the branch. I don't know. Can you tell if its tail is held upright or not?"

"I'm a little out of my element here. I think it's cool that you can even tell it's a wren." Amy looked over Molly's shoulder at the picture. A little map of North America was shaded where each species lived, and the bird shape was colored in the corner, along with dimensions. A paragraph of text presumably described the bird further. A color picture was on the opposite page. "It could be either of those two, I guess."

She tried to hand the glasses to Molly but forgot the strap was around her neck. As Molly took them, the cord went taut and pulled her forward. They almost touched noses.

"Oops." Amy flushed. "Sorry."

"Don't be." Molly gently lifted the cord from around Amy's neck. "I really don't know this bird stuff either. I just thought it would be a nice place for a hike. Relax some. Get to know each other."

Amy realized how close they were still standing. The scent of shampoo and Off insect spray mingled in her nose. "It is nice." She reached out just a little, lightly touching Molly and then dropped her hand.

Molly was still, her soft brown eyes questioning. She hung the cord around her own neck and started to pull away. A loud crack of branches in the distance caused her to spin around, pushing the glasses to her head. She followed a sweeping arc around the far side of the lake.

"There, just to the right. Here." Molly left the strap on her neck and raised the glasses to Amy's face. Their heads almost touching, Amy felt her pulse speed up as the blood rushed to her groin. She once again was looking at leaves and twigs. Then a full eight-point buck stepped from the woods, his golden-brown coat shining in the last of the evening sunlight.

"I don't need a book to identify that one. I hope he survives next fall. About everyone hunts around here, mostly the men I mean. The odds are not in his favor," Amy said. She rested her hand on the binoculars, Molly's fingers barely touching hers. Amy felt herself shiver. *I wonder if she believes in love at first sight. I mean, I hated her at first, well not at first, because that was at soft-ball. Really, I hated her at second, and then how many times in the Jeep? Is she stalking me? Stop thinking too much.* She pushed the glasses toward Molly. "This is great."

Molly lowered the glasses and touched Amy's face. "The view here is spectacular." She leaned over slightly, touching her lips to Amy's.

Amy felt the blood leave her head as she tasted the mint toothpaste. She tenderly kissed back. Molly shoved the book she was still holding into her pocket freeing her hand. She reached and pulled Amy closer, kissing harder, the binoculars crushed between them. Amy responded to the warm touch, her breath catching in her throat. Goosebumps popped up on her arms as Molly's hands brushed against her back. *My pants are going to burst into flames.* Amy reached both hands and cupped Molly's face.

"You are certainly right about the view." Amy smiled.

"I'm sorry to be so forward," Molly said, pulling back.

Amy faltered for a brief moment. "Forward? Damn, if it wasn't for the risk of a poison ivy rash, I'm ready to jump you on this trail." She took Molly's hand, loosely, and squeezed. "You are just so chivalrous."

Molly looked like a deer in headlights.

"And now it's my turn to be sorry," Amy whispered. "I just like you. That's all."

"Maybe we should head back. I forgot to bring my flashlight." Molly turned toward the trail, but still held Amy's hand.

The stroll back to the car was slower, their hands linked together, swinging easily between them. Amy felt the air chill as the sunlight faded, cool shadows appearing through the trees. Near the parking lot, she reluctantly dropped Molly's hand. The Mustang was the only car.

Molly fished in her pocket for keys, popped the trunk and put in the binoculars and the bird manual. She shut the trunk with a smooth motion. Amy reached around Molly's waist, turning her and pinning her to the car. She pressed her hips against Molly, her hands caressing the soft hair by Molly's face as she kissed her.

Molly stiffened at first, then reached into the hug, kissing back. Amy was lost in her own breathing, the way Molly's body fit into hers, and the soft chirp of crickets off in the distance. Time seemed to stop as their mouths explored. She felt Molly grab her belt loops on her shorts and push back.

"I feel like a kid in high school again, necking on the hood of a car." Molly winked, the moonlight reflecting off of her face.

"Spend a lot of time necking on cars?" Amy tipped her head, a naughty smile flickering on her face.

Molly's face turned red. "Actually, yeah, down at the baseball fields. We'd park and watch the kids play. The girl would sit on the hood, you know, and the guy would stand between her knees. My best friend would be with her boyfriend and I'd be with mine. We tortured those poor guys."

They both laughed. A car backfired in the distance. Molly twitched and got a faraway look on her face. Amy peered into her eyes for a moment, and then Molly was back.

Amy hopped onto the car hood, and Molly stood between her legs. She gently brushed the hair from Molly's face. "Now, where were we?" She leaned over and lost herself in the heat of Molly's mouth. Feeling bolder, she let her hands drift down and rub her back, tingling herself as she felt Molly shiver. She felt a pick at the back of her arm and swatted at it. *Fucking bloodsuckers.* She focused on Molly again, tracing her lips with her tongue, sliding her hands lower across her back, edging them forward. But this time the image of her card on the hundred-dollar bill popped into her mind. *I'm not forcing her to do anything.* She swatted at another bug biting the back of her neck. The soft drone of a lone mosquito echoed in her ear.

Molly slapped her calf. "I hate to say it, even with the bug repellent, the bugs are winning. Shall we head out?" She opened the car door and hit the power lock button unlocking the other door.

Mission failure thanks to those fucking mosquitos. Amy pulled the handle and sat down. "Would you have rather been with your best friend?" Amy looked over at Molly.

"Pardon?"

"On the hood of the car. You know, in high school."

Molly froze mid-air, about to push the key into the ignition. "You know, at the time, it didn't really occur to me that I could.

But no. I guess not. It would have been like kissing a sister." She fumbled with the keys. "Dang it." The key hit its mark, and the engine burst to life.

Amy said, "I dated girls my whole senior year. Man, did I get into some trouble." She sighed at the memories, then cleared her throat. "Parents don't give a shit if you sleep over, you know, because you're girls."

"I guess I was a bit of a late bloomer, then." Molly put the car in gear, and they rode through the darkened woods.

Details, woman! But none were forthcoming. "I bet you left a trail of broken hearts behind you."

"A lady doesn't discuss those things." Molly dropped her right hand off the steering wheel, then drummed her fingers on her knee. "Not really, no trail."

Amy watched to see if she moved her hand closer, then she'd pick it up. Nope. Molly grabbed the wheel with both hands. *I really have no game tonight. That's the problem; this isn't a game.* Amy reached for the radio knob.

"Put on whatever you want. There are some tapes in the glove box." Molly gestured toward the instrument panel. "Shotgun picks music. I like about everything."

Amy opened a box packed with plastic cassette tapes. She wasn't kidding. Heavy metal, country, dance music, soft rock. Everything was a current release and the boxes looked brand new. At the front were some Sony cartridges, probably mix tapes. She picked one up and slid it into the cassette player. Thumping bass rocked the back speakers, and Molly started bobbing her head. Amy had never heard the song.

"You don't listen to Salt-N-Pepa?" Molly asked.

"Who? Uh, no. That sounds like stuff they listen to in De-troit." *Oh good. Say something else racist, why don't you?*

"Really?"

"Wait, that came out wrong. I uh, guess I go more for classic rock." Amy looked up at the lights as they passed the ball field. "I think we have only two more games and the season's over. I hate fall ball, it gets too cold."

"Too cold to ride a motorcycle on the diamond?" Molly asked.

Amy said. "Touché, I deserve that one."

Molly slowed by the Dairy Queen. "Do you like ice cream?"

"Sure." Amy wistfully looked up the street to the Lounge. "That'd be great."

Molly ordered at the window while Amy sat at a cement bench. Molly returned with two soft serve cones dipped in chocolate. Handing one over, she said, "I hope it's not as buggy here."

"Doesn't seem to be." Amy tried to eat the cone with some amount of grace. "I can't think the last time I had one of these."

"I was pretty happy to see the town had a DQ. I mean, I've got some standards." Molly grinned. "All present company excepted."

"Oh yeah? And I was just going to say what a good time I was having on our teenager date. Maybe next time we can play Putt-Putt?" Amy bit at the sugar cone.

"I thought maybe we'd drive to Grand Rapids and go to the Club," Molly said.

"You go to the Club?" Amy asked.

"Not in a while, but it's still a women's bar?"

"Yeah, some guys but only on Saturday. The DJ is killer." Amy grinned. "You can tell a lot about someone by how they dance."

"Alright then, next time I'm off on a Saturday, prepare to be amazed." Molly rocked her shoulders while humming her own beat.

Amy wadded up the paper and made the shot to the trash can. Molly copied the move. Once in the car, Molly took her hand as they drove the short trip to the apartment building. She slowed the car and pulled up near the sidewalk.

Amy reached for the door handle and hesitated. Goodnight kiss or try to get upstairs? "Thanks for asking me to join you."

Molly popped the cassette out. "Maybe not an exciting evening, teenager date and all."

Amy touched Molly's arm. "I meant it. I had a good time."

"If you'd like to go on a longer hike, there's a cool homesteading site in the Blackstone forest. Sometimes people dress up in costumes. The rangers and that. Not the hikers, although I guess you could? Maybe you might want to go?"

"Actually, yes. I would like that a lot. A hard pass on the costume though," Amy said.

Molly frowned, "And I was hoping you'd go for the whole old-fashioned backwoods look." She winked.

Amy grinned. "If you just want a short hike, there's also a new trail along the river. They just finished a wood access bridge." She pulled open the door handle.

Molly said, "That sounds good, too. I'll call you. Good night." She got out and shut her door, waving as she went toward the lobby door.

Clearly, Amy was not headed upstairs with Molly. "I'll see you later."

Amy pulled out her keys and headed toward her Jeep, the custom chrome reflecting the light from the street lamp above. She heard the door to the apartment stairwell bang shut and knew that Molly was headed upstairs. She cranked the engine and slowly drove home.

At least they might go hiking again. *I hate hiking.*

CHAPTER 17

Amy wandered down the sidewalk of Main street carrying the red cardboard box with her new boots under one arm. The flower shop caught her eye and reminded her of Molly. She considered getting flowers and decided it might look too clingy. Maybe they wouldn't even go out again. They had a pretty good time hiking, but she'd called twice and Molly didn't have an answering machine. Pretty odd since she had so many other electronic toys. At any rate, Amy couldn't really call the police department and leave a message about a date. The parking lot was nearly empty at the beauty shop, so it might be a good time to see if Winnie could do a walk in.

Winnie called out, "Hey darling, good to see you. How's little Miss Meow?"

"She's good. A little hateful, you know, typical cat." Amy grinned. "Do you have some time for a lost cause?"

"Oh honey, I always have time for you. Just not always right away. But today I just had a cancelation. Mrs. Combes is sick. Come on and sit down." Winnie closed the tablet on the desk and plopped the pencil on it. She walked behind Amy in the chair and looked at her image in the mirror. "What are you thinking?"

Amy considered Winnie, her hair currently a hot red with tight curls. Nothing ventured. "Big. Bold. Whatever you think. I need a change. No holds barred."

Winnie ran her hands through Amy's hair and then leaned down. "How much time do you have, darling? We're going to go all out."

Immediately Amy felt her stomach drop and flip. Winnie threw a cape around her neck and snapped it. She spritzed a bit with a water bottle, then picked up the scissors. Amy watched her work in the mirror, a happy look of concentration on her face. "And how's the season going for you guys?"

"You know I just keep the books, but I think that new gal is really helping. She plays shortstop. Did you know that she's a policewoman?"

"You don't say?" Amy felt the pink creep up her neck and across her face.

"I see you do know who I'm talking about." Winnie spread some solution onto Amy's head and covered it with a cap. "You guys should meet. She's cute. And sweet."

Amy felt her neck heat up, certain a red flush crossed her face. "I have. Met her I mean."

"Oh, good. So, ask her out, already."

"We did. I mean, go out. We went hiking." Amy could feel the crimson heat across her cheeks.

"And?" Winnie pressed.

"She is nice." Amy watched in the mirror as Winnie sorted through the chemicals on her table.

"Are you two going out again? I don't care much for your ex, just between us." Winnie nodded. "You and Molly would be a good match."

"Uh. You think?" Amy stuttered. "I kinda thought it was too soon, you know."

"Nonsense. You just need a fresh look and a little confidence. Come on into the dryer while I get ready for the bleach." Winnie said.

Amy's face scrunched.

Winnie lowered the chair. "You said I could do anything. Trust me. You're going to love it."

Amy spent almost four hours at the salon. First Winnie bleached it out, then did some highlighting that required several more trips under the hair dryer. She had to admit that Winnie was amazing. Dirty blonde curls piled on top and then fell shoulder length, and if you didn't know it, you would never suspect the natural dark shades.

"Winnie, I am stoked. I look like a rock star. You are a wizard for sure." Amy tipped her head and watched the hair bounce across her shoulder.

"You are so sweet to say that. Before you go, I need to get you some product."

"Some what?"

"Product, you know, shampoo and stuff for your hair now that it's colored." Winnie started toward the shelves behind the desk. "What do you use now?"

"Prell?" Amy shrugged.

"Dear Joseph, Mary, and the wee donkey." Winnie began clutching bottles off the shelf. "Let me know if you need me to write this all down. Prell. For the love of Pete."

***

Amy was in the Gilbert and Son Garage combination snack room/waiting room when she overheard her mother. "I'm just saying that we should have talked about it before you installed a new security system. I actually agree with you that we need one since you didn't ask."

Her father grumbled something.

"And you need to be nicer to Amy. All you do is fuss at her. You need to be nice about her new hairstyle. It's quite a change."

"What have I ever said about her hair?"

"Now Frank, I am not kidding about this. Amy is a little sensitive about it. Do not tease her or I swear to god you'll sleep on the couch for a month."

"How bad could it be?" Frank answered, a slight lilt in his voice.

"I didn't say it looked bad, actually she looks pretty great. I expect a new flood of phone calls for her. Just don't say any-thing." Her mother probably thought that she was whispering.

Amy smiled. She tucked her hair into a ponytail and put on a cap to help keep grease out of her honey streaked tresses. She wasn't quite sure all that stuff Winnie sold her would actually clean her hair, despite the outrageous price she paid for it all. Beauty isn't cheap. She walked across the garage, her new boots stiff as she moved.

"Well, well! We must be paying you too much! New boots and a new hairdo." Frank carried an armload of boxes and set them on her work station. He smiled at Amy. "You look great, doll baby. I might need to bring my shotgun to the shop."

"Thanks, Pop. What's in the boxes?" Amy poked at the pile.

"A bunch of crap. Your mom signed us up for the town busi-ness league and the city hall guys sent all this stuff. Help your-self and throw out whatever you don't want. Who the hell puts drinks into a little foam jacket?" Frank flopped his hands forward. "Your mom took the frisbee for Rascal. Like that dog would chase it."

"Amy, phone," Rosie called across the shop.

Amy carried over a little spinning toy labeled "We're tops at Diamond Lake" and picked up the phone. "Amy Gilbert."

"Hi Amy, this is Cheryl. I wondered if you had some time this afternoon to talk to the boss. He seems pretty interested in add-ing you to the staff."

"Maybe after three?" Amy looked around to see where her mom was. "Let's make it 3:15 in case there's traffic."

Cheryl cooed, "Perfect. Will you have time after to go have a drink to celebrate?"

"Maybe. Let's see how it goes. I'll see you later." Amy hung up the phone.

"Do I understand that you're taking off early today? I hope our schedule isn't interrupting your busy social life?" Rosie snapped the ring on her Diet Coke can. "Dang these new ones that stay on the can. I broke my nail."

Amy tipped her head. "Maybe you can take time in your busy

schedule to file it down."

Her mother took a drink from her can, glaring over the top. "I'm just saying you aren't pulling your share. Your father depends on you."

"He depends on me so much he's just selling the shop. Is he going to move, because I for one wouldn't want to look out my window every day at someone else running Grandpa's garage?" Amy turned on her heels.

"Amy, come back here. You don't know how much it hurts him to sell. Amy!"

Amy picked up the orange airline and connected it to her drill. She squeezed the trigger and nothing happened. She glared at the drill, and then stomped to the air compressor.

Her sister came over. "What'cha doing?" Tina was the same height as Amy but maybe had twenty pounds on her.

Amy said, "My shit drill isn't working."

Tina walked behind her as they observed the lines on the way to the opposite side of the garage. When they reached the far side, Tina reached out and turned the lever. "Amy, it's not like you to miss this one. What's up?"

"Nothing is up."

Tina put her hands on her hips. "Been a few weeks since you moved in with Robin. You good with that?"

"Yeah, it's good." Amy squinted her eyes.

"I like your hair, by the way. It's really pretty."

"Thanks, Tink." Amy used her childhood nickname. She took a deep breath. "Can I ask you something? Does it bother you that Dad is selling the garage?"

"There's the elephant in the room. Yes. It does. Bother me. He hasn't asked me what I think. And I assume he doesn't care." Tina shrugged.

"Dad's a douche." Amy dropped her drill and picked up a rag.

"Dad just wants us to be a family. Not just because we work together."

"It was fine when he planned to hand it over to Michael," Amy alleged.

"I don't think he even considered asking us if we wanted to run the shop. He is a misogynist at heart." Tina put a hand on Amy's arm. She perked up. "But you know you could make a lot more down the road at the Ford place."

"I don't give a shit about money."

Tink laughed. "Well, I sure wouldn't be here if they didn't pay me."

"You have a good point." Amy dropped her rag on the bench. She knew she probably could make a lot more. But it wasn't the family business. Her family.

Tina picked up one of the foam can wraps. "What are you doing with these?"

"Giving them all to Robin. She loves those things." Amy bounced one. "What are you going to do once the shop is gone?"

"I assumed the new owners might keep us on for a while, but either way, I guess I'll finish my classes. I sure don't plan on turning wrenches forever." Tina squeezed a foam ball from the collection of promotional items.

Amy said, "I guess I haven't ever thought about not working in a garage. I'm just a grease monkey. I'm not book smart like you."

"You know, with the old gasoline tanks rusting underground, the new owners might just tear the place down." Tina tucked a lock of hair behind her ear. "Act cool. A cop is here."

"What?" Amy turned. "Oh, hi Molly. What's up?" She looked at Tina who's face showed mild amusement.

Tina put her hands in her pockets. "I'll just go build a bonfire in the parts room."

"Okay, good idea," Amy said oblivious, hurrying toward Molly.

"Your hair looks nice," Molly said.

Amy yanked off the ball cap and blushed. "Thanks, just felt like trying a new me."

"It's a change for sure." Molly stared.

"How's the car running?"

"Fine, just fine. Just you being in the car fixed it, you're magical."

"And delicious," Amy teased.

A blush started at Molly's collar, and a little nerve twitched on her face. "I got a concert flyer from a guy at work. He's in a band. Well, sort of thrasher music really."

"Who else is playing?"

Molly handed over a colored paper. "Husker Du is the headliner. I thought you might be interested. It's an all-day mosh."

"Cool beans," Amy said. She reached for the flier and just as she was about to take it, Molly dropped it and they both bent to catch it. Amy snagged it. "Must be a draft."

"Must be," Molly said. She stuck her hands in her front pockets. "I thought maybe we could both go. If you don't mind being out in the heat, it's outdoors."

"What if I get sweaty?" Amy winked.

Molly hesitated. "I could bring a cooler?"

A long silence fell between them. *Come on, think. Ask her something.* Amy tucked her thumbs into her back pockets.

Molly asked, "Are you free later tonight? I get off the clock early today. Maybe grab a bite?"

Amy scuffed her boot. "Sorry, I have plans." She panicked to realize she was going for drinks. "To golf. Don't tell my coach. She'd kill me."

"Yeah. Jams up your softball swing. Okay. Um. See you." Molly turned and walked out of the garage.

Amy watched her walk out. *Why didn't I ask her if she could go out another night?* She glanced at the flier, then absently folded the paper and stuck it in her shirt pocket.

Tina skittered over. "And who is that?"

"Molly," Amy said.

"You like her, don't you?"

"Well, I do love the way those pants hug her ass. It must be the cargo pockets."

"Too much information." Tina held up her hands. "I think you need someone with a kind heart this time. Just saying."

"I don't know what I need, but I think I know what I want."

Amy rubbed her chin.

Tina smiled. "That's a good start. I have a job to get off my hoist." She turned and walked off.

***

She looked at her watch and headed toward her car. She parked under Robin's carport. She ran up the stairs. With no thought, she grabbed some casual clothes. A job interview at a garage wouldn't require a suit. After a quick wardrobe change, she went back down. She grabbed a Coke from the fridge and went down the back steps. As she passed the garage, the sun reflected on the sign: Gilbert and Son. She jammed the accelerator and headed to the highway.

CHAPTER 18

C heryl's suggestion to work at the Ford dealership had seemed just polite conversation the last time they hit golf balls at the range. If Amy's dad sold the place, she'd need a new job anyway. What else did she know how to do? Might as well get a jump on it.

She steered into the parking lot where her Jeep stuck out as the only non-Ford in the row. She slid out and Cheryl appeared at her side. Amy had known Cheryl forever, in that small-town way that everyone sort of knows who everyone else is. They hadn't really been friends until recently when Amy found herself single and Cheryl showed up. She was fun; and as Robin said, there was no harm in hanging out. Amy smiled. Looking over the lanky frame inside a summer weight skirted suit, there was no harm at all. The silk blouse stretched in just the right places. Cheryl was hot.

Amy said, "I hope you haven't been waiting on me."

"Oh no, I just was right here when you pulled in." Cheryl grinned at her like Amy was made of hot fudge and Cheryl was on a diet. "Look at you with your new hair. I just love it." Her voice had raised at least an octave. "So sexy."

Amy smiled back, although her mouth was suddenly like cotton. She was a little nervous about the interview, a little more than nervous about her family finding out about the interview, and truth be told, a lot nervous about Cheryl. She took a deep breath, one step at a time. They had time at the bar to flirt.

"You go on inside and I'll go find Ray," Cheryl said, heading toward a side door.

The lobby of the dealership was all glass with a number of shiny new vehicles parked at angles. The new Mustang really was a good-looking car.

A voice behind her said, "You'd look great in that car, not that you don't look great now."

Amy felt herself stiffen. She had been insulated from the harassment that comes with being a woman in a man's world. At the family garage, it was a non-issue. It caught her off guard. Maybe it was a salesman and not Ray, the owner? She turned and looked into the face she saw on the TV commercials, same primped hair, same glowing smile. Owner. "I'm afraid I'm more of a truck kind of woman." *Can I really work for this jerk?*

His smile froze. "We sell those as well. Ms. Gilbert?"

"Yes," she answered, pasting on a warm smile.

"Call me Ray. Let's chat some, shall we?" He opened the door behind him and held it. "You can see the entire garage from this office."

It was an impressive facility. There was a service desk with three advisors, and a line of mechanics, ten stalls on each side. On the distant side, an alignment pit allowed for two vehicles at once, and a staffed parts window could be seen on the near side. The cashier's office had two ladies who both waved to the boss. There was a full two-lane write-up area, where at least 20 cars could park. Amy knew he wanted her to be impressed. She was. He was quite clearly pleased with himself.

Amy asked, "How many vehicles do you turn a week?"

He shrugged. "I'd like you to meet Bob. He's the manager." Bob came through the door as if on cue. "How many units a week?"

Bob smiled and reached for her hand to shake it. "Glad to meet you. Summer hours, about 300. Winter, less."

Amy nodded. "And how many hours do the mechanics usually turn?"

"Most are here about 45, and usually clock 40. The front-end guy is a beast and he turns 55 every week. I had a chance to look at your file, you're a Jack of all trades, excuse me, a Jill of all trades." Bob rocked on his heels with nervous energy.

Amy smiled, attentive.

Bob waved his arm toward the window. "The shop is arranged by electrical, tune-up, front end, and major engine. Most of the guys can do all of it, it's just more efficient to keep the work areas separated. What do you prefer to work on?"

"Our shop is a little less restricted. I've done it all, but I guess I prefer electrical and tune-up. More diagnosis, more thinking. That's the future."

Ray looked down at Amy and said, "And less physical."

Amy cooly replied, "I assume that you use hoists for engines?"

Bob quickly said, "Yes, but Ms. Gilbert is quite right. The days of the backyard mechanic are almost over with all the fancy electronics and computers. Some of our older guys are afraid to mess with them."

Ray, the owner of three dealerships, looked preoccupied. "Bob, I have a meeting; make her an offer she won't refuse."

Bob walked with Amy back to the showroom floor, going on about health care and retirement. Amy had to admit she was not much of a saver, and maybe a retirement plan was a good idea. He offered her his hand and she shook it. She agreed to call him as soon as she had a firm start date in mind.

Waving at Amy, Cheryl scurried across the tile floor as quick as her high heels would allow. "Ray looks happy. And when Ray's happy…"

"You're happy too." Amy quoted his latest jingle. "This is a really great place. The only issue is timing and that's out of my hands. As soon as Dad sells the garage, I'm switching to Ford." She gazed at the shiny white Mustang, wondering if it came in orange. She'd forgotten to ask what the employee discount was on new vehicles.

Cheryl clapped her hands together. "That's fantastic. Let's go celebrate."

They headed to the local country club where Cheryl was a

member. In the parking lot, Cheryl rolled down her window. "How about we just head to the nineteenth hole?"

That was fine with Amy. Even the driving range would screw up her batting, and she'd been working hard to improve her hitting. She parked and headed toward Cheryl. They walked into the quiet lobby and around to the bar. A big screen TV was on every wall, each playing a different sporting event. The round tables were low with leather rolling chairs. Cheryl put up a finger and a young man in black pleated pants and a tuxedo shirt hustled over to take their order. His piled up curly hair looked like he stepped right out of a music video on MTV.

Amy sat down and rolled the chair back and forth. "Come here often?"

Cheryl laughed. "So cute, and so funny. How is it that we don't know each other better? I don't remember you from high school. You hung out with the jocks, I suppose."

"Not particularly, that was my brother's thing. I was part of the racing team. We had a couple cars we took to the drag strip. Wasn't really encouraged, but we won a lot of money."

Cheryl took Amy's hand. "I just bet you did."

This was a country club, not a gay bar, and Amy looked around. No one seemed to even notice them. She pulled her hand back anyway.

The waiter set down the beverages, each with a teensy paper umbrella and a column of fruit on a stick.

Cheryl picked out the plastic stick and bit down, slowly pulling the first fruit piece off into her mouth. "I'd tell you what these are called, but it's nasty." She giggled and blew Amy a kiss.

Amy felt her throat tighten, and her palms started to sweat. She studied the mysterious naughty named cocktail. She couldn't decide if she was supposed to drink it out of the teensy straw or fight with the embellishments to reach the rim of the glass. Cheryl seemed content to consume the fruit. Out of the corner of her eye, she saw someone headed directly for them.

A middle-aged man with slicked black hair approached their table and reached his hand out. "Cheryl, doll. Great to see you.

Have you met my niece? She's new in town." Cheryl clutched his hand with one hand, his coat sleeve with the other, and winked at him. With his free hand, he waved over a woman that had just stood up. Amy watched as Molly approached the table, looking from Cheryl to Amy. Molly's expression never changed.

"Oh Yancy, don't tell me you have a niece old enough to be in a bar?" Cheryl released her grip on him and twisted around in her chair.

Amy watched in a painful slow motion. *Why is Molly here? Why not, but why am I here with Cheryl and not her? Because I'm a jerk.* Molly walked the span between them like a runway model, confident and cool. *Shit.* Her hand shaking, Amy grabbed the glass, shoved the decorations to the side and drained the ridiculously strong elixir. She sat down the glass and looked up at Molly who had a troubled look on her face.

Yancy adjusted his tie and then put his hand on Molly's back. "On my wife's side, of course, all the Hepscott women are beautiful. Molly this is my friend, Cheryl." Molly nodded. "She works at the dealership. Great salesperson. I'm sure she can take care of things if you decide to upgrade that Mustang. The new one is super sharp if you know what I mean."

"I do take care of things," Cheryl cooed. "And this is Amy. Soon to be from the dealership as well."

Amy sunk lower in the chair; her dad was sure to find out before she could tell him. "Nice to see you. Aren't you on the city council?"

"Sure am, Yancy Wilson, always at your service." Yancy seemed pleased he was recognized. Amy was surprised he didn't whip out business cards. He pointed to his niece. "You don't want to see Molly at work; she's the chief of police."

Cheryl frosted over. "How interesting."

Amy sputtered, "Hi, Molly. Maybe we can golf sometime?" She cringed. *Neither of them is dressed for golf. Maybe she doesn't even play.*

Molly waited for a beat to answer. "It's not good for your softball swing."

Yancy took Molly's elbow and they both headed toward the door. Amy's stomach churned as she watched them leave.

As they walked away, Cheryl picked up her glass. "Maybe at the public course. Her uncle is the member here."

She's catty. She knows I don't have a membership either. Amy asked, "How do you know I don't want to golf with Yancy? He's a councilman after all." She laughed. To her relief, so did Cheryl.

"Where were we? Oh yes. This drink." Cheryl lifted her glass and took a sip. "Your glass is empty. Waiter?"

Another glass appeared in front of them. After the third round, Amy was starting to wish that she'd eaten more at lunch. After the fourth round, Cheryl took her hand again.

This time Amy pulled it back and put it in her lap. "I think I may have given you the wrong impression."

"No, you make an excellent impression." Cheryl didn't hide the sweep she did of Amy head to toe. "Would you like to see the place? Or maybe head to mine?"

"I'm sorry, I have to go. I shouldn't have come with you in the first place. But thank you for asking." Amy's head swam when she stood up. She hoped she didn't look as drunk as she felt. She just missed whatever Cheryl said as she followed her up the hallway, but it sounded a little sharp. The blast of the cool night air on her face didn't change her stagger. She could hear Cheryl's shoes click as she tottered off to her car. Amy went to her car door and dropped the keys as she went to unlock the door.

A voice behind her said, "Well, good evening."

Amy turned half bent over and rammed her head into the mirror. She grabbed her head and stood upright, her elbow bent upwards. "Ow. Oh, hi. I was surprised to see you here. How come you're by my car? Did you wait for me?"

Molly grabbed her before she wobbled backward into the Jeep. "Yep. I assume you weren't going to try and drive yourself home."

"It's just a couple miles up the road." Amy put her hands on her hips. "But you know what? I think that may be a bad idea."

Molly asked, "Why?"

"Because Cheryl is really mad at me because I left and wouldn't have sex with her. Shhh. Don't tell, but I like somebody else. She's a cop. And Cheryl is super mad and she might ram my car."

"That's your reason?" Molly shook her head. She opened the door to her Mustang, and half shoved Amy into the front seat. Molly went around to the driver's side door and climbed in. She cranked the engine and drove off. "You have to promise me you'll say something if you're going to barf."

"Oh, I don't ever get sick. I'm really healthy." Amy took Molly's hand. "I should have just gone out with Molly, I mean you. I got a new job and now I feel bad."

Molly pulled her fingers away. "Why do you feel bad?"

"Well, my dad will be sad I don't want to work there anymore. And I feel bad I had drinks with Cheryl and I wanted to have drinks with you." Amy started to paw the interior door panel.

"What are you doing?" Molly asked.

"Trying to find the window crank. I need air." Amy's head bounced off the glass as Molly abruptly pulled to the side of the road.

She reached over Amy and grabbed the door handle. She pushed the button to release the seat belt.

Amy belched. "See, I told you I don't get sick." And with that, she threw up.

When Amy opened her eyes, she was laying on a couch with a blanket over her. She was still dressed, but her shoes were off. She spotted an Eastern Michigan cup on the table, next to a plate with toast and a bottle of aspirin. *Shit, I'm at Molly's place.* Her Jeep keys were laying next to the plate. A tiny marmalade ginger kitten stared at her from on top of a kitty tower.

"Hello, little kitty. How did I get here? Where is your mommy?" Amy said.

The cat blinked his tiny blue eyes. There was a note.

Good morning,

Stay as long as you need to. There's more juice in the fridge.

Cheeto is my new cat. Call me when you're up to it.

Molly

Amy sat down the note, and took two aspirin, forcing herself to drink the juice. Sugar helped a hangover.

"I don't get your mommy. I thought she'd be mad." She managed a bite of toast before she fell back asleep.

CHAPTER 19

Molly was starting to think she spent more time in her police car than in her office. In a small-town department, she wore a lot of hats, but this was getting out of hand. She would have to look at the schedule. She heard the voice over the radio and knew it was Doug. He had been on the force right out of the academy, just a year behind her. Another wreck out on the back highway. Single car. She reached over and flicked on her lights and floored the accelerator. She slid the car behind the other rescue vehicles, blocking the lane at an angle. She pulled on her reflective vest and adjusted the strap around her.

The car was sideways against a tree, the windshield blown out where a driver had exited the vehicle. *Why couldn't people wear a seat belt? It's not that hard.* She looked toward Doug. "Is a bus coming?"

Doug shook his head. "Yeah, but the coroner is coming too. Stupid kids dragging. If you see a brown G van pull up, that's his dad. Stop him. It's not pretty."

"Roger that." Molly scanned the scene, and the two rookie officers were already taking pictures and measuring tracks on the pavement. Not much else to do except wait for the coroner to call the death, and then finish the investigation. The tow truck was waiting to clear the wreckage from the scene, if possible, without civilian interference. "Hey, put up some tape. We don't need the Courier photographer getting a nice grisly photo for his family to see in the paper."

Her pager went off and she peered at the number. She walked back to her cruiser and flicked on the radio. "Dispatch, connect me to the Fire Chief."

After an eternity, a voice came back. "He says the water rescue team is at the lake park. They got a floater. Been a while. They need a police report; should he call the sheriff?"

"No, I'm on my way." Molly stepped out of her car. "Hey Doug, the coroner needs to head to the park beach when he's done here. Tell him to dump his lunch box before he heads out. We have a floater."

At the lake, it was obvious the body was dead; it must have been in the water for weeks. Molly canceled the coroner and headed back to the station. Not much could be done until an autopsy was completed.

In her office, she doodled on the pink message sheet. *If it walks like a duck and quacks like a duck, it must be a duck. Amy. 555-2932* It's easy to give up drinking while your puking on the side of the road. It's harder in the middle of a bar. She picked up the phone.

"Hi, how're you feeling?" Molly asked.

"Like an idiot. I'm not sure I even want to know what I did last night," Amy said.

"Before you threw up or after?" Molly asked.

"Oh no. No. No. No. Don't tell me. Thanks though. For everything."

"I've had a lot of practice picking up the pieces. What's with the duck thing?"

Amy paused a while and then said, "I was thinking about some of the stuff from our chat. You know. Drinking. Maybe I do need to cut back."

Molly sighed and started doodling again. "Only you can decide that."

"Well, I'm cutting back," Amy insisted. "I was wishing I'd gone with you instead, but Cheryl helped me get a job. I messed up."

"Actually, I agree with you," Molly admitted. "It's okay. I like you, and I just don't want to see you get hurt."

Amy sniffed. "Even after all that?"

Maybe especially because of all that. "Yeah. But don't do it for me." Molly shifted in her chair.

"Well, okay, I can just stop for a while and prove I can," Amy said.

"Your call."

"Shit, I gotta go. Robin just walked in the house. Thanks again for everything."

Molly looked at the doodles on her paper. A little cowgirl was shooting bottles off a fence. *Now I need a drink.* Her phone rang. "Chief Gorman."

"There's a Lady McKenzie here to see you."

She pinched her nose between her eyes. "I'll be right there."

***

The next morning, Molly was surprised when she got the papers in the fax machine from the coroner. He had already completed the preliminary report on the floater but did not want to give the identity except to the police, preferably her. What better way to start the day than a trip to the morgue? She grudgingly drove over to the hospital. At the front office, she confirmed the room number of the morgue and walked to the end of the rear hall. She stopped at the nondescript door, no number, just a sign reading 'staff only' in small letters.

Molly braced herself before she knocked on the door. Even with the sanitizers of a morgue, the smell of the dead bodies still choked her, and she suspected the floater, half decomposed at best, was going to be pretty ripe.

She pushed open the door. Two sides of the room had silver metal countertops, a fish scale hung in one corner. Through a glass cabinet, she could see shelves with trays with surgical tools. In the back, a few hinged doors covered the refrigerated storage areas. A typical surgical table stood in the center of the room. An older man sat at a stool at a small table writing. "Dr. Eastman, good morning."

He looked up. "Molly, yes, yes indeed. I'm sorry, I mean Chief Gorman. Been a few years since I said those words. Your grandfather was a good man. We used to golf together. Gurmond means protector *auf Deutsch*, am I right? Well, never mind all that. Welcome." The doctor had a white shock of hair tufted on his head, his eyes glistening behind thick glasses. Dr. Eastman opened a door and slid out a tray holding what was left of a human body.

Molly felt her stomach tighten as the smell hit her nose, sort of a rotten scent with a weird sweetness. "Thanks for letting me stop by."

"Take a couple of deep breaths through your nose. I know it seems contrary, but you won't smell it after a moment or two." He flipped a sheet back off the top half of the corpse.

She forced herself to take a third breath in a row. "The body has been here only a few hours and you already have a preliminary report?"

"Yes. I'm fairly certain that this is Barry, I mean Chief Tristan. Right height, been in the water since sometime this winter. Bits of orange hunting clothing."

She stared at the bluish bloated corpse on the table. It was grotesque in shape, the stretched skin from the decomposition lay wrinkled and slack as the autopsy cuts let the gasses out of the abdomen. Where the skin had split, a waxy substance showed. The facial features were unidentifiable. One hand was missing. Her stomach lurched again at the ghastly sight, but she forced it down.

"How do you know how long it's been in the water?" Molly asked.

"In layman's terms, the corpse wax. The fatty tissues turn into a substance, not unlike soap. Preserves the body. Somewhat." He lifted a piece of chest muscle and pointed to a section. "All this tissue would be gone in a month or less in warmer water."

Molly furrowed a brow. "Why did it come up now?"

"Oh, it's probably been up and back down a time or two.

Eventually, the critters clean it up and the bones stay down." He casually pointed to another area. "This is a clear nick, though. I am afraid this man was shot. Large bullet, likely a heart shot. Shattered this rib on the way out. There's too much decomposition to be sure if he was dead or alive when he hit the water."

"Why do you think it's Barry?"

"Two things. One, he's missing. And two; I've been the doctor in this town for a long time. He has a wicked scar across the back of his head. I sewed up a young minibike rider once upon a time, about half his scalp was torn up. I'll call the Sheriff once I confirm the identity with dental records." He squinted at Molly. "You favor your nana, but you act like your papa. He was a good man. This is pretty exciting for a little town like ours, but it'll take the clerk at the office a while to find the records. I want to be sure."

Molly nodded. "Thanks, Doc. I'll call the Sheriff and let him know we found the body."

"Only if you think it will be helpful for him to know sooner than later." He lightly touched her arm. "I asked for you to come for a reason. You might also be extra careful. If this wasn't an accident, you might be in danger too."

She scoffed, "I highly doubt that. Thanks for the info. And for the record, I don't golf as well as my grandfather, but I would be happy to hit the links with you sometime."

She strolled down the hall lost in thought. She hadn't really considered what would happen at the end of her stint as interim police chief. Chief had been her first professional goal. At her car, she looked around the parking area of the small hospital, with cement benches placed under trees and planters full of annuals. This small town isn't too bad. Maybe things will work out with Amy. She took a deep breath of the flower-scented air and got in the car. She drove around the perimeter of the town to the police station, the whole way thinking about what Dr. Eastman said about her safety. It's time to be proactive.

Molly headed for her office, then locked the door. She picked up the phone and dialed.

"Sheriff's office, this is Reed." His deep voice suited what she knew was a large frame.

"Sheriff Reed, this is Gorman over at Diamond Lake. I think we have the remains of Chief Tristan in the morgue. I thought you'd want to get the medical examiner to pick him up."

"Of course. Where did you find him?" he asked.

"He was a floater in the lake." Molly paused. "He's been there a while."

"Man, he deserved better than that. He was a good man. I'll make sure Harley gets him right away. Did you call his wife?"

"No, I thought you might stop by since you know her better than I do. There's no rush. She won't be able to make an I.D. and Dr. Eastman is waiting on dental records." Molly cleared her throat. "Hey, you got a minute?"

"For you, always," Reed said. "What's up?"

"I wonder if you could tell me how these small towns handle internal affairs?"

"Huh. I didn't expect that but I know better than to ask questions." The Sheriff paused. "We have a regional guy, ex-cop, he's straight up. Carlton Jeffries. He conducts what they call professional standards reviews. Same as IA basically. Need his number?"

"If you have it."

"555-RATS."

"Really?" Molly said.

"I am serious as a heart attack." Reed paused. "Is there anything I can do to help?"

"I have a situation brewing here," Molly said. "Can you keep it under your hat that I even asked?"

"Asked me what?"

"Exactly." Molly smiled. "Thanks." She touched the button to hang up the call, then dialed the number. "Carlton Jeffries, please?" She picked up a pen, absently tapping with the Muzak playing. She was about to hang up when a stuffy voice answered.

"Jeffries here."

"This is Molly Gorman, interim Chief at Diamond Lake. I need to start a formal investigation."

"Can you speak freely?" Carlton asked.

Molly stood up and turned up the radio sitting high on the file cabinet. Al Greene floated around her office. "Yeah."

"Okay, I've got some paperwork you need to fill out. What is the nature of the alleged violations?"

"Burglary ring, involves at least two officers, maybe more." Molly stared at her fingernails. "What's the protocol?"

"We need pictures, otherwise it's pretty hard to prosecute. Can you set up a sting?" Carlton coughed. "Sorry, seasonal allergies are killing me."

"I'm concerned about the costs going through financial, and more importantly of tipping them off." Molly tapped her fingers on the desk.

"I can get you video cameras, but you'll have to set it up. Do you want the fence too?"

Molly answered, "Yes, but if I set up a sting shop, they'll know something's up. I might be able to get the sheriff to put someone undercover in the pawn shop for a while."

"Up to you. There are other ways to get him. Can you meet me in Two Rivers police station at three? I have an office on the second floor."

"Sure thing. Thanks." Molly hung up the phone as Elvis wailed about "Suspicious Minds." *What are these guys up to?* She tapped her fingers on the desk, lost in thought.

CHAPTER 20

The main shop at the Gilbert and Son Garage was unusually quiet for the middle of the afternoon. Her mother had left and Tina had been working in the office for a while. Amy wiped the last of her wrenches with a light coating of oil and laid it on the tray. She slid the drawer shut, and wiped the front of the toolbox. Using the broom and dust bin, she swept up the cat litter soaking up the earlier coolant spill. The rotted hose had split just as she had reached for the loosened clamp. The scent wasn't that different than those drinks at the golf course. Her thoughts drifted to Molly. Using the garden hose hanging on the post, she sprayed off the floor and finished with a squeegee on a long pole.

Tina broke the silence. "Amy, can you come in here for a minute?"

Amy wiped her hands and dropped the towel into the trash. "Be right there." She drank the last of her Sprite and tossed the can into the recycle box. She clicked off her radio and took a dozen steps to the office. Her sister was tapping the keyboard by the computer.

"Hi Tink, what are you doing? Taking over for Mom? You know she hates when you dig around in her files."

She spun away from the computer. "I'm not just digging. I've been helping mom with the payroll and I noticed something. I made a little chart of everyone's actual clock hours and work turned hours for the last two months."

Amy studied the chart Tina slid in front of her on the desk. "Wow, I am looking at total chaos."

Tina sighed. "Here is your line. You turn in about two hours a week more than you clock. I do the same. Olivia kicks both our asses and does more than eight over. Donny was here almost 60 hours and I think that he's skimming off the shop."

"I still don't follow; you know I hate math." Amy frowned.

Tina tapped the paper. "Look, he turned in thirty-five hours last week. He was here until 7 every night. Olivia left by 6 and turned 55 hours."

Amy scratched her head. "I don't see what you're saying. He's here longer and turns in fewer hours. Maybe he botched a job? How would that be skimming the shop?"

"Donny doesn't botch jobs." Tina looked around. "I think he's taking payments directly from customers and passing the books."

Amy leaned back. "Donny's family. He wouldn't steal from us."

"Maybe. Maybe not. But something is going on back there. I just know Olivia would be really pissed if I accuse him of something and don't have any proof," Tina said. "Redheads and their temper."

"You want me to go look around for work orders or something?" Amy asked. "Do you think Mom is on to Donny too?"

"Maybe I should ask her?" Tina closed the computer down.

Amy studied the rows and columns. Tink had colored the over clock hours with pink and all the shortages in neon yellow. They all had a spot of yellow or two, but Donny had yellow in every column.

Tina covered the chart with blank payroll paper and abruptly stood as she looked behind Amy. "So then if Mom isn't here, you just put it in this column."

"Huh?" Amy asked.

"What are my girls up to?" Frank reached out and squeezed Amy's shoulders. "I thought you didn't care about this place anymore?"

Ah, that's why she changed topics so fast. Amy shrugged. "It wouldn't hurt to pay a little more attention."

He looked her in the eye. "I thought you'd already be at the dealership looking for a job. They got a pretty sweet set up."

Amy shrugged again. *He knows. How?* "The sign still says Gilbert, and as long as it does, I'll be here."

Tina added, "We all are in, Dad. Except you. You want to just sell it."

"I do not. I'm getting too old for this business. It's either sell it or hire someone who wants to actually work around here," Frank said.

"That's not fair," Amy said. "You know we all work hard. It's our family, not just a job. We are loyal to Grandpa and his legacy. Family first."

"As long as you are loyal, I will be." His voice was chilly. His eyes shifted. "Your mom wants you all to come for dinner on Sunday."

As he walked off, Tina hissed, "I'm telling you, something fishy is going on here."

Amy nodded. "Yes, for damn sure. I have to go. Don't say anything to Mom yet. I'll try to keep a better eye on what's happening in the body shop."

Amy thought about Don as she walked home. He and Olivia had been together forever. He was a know-it-all, but generally nice enough. Stealing? There must be some other explanation. She keyed her way into the house, dumped some kitty bitties into the bowl for Meow and headed upstairs. She still smelled sweetly greasy from the coolant. She stripped and tossed the uniform into the bin, and turned on the water to the shower. Meow wound around her feet as she waited for the water to warm. "I'm excited too. I didn't expect Molly to call me after the other night."

The cat rubbed her leg and started to purr.

"I'm not going to blow it this time. Be prepared to be charmed off your feet, Molly Gorman."

Meow stared at her with a slow blink. She walked around the mat twice and curled into a ball on the corner of the bath mat. Amy smiled.

Amy tested the temperature and then stepped inside. She let the hot water steam all the shop smells from her skin. The first product smelled like a fruit salad, and the follow-up product had the same general scent. *I better be on the lookout for bees. I smell like a meadow of wildflowers.* She shaved her legs, all the way, just in case. Everything south seemed trimmed enough, she patted herself dry, still amazed to see the mountain of curly blonde hair on her head. Winnie was a magician. She gently blew it dry, spraying the can of hair product three as she went along. One more scrub of her teeth and she was fully transformed from greasy car mechanic to vixen.

When she called, Molly surprised her with the last-minute invite to watch a movie at her place rather than more hiking. Amy was going to make the most of her opportunity. Already in the skimpiest underwear she owned, with matching bra, Amy stared in her closet for a while, considering her options. Comfortable, easy to remove, and soft. Good color…what was best with her new hair color? Maybe a hot pink. Something playful to strip out of, not a t-shirt. She held a flowered shirt against her favorite parachute pants. Nope. Acid wash? Nope, the major damage jeans. Maybe. She hung up the shirt and picked up the shirt that matched the patches in the knees of the pants.

"What do you think, Meow?"

The cat lifted her head from her pillow.

"I agree, this is it."

She rummaged around the floor of the closet and picked up her tennis shoes.

She pulled on the selected clothes, blousing the shirt and adjusting the fluff of her hair. She spritzed a cloud of perfume and walked through it. Amy added a dab in the hot spots behind her ears for good measure. She hadn't even reached her car yet and her pulse was pounding.

CHAPTER 21

Molly whipped open the door to her apartment before Amy could knock. "Hi, come on in." She stepped back to allow Amy to enter. "I got a couple movies from Blockbuster, one's a comedy and one's a thriller. I didn't know what you liked."

As the stereo was playing, a low buzz emanated from the right speaker.

Amy tilted her head. "I think you blew that speaker; do you hear the buzz?" she said as she kicked off her shoes.

"What?" Molly said.

"You don't hear that?" Amy asked again.

"Hear what?" Molly grinned.

"I said, oh wait. That was funny. Do you want me to look at it?" Amy was already touching the cabinet.

"I was hoping to not share your attention with a speaker, but if you must." Molly sat on the couch. "What's the deal with that lady at the golf course?"

Amy was tipping the cabinet, tapping the fasteners. *Uh oh. I wish I could remember what the hell happened that night. Sound casual. Deflect.* "Who? Cheryl? She's just someone I know. Helped me get an interview at the dealership."

"You really are leaving your family business? That surprises me," Molly said.

"They've made me an offer that's hard to resist."

"Look out!"

Cheeto took a flying pounce and landed on Amy's back.

"Wow, naughty kitty." Amy reached around and plucked the cat off her shirt. She then rubbed her nose on his. "You didn't mean it, did you? Here, you sit right there." She put the little orange terror onto a pillow on the floor. He tipped his head and continued to watch her.

"I'm sorry, we haven't had much time for training."

Amy laughed. "You think you can train a cat? That's ambitious."

"Well, he's a really smart cat." Molly shrugged.

With that, Cheeto ceremoniously began to lick his privates.

"I can see." Amy said, "Cheeto is a perfect name. He's adorable."

"It's a good thing. He was up half the night meowing until I let him sleep with me," Molly grumbled.

"Uh oh. You've already ruined him." Amy scooped him up and rubbed his head. He responded with a full claw attack. "He's a little stinker, isn't he?" She sat him back down.

Molly tapped the carpet and he scampered to her. "When do you start at the Ford dealer?"

"My dad is trying to sell the place. I don't really want to leave." Amy sat the speaker down. "I'm not sure I want to run it either."

"Nothing ventured, nothing gained." Molly leaned back into the couch, then jumped up. "Can I get you a drink? I got both Coke and Sprite." She laid the now sleeping kitten on the cat tower next to a little stuffed toy.

"A Sprite would be great." Amy followed Molly into the kitchen. The entire refrigerator was blank, no pictures of family. Not even a magnet. No clues there. "I wasn't one of the kids that always knew what she wanted to be. I just sort of became a mechanic. How about you?"

Molly twisted the lid off two bottles and handed one to Amy. "My grandpa was the police chief here when I was a kid. My brother and I used to spend a week or two up here every summer. I adored my grandpa, and I wanted to be just like him. Even if he thought women belonged in the kitchen."

"Old fashioned is a pain in the ass." Amy took a sip from the bottle. "Wow, this is so much better plain."

"Should I have given you a lemonade instead?" Molly smiled.

Amy's pulse raised a notch. *Who's chasing who*? "I'll behave," Amy said. "If you want me to."

Molly reached out and took Amy's hand. "I'm still undecided."

Amy smiled her best flirty smile. "Can I help you make up your mind?" She leaned in and laid a smoldering kiss on her mouth. Amy felt Molly resist for a moment, and then shivered as Molly kissed back. *Damn, this woman is delicious.* Amy pulled her closer, and their bodies curved into each other perfectly. Only slightly taller, Amy looked up into her eyes, always her go-to move. "I'm so glad you gave me a chance, after how we first met."

Molly's face was starting to flush. She took Amy's face in her hands. "I believe in second chances." She kissed Amy softly. "And third chances." Another kiss. "Sometimes as many as it takes." She buried her hands in Amy's hair, kissing down her neck to her open shirt collar.

"Oh, I am so glad." Amy sighed. She closed her eyes. Molly smelled of some fruity shampoo, with a hint of something spicy and exotic. Her shirt had the softness of cotton after about a hundred times through the wash. The stereo started playing an old Chicago album. She pulled Molly closer and began to sway with the tempo. As they slowly twirled around the room, Amy listened to the lyrics of "Colour My World" and choked up. *I can sleep with her because I like her. It doesn't have to be because of Robin and her stupid bet.*

"I don't mean to rush or pressure you, I just really like you," Molly said. "Sometimes I jump in a little too fast."

"Should I put on a seat belt?" Amy asked.

Molly stopped dancing. "How about I give you a kiss and you can return it if you want."

"Wow. That's as smooth as a well-aged bourbon."

"Better than admitting I don't have any condoms?" Molly laughed.

Amy said, "I was going to ask what you wanted for breakfast in the morning."

Molly snuggled in closer. "How about we stop talking so much?"

Amy pecked her cheek. "I was just thinking the very same thing." She went in for the finish, touching her mouth firmly onto Molly's, her tongue probing into her mouth while her hands roamed down to her backside, pulling her hard against her body. Her mind was only on Molly, how warm she felt, how she tasted like the lemon-lime pop. Dizzy, she swayed into Molly until there was no space between them at all.

Molly brushed fingers along Amy's sides, adding a torrent to the waterfall below. Amy thought her knees would buckle when she touched her breast, cupping it then rubbing against her through the shirt.

Molly's voice seemed far away. "Do you want to go to the bedroom? Otherwise, I'm afraid we'll end up on the kitchen table."

Amy caught her breath. "Table? Maybe another time." She winked at Molly. *We could be on the balcony and I wouldn't care.* "I want to be totally up front. I have very little self-control on a good day."

Molly grinned. "I was sort of counting on that." She took Amy's hand and led her to the back room, a queen size bed took up the wall under the window. The multicolored quilt looked hand made. The evening sky was a red glow through the window sheers, casting a soft pink around the room. The ceiling fan turned, barely moving the air. *Is it hot in here? I'm already sweating.* Molly sat down on the bed and scooted her shoes off. Amy stepped between her knees and pushed her flat back on the mattress. She slid her thigh against Molly's crotch and pushed against her as she buried her face in her neck.

Amy rolled next to Molly and started to unbutton her shirt.

Molly took her hand. "You've done this before, right? I'm not sure I'm up to listening to you talk about it half the night."

"Are you kidding me?" Amy said. Molly started to tickle her. Amy giggled. "Yes, maybe a few times."

Amy's pants were about to soak through, and she would start getting cramps soon if she didn't get some relief. *So many dirty thoughts at one time. I am going straight to hell in twenty religions.* She smiled. "I'm a fast learner. And I think we're overdressed for this party." She stood up and started to undo her pants.

Molly had already shed her shirt and was unhooking her bra. At least a C cup. Her flat stomach had just a hint of a six-pack. *Damn, she is perfect.* Amy froze just watching. Molly dropped her pants, and Amy's breath caught as she slid down her bikini underwear, the dark triangle of hair beckoned her forward. Amy realized she was still dressed and jerked off her shirt, popping a button. Molly's hands were on her breasts, her hot mouth breathing warm air onto her skin as Molly slid her hands around to unhook her bra and free the girls. Amy gasped as Molly's mouth consumed her breast, and her hands rubbed her belly as she pushed her pants down around her knees.

Amy shimmied out of her pants and Molly leaned her back onto the bed. Used to being more of the aggressor, Amy relaxed and groaned as Molly laid over her, kissing her neck.

"Pretty sure I will die if you stop," Amy whispered.

Molly rolled off of her. "I am pretty sure you won't have to take that chance." She slid down and sucked a nipple into her mouth and grasped the other with her fingers, squeezing and stroking. Amy writhed under her touch, aching for attention a little further south. Molly tickled her ever so slightly as she moved across her stomach, past her hip and to the inside of her thigh. Amy shuddered as Molly bit her nipple, her hips twisting toward her hand. Amy reached out and cupped Molly's breast, flicking her thumb across the nipple, urging her back up. Molly kissed her way up her chest, nibbling her neck. Amy caught her breath as Molly rubbed against her, their bodies tangled, time stopped as all she felt was the throb between her legs and the teeth against her neck.

Molly stopped and looked her in the eye. Amy's eyes fluttered closed as Molly's fingers explored her drenched folds, passing up one side and down the other before they slid inside her. It was as if her entire body collapsed into her pelvis, the only sensation bursts of pleasure as Molly explored inside of her. Amy pushed against Molly, her hips rising to meet Molly's thrusts.

Amy forced her eyes open, watching the concentration on Molly's face. "Oh, yes, that's…" Amy gurgled out until Molly's thumb pushed against her hard clit. "Jeee." Amy froze, her entire mind focused on a small explosion starting in her belly. Each flick brought her closer until her shoulders raised off the bed, her muscles frozen and an animal growl left her throat. *Uh oh. Too loud.* She dropped to the bed, her skin coated with sweat.

Molly smiled at her. "You are so passionate. I love it." She gently pulled her hand from Amy, resting it on her mound, absently twirling the dark hairs.

Amy took a deep breath and sighed. *Damn. This woman is awesome.* She smiled at Molly and hesitated. *What is the matter with me? I know what to do, what I want to do. Why is it so important I do this right?* Amy traced her way across Molly's hip, teasing her way across the top of her thigh, slow and easy. *Because I like her and I really want her to like me, too.*

Molly started to twitch under her touch. Amy smiled, confident. She kissed her way from one ear, down her neck, and up to her other ear. Molly was pushing against her, clutching Amy's body. Amy whispered, "You are gorgeous."

Molly skin flushed, her pupils dilated with ancient human urges. Amy pressed her hand flat against Molly's crotch, grinning as she felt the heat. Molly sucked in a breath as Amy slid one finger between the drenched folds. "Oh, my. So wet." Molly shuddered. Amy lightly touched her deeper, pausing just over her opening, exploring, touching.

Amy shifted on her side and raised a knee as Molly slid her hand back between her legs. Amy watched Molly's face, her eyes shut, her mouth slightly open. Amy focused on the sensations and tried to match each flick she felt with the ones she applied to Molly. Molly's hand drifted to a stop as her breathing got shallow and fast. Amy grinned as Molly's legs lifted and a soft moan drifted from her mouth. She laid her head on Molly's shoulder, drunk on the scent of sex in the air, the only light in the room now a soft green glow from the alarm clock.

Amy woke with a start. She stared around the room for a moment before she remembered where she was: in Molly's bed. Well, on it. And she was freezing. Amy wandered to the bathroom, and when she came back, Molly was up getting dressed.

"Hi, beautiful." Molly slipped a shirt on, braless. "I just want to apologize, for rushing things. I really think things work better long term if you're friends, I mean, we are friends, but you know what I mean."

Amy touched her arm. "And I am forever a romantic. When it's the right one, it's the right one."

Molly furrowed her brows. "Well, I guess I figure if people spent more time trying to be the right one, instead of chasing after 'the right one' it would develop naturally instead of all sparks and no fire."

Amy realized her mistake. *Don't scare her off. Hold on loosely... wasn't that a .38 Special song?* "Pretty sure I saw flames. I really like you." She gave her a quick kiss and picked up her shirt from the floor.

"I'm glad to hear that. I'd hate to sleep with an enemy." Molly opened a drawer and rummaged around.

Amy's mind went straight to sex toys. Instead, Molly pulled out a pair of gym shorts and slid them on. *Of course, slow things down, not go crazy the first time together.* "Let's be better friends, then. When's your birthday?"

"November 15." Molly bent and took her dirty clothes and flicked them toward a basket.

"OOoo, a Scorpio...sting." Amy laughed.

"Maybe, but I always think of it as the first day of hunting season. My mom played hell keeping my dad around on my birthday." Molly asked, "And yours?"

"April first." Amy expected it. A little smile crept onto

Molly's face. And there it was.

Molly quickly erased it. "That sign is what?"

Amy touched Molly's leg. "It's okay, it's not like you're the first person to remind me of April Fools' Day. I'm not too keen on tricks for my birthday, just so you know that up front."

Molly took Amy in her arms and laid her back on the bed. "I wouldn't dream of it. I take birthdays very seriously." She kissed Amy softly.

Amy slid her hands under Molly's shirt, rubbing her back, disappointed that she had clothes on again. *This woman is so damn hot.* "Aries."

"What?"

"April is Aries. Impulsive."

Molly smiled like a Cheshire cat. "I can't disagree." She moved in for another kiss, this time smoldering. She pulled off her shirt and wiggled out of her shorts.

Amy grinned. So much for taking things slow. She stood up to strip and Molly started to help her. This time she took the lead and pushed Molly back onto the bed. Her slight frame was muscular, but still soft enough in all the right places. Amy kissed Molly's neck, gently teasing her way south. She pulled a hard nipple into her mouth, biting just a little. Molly pulled back. *Too hard, oops.* Molly stroked her shoulders as she slid to the other breast. Amy trailed a hand down her stomach, following it with little kisses. Molly jerked as she kissed her inner thigh and groaned when Amy slid up and exhaled on her wetness. Amy loved this moment of anticipation, smelling the musky scent turned her on. She noted that Molly kept things under control, and she didn't have to wade through a forest. She slid her tongue flat across the entire dampness, clutching Molly's hips to keep her close. Molly stiffened as she rolled around the hard nub, and Amy matched her strokes to Molly's hip movements. Molly shuddered, this time shouting as she came, and Amy smiled.

She softly kissed her pale skin just below her navel and grinned when Molly twitched again.

Molly sighed, "Impulsive."

She suddenly lunged and lifted Amy up off the bed and flipped her onto her back. "I raise you one and call."

Amy laughed, and drug her hands down Molly's back as she started to move against her. Her mind wandered back to the contents of that drawer, then totally back to just the ache in her belly as Molly stirred her animal lust back to a frenzy. Amy shifted her thigh just enough to get firm contact and the whole world disappeared into a blackness filled with only hot sensations between her legs. The tingling started almost at her toes, her right calf cramping, slowing the rise. With a sonic boom, her pelvis exploded and she heard herself cry out. When she lay still, she stroked Molly's neck.

Molly whispered in her ear, "I love hearing you, but can you keep it down." Her eyes twinkled inside creases as she beamed.

"I can try, but it's all your fault. You're the one making me scream." Amy looked in her eyes. "Your eyes are so dark and mysterious."

Molly laughed. "Oh, you think so?"

Amy nodded. "Yes. And I am not doing well on this 'take things slow' plan of yours."

"Excellent."

CHAPTER 22

The police station had been a zoo all morning, but still nowhere near the chaos every day in Detroit. Molly leaned back in her desk chair, quite content. She stretched and rubbed her nose, smiling at the scent of Amy still on her hands. She caught herself yawning. She walked to the break room, dropped coins into the machine and listened as the can banged through the bends and twists and dropped at the bottom latch. She opened the door and took the Coke. She tapped the lid so it wouldn't foam over. *Does that really help?* She flipped the stay-tab and took a drink. Molly went into the workroom and picked her mail out of the box labeled 'Chief.'

She walked past the reception desk, sorting through the papers in her hand. She saw the label to Barry Tristan and thought about his disappearance. Absently, she stopped at the file cabinet. Officially the sheriff had jurisdiction on the murder of the chief. She had her suspicions that it went farther than a hunting accident. In a big city, retribution was certainly a possibility, but here? What could he have been on to?

The receptionist peered over her glasses. "Lost?"

Molly startled. "No, sorry, just thinking."

The phone rang, and the receptionist answered. "Hello, Diamond Lake Police. Yes? Again? Okay. I'll let him know." She banged down the phone. "Molly do me a favor and tell Sarge that Secureahome says that the lines are down at the Wilson's place.

Can he run a car by?"

"Sure. Give me the address." Molly walked down the hall, her pulse rising. *Does Charley actually get calls about the security system being down? Was he involved with the burglaries? What if the chief was on the take? Shit. Be cool.* She tapped on the door frame of his office. "Sorry to bother you. Wilson place needs a drive-by. Security down."

Charley said, "What a shitty service. I swear to god they couldn't guard a German shepherd. Okay, I'll make sure Doug adds it to his route."

"I could go," Molly offered. "It's not that far from the commercial route I was going to run before I leave."

"Sure, if you want to, but it's not necessary. Half the houses in town use that service. If we watched every time a line was down, that's all we'd do around here."

Molly walked down the hall, trying to keep an even steady walk. She flipped on the radio and dialed the phone. "Jeffries, yes, this is Chief Gorman. We're a go in Diamond Lake."

She passed the break room, made a small waving gesture to the men sitting at the table, and kept walking.

She slid into the car. What if the chief was closing in on the robberies? He might have been putting things together. Maybe he just got too close to something even bigger? Back in the day rum runners ran through this town. They said even Al Capone had a big house on Diamond Lake, complete with underground tunnels. But nothing that exciting had happened in decades. She cranked the engine and eased the car down the main drag. She turned at the corner. *Charley didn't ask which Wilson.* She parked the car at the back alley behind the flower shop and opened a pack of gum. Her mouth flooded with saliva when the wintergreen hit her tongue. She smiled thinking of Amy. A little twitch started in her belly. *Focus. Slow down. He said he'd tell Doug. How many guys were in on this?*

Molly decided enough time had passed and started the car. She drove the street at the speed limit, passing the Wilson house. It was a Tudor two story, a basketball hoop in the driveway, with a boat parked on the side of the garage. A metal sign with the alarm company logo in blue poked through the front bushes. The neighbor's yards faced each other in the back over a chain link fence. The only possible entry without casual observation would require a ladder on the south side.

She eased the car around the corner, eyeing which houses already had lights on in the windows indicating someone might be home. With all the people using timers on lights, it wasn't a sure sign of occupancy. She peeked in her rear-view mirror, and as she suspected, the Wilson house was still dark.

Molly parked next to the flower shop again; all the businesses were closed for the night. The sidewalks of Diamond Lake practically rolled up at six o'clock. As the sun dipped lower in the sky, she hoped the easy mark was too tempting for the thieves to pass up. The Wilsons were related to Carlton Jeffries and had agreed to let him install video surveillance in their home. She didn't really understand everything he had explained about the system, but it would provide good, solid evidence, something sorely lacking in most burglary cases.

Her Spidey sense was going off. She radioed in an all-clear for Market Street. She hadn't been there for long when a large white van went right past her. There was a Secureahome logo on their van, hand painted. Molly cranked the engine and pulled out onto another side street. As she circled the next block, she caught a glimpse of the van headed east.

The driver would have to approach from the west end of the garage and she would head east about three blocks behind them. It was only a hunch. And she really hoped it was wrong. She spotted the van as she passed a gas station. She went into the parking lot, looked over the dark building, and then continued her path. At the Gilbert garage, the van was parked in the back, and on closer inspection, the painted logo had been covered with a plain white sheet magnet. She could hear the pings of the metal under the hood as things cooled down. The hood was still hot. The place seemed deserted, so she walked the perimeter. Almost back to her car, she heard a deep voice.

"Hold up," Frank Gilbert said. "I don't remember calling for the police. What's going on?"

Molly turned her mag light, shining it in his direction. "Good evening sir. I don't know who called it in to dispatch. Someone reported a burglar in the area."

"It's probably just a neighbor kid sneaking out for a smoke. People need to mind their own damn business." Frank ran his hand through his hair. "It looks secure. Want me to open it up?"

"I'm already here. It's up to you, of course, but I'd be happy to look around." Molly considered the assorted barrels and stacks of tires at the rear of the building. You could hide a refrigerator back here and no one would notice. She scanned the parked vehicles. "Do all these cars belong here?"

Frank shrugged. "Probably. My wife Rosie keeps up the calendar, but I can check. If they have a white tag on the mirror, they have already been checked in. Once in a while, people drop them off the night before so we can work on them. They might not have a tag yet."

Molly glanced around, and sure enough, the white van had a numbered tag hanging from the rear-view mirror. She doubted it was there for service. She followed Frank in through the back door. He punched some numbers into an alarm code box and he flipped on the lights. They passed through a body shop, a few Bondo prepped cars sat taped and waiting for paint. In the main garage, the hoists were all empty. The front office was dark except for the orange glow of lights on the power strips under the desk and the red eye of a security camera.

Frank flicked on the office light and opened a leather log book. He ran a finger down the list. "I don't see anything unusual. Shall I have Rosie call you?"

"Just when she has a chance. I might stop by in the morning if you think she'd have a few minutes." Molly watched his face. Still anxious. No change. He didn't seem to be aware of anything going on.

"That would be fine. Anytime." He reached blindly and turned off the light.

They walked through the dim garage, their shoes making the only noise. A huge crash came from the side room.

Frank screamed a high pitch, little girl scream. "Holy shit, what was that?" Frank jumped back behind Molly.

Molly flicked her light and saw a set of glowing eyes.

Frank picked up a broom and swatted. "Just a damn possum. Don't mind me. Too much coffee. I think my daughter is feeding that fleabag."

"No problem. Thanks again for your cooperation." Molly tried to hide her smile.

***

Amy came by the office window, right on time for work. "What's up, Ma?"

"Somebody got flowers!" Rosie waved like Vanna White on Wheel of Fortune.

Amy took the small envelope, happy to see it was still sealed. She opened it and it simply said 'Impulsive is good' next to a really good line drawing of a Carolina wren. So, Molly was an artist...what other talents remain to be discovered? Amy's mind went right into the gutter.

Frank closed the lid on the coffee machine with a snap. The water hissed and gurgled through the paper filter, releasing a stream of dark liquid into the glass pot below. "I don't miss the percolator, but the coffee was better."

"It was not. You left it until it was like tar." Rosie picked up her mug anticipating the last snorts of coffee. "Go on and pick us up some donuts, why don't you?" Rosie tapped her fingers as she waited. "Of all mornings to switch to decaf. The whole shop is going to be crazy in a few hours without caffeine. Maybe sugar will help."

"Good idea and I can get some regular coffee while I'm there." Frank kissed his wife's cheek.

Amy shuffled through the work orders. "Decaf? Mom, really? That stuff tastes like crap."

"It does not." She leaned in toward Amy. "The new police

chief walked through the shop with your father last night."

Her heart leaped in her chest. "Oh yeah? What for?" Amy asked.

"Someone called in a burglar report, but your father thinks it was just kids smoking. She asked if we could make sure all the cars out back belong in our lot." Rosie looked around and whispered, "Take this list and make a note of any tags out back that aren't on it." She slid a paper forward and then used her regular voice. "I think it's been there a while. You may have to move a few to get it out."

Amy looked at her mom. *Why the ruse? I'll play along.* "I hate when I start the day with a wild goose chase."

Amy cut through the body shop, where Donny was busy in the paint booth, a cloud of red fumes around him as he worked.

Olivia was masking a hood. "Glad you're on time. Dad has been a real pain in the ass about getting more hours done around here."

"Don't I know it." Amy shoved open the back door, jumping when a possum stopped mid-stride crossing the walk. "Dammit stop feeding that thing. He scared the hell out of me!"

Olivia laughed. "It's not me. It's Donny."

Amy trudged to the back of the lot and started to go through the list. There weren't really that many vehicles out back at first glance, but they were parked in as close as possible. A few were half done family projects, some were waiting on parts. More than a few were waiting on insurance claims to go through. Behind a beat-up Camaro, a shiny black Caprice had no tag. She marked it down. An old Volkswagen sat on blocks, and she knew it wouldn't be on the list. It had been her first car until the incident at the beach. It took almost an hour to calm her dad down when he found out she'd been racing on the sand. He pulled the engine the next day.

At the near side, Amy noticed the white van. The tag said 607 but they were already up in the 900's. She glanced and her suspicions were correct. No van. She made another note and headed toward the shop.

Donny was standing under the awning, a cigarette in his mouth. "What are you doing?" He sucked in the smoke as the tobacco flared scarlet.

Something in the coldness of his eyes creeped her out enough to be guarded. How long had he been watching her? "Mom thought maybe a car was abandoned here. Just checking to see. So we can tow it." Amy watched his face for a reaction.

"Was there?"

"What?"

Don flicked the cigarette on the ground, crushing it out with his boot. "Was there an abandoned car?"

"Looks like a couple been here a while, but Mom can follow up."

"Why does she think that there is?" Don looked down at her clipboard.

"What?"

"An abandoned car? Seems there'd be a left-over invoice. Never searched the lot before." He stared through her.

"Maybe part of the process for selling the place?" Amy tipped the clipboard against her chest so he couldn't read her list.

Don puffed out his cheeks. "Sometimes I get a friend that drops his car by. Let me know what you find. So Rosie doesn't tow it. You know."

Amy nodded. "Of course." *He is skimming.*

CHAPTER 23

A team of little league kids was at the far end of the batting cages. Amy was glad because she had trouble watching her mouth when she and Robin got to talking. She had let Robin convince her to spend yet another night at batting practice. She had to admit they were both place hitting better.

Robin connected with the bright yellow ball, sending it high over the pitching machine. "How's things with Cheryl?"

Amy tried to seem unphased. "Just work stuff, I told you that."

"Work stuff." Robin wiggled her eyebrows and looked closely at Amy. "She's not too bright, but she's a looker."

"Yes, she is," Amy agreed.

"Second base? Third? Come on, don't leave me hanging." Robin swung and launched a solid hit to the back of the far net.

"You don't get enough action yourself so you need to hear about me? Please. If you put notches on your bedpost you'd be on the floor by now."

"You know I have a water bed. I'm just trying to make sure I understand." Robin stood flat-footed as a pitch passed and cracked into the chain link fence. "Did you get busy or not?"

"What's your point?" Amy asked.

"Just wondered. That's all." Robin shifted her feet in the batter's box painted on the concrete. The ball came in a slow arc and she plinked it across the ground. "I like her little tattoo."

"I'm not falling for it, I didn't sleep with her." Amy felt the hot blush across her cheeks. "Why do you always interrogate me?"

Robin opened the door to the batting cage and punched her shoulder. "Still on the hunt. You dog. You don't need to keep secrets from me!"

Amy mumbled, "I think I was the rabbit on that one." She shut the door to the batting cage and dropped some coins into the machine. Lights flickered on the front of the pitching mechanism. Amy took her stance.

Robin asked, "How's the situation with the cop?"

Amy turned and missed the first pitch. "You mean Molly?" She rested the bat on her shoulder.

"Ball. Watch what you're doing in there. You're going to get hit."

"Actually, we talked some the other day." Amy smacked the bat at a pitch, the ball skipping across the concrete floor.

"That'd be a double if it cut through the infield. Am I about to lose the hundred bucks?"

"I wish that we hadn't made the bet," Amy said.

"I did lose the bet." Robin asked, "You like her?"

"I think so. Yes. Definitely." Amy swung and chipped it up. "I like her. I'm taking things slow."

"My slow?" Robin asked.

"Ha. That's like giving her a hotel key when you first meet her." Amy looked at Robin. "I'm still on the rebound. Don't you think?"

"It's not too soon. The right one could slip past you if you aren't paying attention." Robin put a cigarette in her mouth. "I'm glad you put yourself out there. See what I did there? Put out."

"We went hiking," Amy said. "And things got moving a little fast."

"Since when do you go hiking?"

"Since now."

"Damn, that's the way to hunt. You're frickin' unstoppable!"

Robin flicked her lighter and took a long pull. "It's a good thing I'm your friend, or you'd have tagged me. You dog. You just needed some motivation."

Not as much as you think. "It was too soon. It didn't seem right, because of your stupid bet. I don't know." Amy let the last ball go by and stepped out of the box. She unzipped the end of her bag and slid the bat inside.

"I know. Trust me. There's only good sex and great sex. It's good for you. You don't want to settle. You need to shop around."

"Shop around, huh?" Amy reached out for a hit off the cigarette.

Robin handed it over. "When did you start smoking again?"

"Just now."

Amy looked at the glowing end. *What the hell am I doing?* She handed the cigarette back to Robin who waved it off and lit another for herself.

"I forgot to tell you I pulled late shift. I won't be home until probably three. Just leave a sock on the doorknob if you have any company." She grinned.

At the parking lot, they each got into their own cars, Robin tapping her horn as she pulled away. Amy drove home lost in thought. Molly didn't believe in love at first sight, or at least it seemed that way. Molly was a beautiful woman and she had Amy's full attention. *Maybe I should call her?* The phone was ringing when she went through the back door.

Amy picked up the receiver. "Hello?"

Her mother's voice came through. "Hi honey, I made chicken parmesan if you want to come get a plate."

"Thanks, mom, I'm not real hungry." Amy pulled open the fridge hoping to score leftovers. There were none that caught her eye. "Hey, I changed my mind. See you in a few."

Amy was going to walk the short distance and then decided against it. She had a funny feeling. Intuition, something. She took her keys and cranked up the Jeep. A little card was on the windshield held by the wiper blade. A little picture of a flower was sketched onto the paper. Amy smiled. Molly was a charmer, that was for sure. She put the car in reverse. If she kept taking one block drives, she'd need to change the oil every three hundred miles. Maybe she should take a long drive this weekend and burn some water out of the engine. Maybe Molly had some time off? She parked and smiled to herself.

She went in the front door and her dad was in his recliner.

He said, "You're front door company now? You know you could actually eat with us instead of just taking the scraps."

Rosie came into the room from the kitchen. "Well, I don't care if you do. We wouldn't see you at all if you never took leftovers."

"Mom, you see me every day at work." Amy took the plate. She picked a noodle from the side and slurped it into her mouth.

"Stop, let me get you a fork. Sit down. And you know that's not the same thing. We don't really talk at work." Rosie rummaged in the drawer, then opened the dishwasher. "Frank, turn off that boob tube and talk to Amy."

Frank struggled out of his chair. "I'm going to order that converter for a remote control."

"You are not. You'd never stand up all night if you didn't have to change the channel." Rosie sat on the couch next to Amy and handed her the fork. "Isn't this nice?"

Amy shoved a full fork of food in her mouth and nodded. Frank rolled his eyes.

"Don't you have anything to mention to Amy?" Rose gave Frank a look.

"A guy can't do anything for a surprise?" Frank carried a beer in from the kitchen. He handed a Coke to Amy. He looked at her expression. "You don't need a beer."

He shuffled to his chair. "I been thinking about what you said, and I'm not saying that I was wrong, but I do want to ask you what you think we should do with the garage. Hypothetically." He dropped into his La-Z-Boy.

"Really?" Amy finished chewing. "Okay, well, first I would get rid of the body shop altogether. Too many chemicals and the cost to dry the paint. People want a great paint job on a Maaco budget. We shouldn't even bother to try anymore."

Frank said, "Oh man, Olivia, she won't care either way. But I want to be there when you tell Don."

Amy took another bite and continued with her mouth full. "I'd maybe cut back to a of couple areas, either just do oil changes and light maintenance or focus on engine electronics and tune-ups."

Frank gave his wife the 'I told you so' look. Rose gave him a cold stare.

He asked, "I'll bite. Why?"

Amy finished swallowing. "There's too much to keep up with all the equipment for engines, front end, and that crap for a small shop. Oil changes are simple and could be a money maker if we did them fast enough."

"There's already oil change places. They rip people off." Frank took a long drink.

"We wouldn't. I mean, we don't now. People would still trust us. Folks don't want to pay too much, but they are also scared of getting ripped off. Our reputation will be the sales point." She crammed another forkful in her mouth and chewed. "But I think there's more growth in the electronics."

"Electronics," Frank repeated.

Amy sat down her half-empty plate. The dog Rascal lifted her head from her pillow and stared at the food. Amy looked to see if she needed to pick up the plate. Rascal must have decided it was too much to walk over as she dropped her head back down.

Amy continued, "Yeah. Electronics give the backyard mechanics fits. They don't have the tools, and even if they do, to diagnose it without a big computer is a nightmare. And they aren't going to make cars with fewer computers, it's only going to get more complicated."

After a long silence, Rosie asked, "What do you think, Frank?"

"Huh?" Her father seemed to be lost in thought. "What about tires? Cars all got tires."

Amy sighed. "Of course, but they're heavy, and they take up a lot of room, and people expect you to change them right away.

It's okay if people don't mind the wait, but not enough margin. Not if we don't franchise."

"Okay. I've heard enough." Frank stood up and looked at Rose. "Are you ready?"

"Yes, come on with us." Rose took Amy by the arm and guided her to the side yard. Across the span of grass, the shop lights in the front parking area glowed a light yellow. At the top of the garage door, a new lighted sign said 'Gilbert Garage' in red letters framed in black with 'since 1931' in yellow script.

"You are fucking kidding me!" Amy shrieked. "You changed the sign?"

"Do you kiss your mother with that mouth?" He waved a hand toward the shop. "Your sister Tina is way smarter than I am with the books and that. You two figure out how to run the place. With Olivia, she can be a tie-breaker."

Amy looked from her mother's face to her father's. "You're retiring?"

"You won't get rid of me that fast, but yes. Your mother is tired of working there, and I thought we might get an RV. Drive across the country."

Rosie asked, "What do you think, honey? Isn't it wonderful?"

"I think it's frickin' awesome!" Amy hugged her parents.

"But…" Frank said, "I see that look."

"Not a big but, just a little but. What if we all get married and change our names?" Amy asked. "Olivia doesn't use Gilbert anymore."

Rose said, "I didn't think you were going to ever get married."

Amy put her hands on her hips. "Well, I…"

"Have you no respect at all for tradition? Buy another sign. I don't care. The shop belongs to you and your sisters." Frank smiled. "The only catch is that you have to tell Big Don. He seems to have been working under the delusion that I would actually sign the shop over to him. Jenkins Garage, probably only do bodywork."

"Come on, you can't be serious," Amy said.

"Oh, I wish I wasn't." Frank headed to the house. "Come on

woman."

Her mother and dad actually held hands as they walked. *Gross.*

"Good night," Amy said. She drove toward Robin's, her mind swirling with the possibilities.

CHAPTER 24

Amy stood at the back of her Jeep, holding her softball bag. The warmth of the day remained as the lights in the softball field flickered and buzzed as they came on. Bugs flew around them, high above the green outfield. Women started to put gear into the dugouts. She changed into her cleats, a new pair for luck, white with a neon stripe. They clicked on the blacktop as Amy approached the diamond.

Robin and Stacy were tossing a ball to warm up. Amy hooked her gear bag in the dugout and fished out her mitt. She stepped next to Robin, who scooted over a bit so Stacy could throw to both of them. She had a great arm. *She could play outfield for sure.* Amy caught the ball and lobbed it back.

"You're blinding me with those shoes. Couldn't you step on them some?" Robin complained.

Stacy said, "I think they're snazzy." Coach Gail bounced between the players confirming positions and the batting line up.

Robin made a catch. "Ready to beat the crap out of Nancy's team?"

"We play Nancy's team first?" Stacy asked.

"Yep," Coach Gail replied. "And it's single elimination so look sharp tonight." She marked something on her clipboard. "Amy, smart bat today. No temper. Just hit the ball."

Robin said, "Amy is hitting big time, Coach. Put her in cleanup. She scored big time this week."

"Robin, come on. Enough. It's embarrassing," Amy said.

"You shouldn't be embarrassed. You didn't do anything wrong. She's a fine lady. And you're single. No harm, no foul." Robin snapped her gum.

"Enough, please stop talking about it," Amy begged.

Gail kept on walking, her eyes focused on the clipboard in her hands. "Right. Cleanup. And we were called the wild generation."

"Did you or did you not win our bet about Molly?" Robin asked.

Coach Nancy was walking past them. "Bet about Molly? My Molly?"

"Yeah, we bet who could tag her first. Amy hit a home run on that one, didn't you?" Robin threw a grounder toward Stacy.

Stacy held the ball and stared at Amy. "You actually made a bet?" She lobbed a soft toss.

"No. Yes. Well, fuckin' A." Amy caught the throw from Stacy and muttered, "I will kill you, Robin."

Nancy said, "Really? That's pretty juvenile, even for you, Robin."

Amy fired the ball to Stacy, who burned it back to Robin.

Robin caught it. "Just the facts ma'am; Amy won the bet. She slept with Molly." She whizzed the ball to Stacy.

Amy froze as Molly stopped just behind Nancy. Molly walked past them, paused, and then headed back toward the parking lot. Robin and Stacy both looked at Nancy.

Stacy asked, "Do you think that she heard?" She steamed the ball to Amy.

Nancy put her hands on her hips. "Not think, dumbasses, I know. How would you feel if you liked someone and they only slept with you on a bet? You're a real piece of work, Gilbert. A real piece of work. I'd expect that shit from a frat boy, but really?"

Amy held the ball in silence, her cheeks red with shame.

Nancy threw her hands up in the air. "Thanks to you I have to settle down my best player. I'll be lucky if I can talk her into playing tonight." She hurried after Molly.

Amy tried to act like it didn't bother her to be scolded. *Nancy is right. I am a shitty person. I don't deserve Molly, but I need to explain.*

Robin shrugged. "I don't care who knows if I slept with somebody. I've dated some sizzling hot women."

Amy said, "Dated implies you see them more than one time."

Robin shrugged. "Some I do."

Stacy took the ball gently from Amy. "I'm warm enough. And for the record, I think you're cute, and I don't care if people know that I slept with you."

Robin smirked. "Amy says the deal wasn't sealed."

"Do you mean that you think we didn't sleep together?" Stacy demanded. She followed Amy all the way to the bench. "Just because I didn't actually spend the night or just because we weren't naked?"

"Look, I don't really think clothes are what's important," Amy said. *What a drama queen.* "Can we stop discussing this. I don't plan on sharing all my private business."

Robin laughed. "Just your privates."

"Oh, so you think only certain things count as sex. I am just hurt, totally devastated. Maimed for life. I wasn't important to you at all." Stacy threw her mitt which hit the bench and fell underneath it.

Gail walked up between them from behind, putting a hand on each of their shoulders. "Ladies, we are going to play a game here. One I would like to win. As enthralling as your tales of romance may be, button it. Now."

Amy turned back toward the diamond where players were milling in position. "She seems cranky."

Stacy said, "Yeah, I bet she didn't sleep with you either."

Robin chimed in. "For the record, I haven't slept with Amy."

"No, dammit. We have not had sex. We're friends." Amy was exasperated.

"You sleep with enemies?" Robin asked, with an odd lilt in her voice. "Maybe we should. I'm not exactly chopped liver."

Stacy crossed her arms. "I feel denied."

Amy hissed, "You are the one who bailed. Can you just drop it?"

"I am not embarrassed to say what we did. And you shouldn't be either. Except for Robin, we are all adults here." Stacy was not dropping it.

"We didn't do anything." Amy watched the runners advance a base, with one runner out at third. *Shit.* Two outs and she was up. She clutched her bat and headed toward the circle for on deck.

Coach pulled her sleeve. "Alright hot pants, can you harness a little of that energy and smack the ball? Or are you too tired?"

"I didn't sleep with her," Amy said, yanking away from Gail.

"You better hope not, Vicky is one jealous woman. She will kick your ass."

Amy choked, almost swallowing her gum, and headed into the batting box.

CHAPTER 25

Amy had sulked most of the day, leaving her bedroom only to get drinks or to use the bathroom. Robin brought her a takeout plate from Denny's and then left her alone. Her stomach hurt too much to eat. As lousy as she felt for betraying Molly, she knew how much worse she'd feel if the situation was reversed. Somehow you don't remember times when other people were humiliated, but every time that you did something embarrassing it was locked into your memory. *Molly must be mortified. And I do really care about her. It wasn't the bet. What if Molly was The One? Dammit, I'm always just pissing things away.* Her shame added to her tears of grief.

Meow nudged the dish in the bathroom. Amy got up to fill the water bowl. "I need a drink myself, Meow."

The cat stared at the bowl and then left the bathroom.

"Alright your highness, you're welcome."

Amy opened the fridge and noticed all the empty beer cans in the recycle box. "Molly's right. I do drink too much."

She took a Coke, and Meow jumped in her lap when she sat down. A few tears trickled, and Meow purred and kneaded her leg. "I suck, but you still love me."

Meow leaped from her lap and went under the bed.

"Thanks, ingrate."

Amy sighed. She should apologize, at least. Amy paced around the room, looked at the phone, lifted the receiver and then slammed it down. Meow crept out from under the bed and watched her. She took a deep breath, dialed the number and waited. No answer.

Last night, Molly had on sunglasses the entire game, so Amy wasn't totally sure if she'd ever looked at her, but Molly's face was like Arnold Schwarzenegger in that Terminator movie. Stiff and unmoving. Amy struck out first up and made an error before Gail benched her. Amy didn't stay to watch the rest of the game.

Amy picked up the phone and slammed it again. Meow twitched at the noise.

"What are you looking at? You might be a little bent out of shape, too, if you jacked up everything like I did. I didn't mean to hurt her feelings. And I like her. A lot. I totally fucked up."

Meow slowly closed her eyelids, her tail flicking back up around her body.

"You're right. I did all this myself. And I better fix it myself."

Amy headed out the back door, carrying her helmet. She slid a leg over the seat and popped the helmet on her head. She didn't bother to strap it, just to be reckless. She kicked the engine to life, popped the clutch and raced the bike around downtown.

At the front of the beauty shop, she rode up next to the sidewalk and flicked off the engine. She snapped off the helmet and crammed it onto the sissy stick.

"Winnie, I need a change," Amy said as she pushed open the door. "I hope you can help me out."

"Maybe." Winnie peered over her reading glasses. "Seems you might need more than I can do, based on what Nancy said."

Amy rubbed her hands, and then took a deep breath. "Not really sure what you're talking about."

"Oh darling, we've known each other way too long for you to bullshit me." Winnie folded her log book shut. "Have a seat."

"I want a haircut. This hair is amazing, but it's too much. It's not me. I need something that won't get messed up with a helmet." Amy waved toward the motorcycle in the street. "After I ride."

Winnie pulled her hands through Amy's hair. "That short?

It'll be dark again in a couple weeks."

"I need a big change. I'm turning a new leaf, and I need to be rid of this me." Amy stared straight into the mirror. "Please?"

"I can change the outside, but only you can change the inside." Winnie snapped the cape and swung it around Amy's neck. "What you did to Molly was shitty, and really selfish, and it was mean. You know, Nancy had to talk Molly into playing the rest of the tournament. She wanted to quit the team. She even talked about leaving town completely."

Her stomach clenched, and she tried to fight it, but moisture welled up in her eyes. The water spritzing around her ears seemed a little harsher than usual.

"Crocodile tears for yourself?"

Amy dropped her head.

"Head up." Winnie spritzed a little more. Then she shook her comb at Amy's image in the mirror. "Don't bother trying to suck it up for me. I won't tell. All beauticians keep the secrets of their clients. You know, like their real hair color, what they confess. It's almost like a priest. Except no Hail Marys and you better be glad I'm not Catholic because if I had any beads right now, I'd hit you with them."

Winnie combed Amy's hair spreading the water and picked up the scissors. "You're not going to change your mind?"

"No, but I sure hope Molly will," Amy whispered.

Winnie started to cut. "I can't really speak to what Molly will do, but you might stop and see Nancy after we're done here. She's better with matters of the heart."

In less than fifteen minutes, pretty much all of the blonde hair was on the floor. Winnie pulled a comb through the short spikes. She handed Amy a mirror. "What do you think?"

"It's great. Really. Thanks," Amy said. She paid Winnie, gave her an extra twenty and went out the front door. Three steps later, she paused just a minute before pushing the door to the flower shop.

Nancy had her head inside a cooler, adjusting flowers. Alerted to Amy's presence by the bell hanging on the door handle, she backed up and stood upright. Her expression flashed a scowl for just a moment. She adjusted her apron and plastered a smile on her face. "What can I do for you?"

"Hi, Nancy. I wondered if you could help me out? I need to send some flowers." Amy rubbed her hand on her pant leg.

"Friend or foe?" Nancy asked, pulling a pencil from behind her ear. She took a small pad out of her apron pocket. "I hear you have plenty of both in town."

"I want to send something to Molly." Amy rushed out the words. She took a breath and slowed down. "I hope you have something for a horse's ass that needs to apologize. I'm open to suggestions."

"Then I suggest you start treating people like they have feelings and not like just a notch on your headboard." Nancy snapped her gum. "Budget?"

"What?" Amy tipped her head.

"How much do you want to spend?" Nancy tapped her pencil on her pad.

"I don't care." Amy peered into the cooler. "I have a lot to make up for; send them right away."

"I can deliver them personally after five unless you're brave enough to do it yourself."

"I think delivery would be better." Amy picked at her fingernail. "Maybe you should deliver some every day until she stops throwing them out."

"Might take a few days, but not any longer. At least I don't think so..." Nancy sighed. "She won't throw them out. She's hurt, not angry."

"Really?" Amy looked up. "There's hope?"

"There's always hope. But I am warning you, I will be first in line to kick your ass if you fuck this up again." Nancy snapped her gum. "Care to write a card?"

"Uh, sure." Amy considered the assorted cards in the rack and selected a simple ivory framed in black. She picked up the pen and wrote *It takes a strong person to say I'm sorry and an even stronger person to forgive. I've been an ass. I don't deserve you.* She took up a second card, this one with a smiley face: *I liked you from the minute you hit me in the ankle at first base. Please forgive me.* She picked up a third card and then sat it back down in the stand. She dropped the pen on the counter and pulled out her wallet. She peeled out six twenty-dollar bills and set them on the counter. "See what you can do." Then she put down three more.

Nancy nodded. "Give it a day or two before you call."

"Thanks, I'm not sure what to say," Amy admitted.

"Start with 'I'm a douche' and work it out from there?" Nancy suggested.

"And Winnie says you're the romantic one," Amy mumbled under her breath as she went out the door. She spotted Don sitting in the parking lot.

He slid open the big door and popped out of the van. He called out, "Hi Amy, funny running into you here."

Amy went over. She smiled. "Hey Don, you here to get flowers? You should hurry, they close soon."

"Yeah? Thanks." He stood next to her, suddenly grabbing one arm over her mouth and the other around her waist. He lifted her, the surprise rendering her still until she hit the floor of the van. Now it was too late. He pulled the door shut, yanked a piece of tape dangling from the ceiling and covered her mouth.

He laughed as she kicked, pulling more tape around her legs above her feet. Her blows bounced off him until one hit him square in the eye.

"You little bitch," he hissed. Pinning her arms with his knee, he taped her wrists.

Amy kept struggling against the tape, rolling from side to side.

"Good. That ought to wear you out." He stepped over her and into the captain's seat. He took the gloves off the passenger seat and slid them on. He opened the door. In a few moments, he was back. "They won't find your bike for a day or two. At least until the trash truck comes."

He cranked the engine, the smell of burning oil drifted into the interior. *It's burning oil, might need more than gaskets with that tick. Forget that. Think.* She forced herself to notice the minute details of the things around her. The van was stripped except for the front seats. The floor was pretty rusty, a number of pieces of lumber were placed across the length to shore things up.

"It's a good thing you headed right for the motorcycle. With the short hair, I almost missed you coming out. Yesterday you looked like LisaLisa and now you look like Adam Ant. I mean, you don't much look like Olivia, but you can tell you're sisters. Did you realize we have been married for almost ten years? But your old man still treats me like an outsider. The last straw was when he took the "Son" off the sign. What the hell am I? SON-in-law. Loyalty doesn't mean a thing."

She shifted her weight; she fell to her side. The view out the windows was just leaves. *What the hell is he doing?* She tried to tug her arms apart, but they didn't budge.

"You know what's the matter with people? They don't think." Don twisted the steering wheel and the van lurched around a turn. "If you want to make money, you have to invest in something solid. Banks, now that's a bad idea. The government knows exactly how much you have. No. Precious metals and property. Gold and dirt. That's the ticket."

The van picked up speed. "I made this trip all the time when I was a kid. I didn't even know my uncle sold it until I got it at a tax sale. Pennies on the dollar. I've got a list of lots and cabins all over the county."

Donny shoved the van lighter against a cigarette. "You don't mind? Speak up." His laugh was maniacal. "I crack myself up."

The van slowed and twisted through turn after turn. Her stomach cramped and Amy hoped she wouldn't get motion sick. The van slowed even more as the tires began chattering across what must be a washboard dirt road. It hadn't rained in weeks and the back roads were rough. The van stopped, and Don got out but hadn't turned off the engine. She heard the metallic scrape of an overhead door opening. Don got back in, the van eased forward, and he turned off the engine.

"Ready for something to eat?" Don asked. He slammed the door down, and then the van slider scraped open. He grabbed her shoulders and slid her out onto her feet. He lifted her on one shoulder and flopped her down onto an old couch in a corner of the garage. He rummaged in a cabinet, pulling out a bag of potato chips.

He crunched and tipped the bag toward her. "Chips?" He pulled the tape from her mouth. "You can holler all you want, no one is around for miles this time of year."

Amy shifted. "Just cut me loose, would you? Stop fooling around."

"Oh, my dear Amy. I am not fooling at all. I have an excellent plan." Don stuffed more chips into his mouth. "One might say it solves two problems at one time."

"You have lost your damn mind." Amy gave him a sharp look. "You're not getting anything for Christmas this year."

"That's the best you got?" He laughed.

"If this is some sort of practical joke…" Amy started.

"The only joke around here is you. I hope you'll forgive me for leaving you here, but I have to do a perimeter check." Don pulled a new piece of tape from a roll on the shelf. He plastered it across her mouth. "No reason to tempt the fates."

Amy watched him leave through a side door, the window painted black. She couldn't begin to guess why or what he was going to do with her. It couldn't be good. She looked around the space. A few tools on some pegboard, a narrow shelf holding cans of oil. *Must have been there a long time, most oil comes in plastic bottles now. That Australian beer came in a can like an oil can. Focus. Okay, I hear waves hitting the shore. And birds, and insects. We're at a cabin in the woods somewhere, near the lake.* The other walls were bare, the roof boards visible from her perch. She couldn't see any way to cut the tape and pulling at it had only ripped at her skin. Maybe she'd have a shot to run if he let her use the bathroom. *Where would I run to? What bathroom?*

Don burst back into the damp garage. "Good news! It's dark so you can move to your final destination for today." He laughed.

"Final destination...get it?"

He cut the tape at her ankles. "If you start anything, I'll cut you."

She couldn't believe he said that to her. But until a few hours ago she would have never believed that he could kidnap her. *That's it! He actually is stealing money from the garage, and he thinks that I know. I'll just straighten this all out. If he ever lets me talk again.*

He pushed her out the door, and there in the moonlight was a typical small lake cabin, maybe one bedroom, heated with a pot belly stove based on the type of chimney pipe poking through the roof.

Ahead of them was a boathouse. The shoreline had been solidified with concrete, a pretty big investment. The low building was made from scrap lumber it seemed, with a metal roof. It had a garage door, probably to pull the boat out? Don opened a side door and pulled her inside. There was a chair on one wall, water ski equipment rested on the rafters, and assorted fishing gear hung on the other wall. A crimson 24-foot boat floated between the dock on each side, it's hull smacking on the water.

"This is it. Have a seat." He pushed her down into the desk chair, not any different than the ones in her parent's office. He pulled out tape and tore off a long strip.

Amy kicked her feet as he tried to tape them to the chair leg, landing a few good blows. Don smacked her upside the head so hard she saw stars. When she focused, her legs were already trapped.

"If you keep hurting me, my patience will run out," Don said.

Amy stared at Don. *What the hell is wrong with him?* She flexed her wrists behind her back, her hands becoming numb in the tape.

"I was going to switch and tape your arms to the chair, but now I won't. You gave me a fat lip. I can taste the blood."

Don took a look around the boat shed. "I think you'll be safe here. No snakes or anything."

Snakes? Besides Don? She wriggled on the chair, causing it to scoot.

"I'd be still if I were you. Wouldn't want to fall in the water and drown." Don stepped out and she could hear the deadbolt click on the latch of the door.

CHAPTER 26

The bedroom was still dark when Molly heard the alarm clock and reached over blindly to shut it off. Between the nightmares and thinking about Amy, it had been a long, sleepless night. She rolled out of bed and sat for a minute. *After all I did for her. All the talk about love at first sight. All bullshit. Damn it. I have no reason to be embarrassed. I was just tricked. Robin and Amy are both jackasses.* She looked at the clock and hurried to get out the door.

She stopped at the bakery on the way into work. She needed sugar, and it would be a nice gesture for the crew. She balanced the box on her hip as she shut the car door.

Doug opened the front door for her when she approached the building. "Someone got flowers."

"You or Charley?" Molly stopped at the receptionist desk. A cut-glass vase held a stunning display of purple hyacinth, the flower of regret and forgiveness. Deep inky colors in each petal faded to almost white at the center. The scent was amazing even across the room. "Give me the card, but you can keep the flowers out here. They look nice on the desk." She sat down the dough-nuts and put the card into her pocket without reading it. Doug watched without a word. "We start in ten minutes." She took the lid off and sat the box inside it. She stopped and just looked at Doug.

"Right. I'll get everyone." Doug scooted down the hall.

She waited in the hall as the troops filed in, Charley, Doug, the two rookies Tracy and Duncan, followed by Jeff. She waited for a few beats to let them shuffle around into the chairs. *Strong entrance.*

Molly walked into the conference room and went to the head of the table. *You get more bees with honey than vinegar. That was stupid. Bees made their own honey. Speak softly and carry a big stick.* "Good morning."

Charley had a mouth full of doughnut "Yes, it is."

"I'll make this quick. We all have work to do." A file on her podium read "Wilson burglary" and it was open to the statement that the Wilson's gave when they came home. "Look, I know we do a lot of burglary reports, twice as many as the next two towns as the Courier has repeatedly pointed out. Thankfully, most are not active felony scenes, so they are pretty routine. Here are some of the highlights in this report on the Wilson house: 'No apparent entry, place not flipped. Jewelry taken, and entire fire safe box.' There are no pictures, notes, sketches, no neighbor interviews. That is not enough effort. We aren't making any headway on solving these crimes, and I've been through the files myself." She scanned the room for any response. None.

"It's easy to get complacent but remember this type of thing makes people feel violated. A stranger was in their home. These victims deserve our best investigation every time. We know that the chances of getting their property back are slim but taking a thorough report helps people get back the biggest item stolen: their sense of security."

"You guys know how to do this, I should hope. If I need to make a check sheet, I will. Step up your game." Molly stared evenly around the room.

"On a more personal matter, I didn't know the chief like you did. I really am sorry it turned out to be a homicide." Molly wished she had something profound to say. "I expect the funeral to be a media circus. Formal attire for everyone, yes gloves. Pick one award for your lapel, otherwise, you look like a Boy Scout with badges all over. We will meet up at one o'clock and proceed to the church en masse. Charley has been asked to drive the widow in one of our units, so he will leave earlier. Any questions? Thank you."

She went back to her office. She sat and stared at the little envelope for a few minutes, then tore it up unread and threw out the pieces. *Amatta Gilberta. Mafia. Who said that anymore? The Syndicate. Here in Diamond Lake? Ridiculous.* Molly headed out to the Wilson house. *Damn. It was right down the street from Charley's house. Bold fuckers. What neighbor might be home*?

Molly selected a white Tudor because the car in the driveway was a Buick. Stereotype or not, she had been correct and a little white-haired lady stood at the door. In the background, a little dog barked like a chainsaw...rrr rrr rrr rrr. The woman leaned back. "Shut it, Precious. Mommy is talking." The barking stopped.

"Ma'am, I'm Molly Gorman from the Diamond Lake Police Department. I am sorry to bother you, but I wondered if you had a few minutes to talk with me about some recent burglaries."

"Come in, please, have a seat. I'm Betty, Betty McIntire. Would you like some coffee or tea?"

"No thank you. I just ate." Molly studied the room.

A medium sized, gray-muzzled beagle studied Molly from the kitchen, not concerned enough to stand up. The front room was bright, despite the dark green carpet and oak paneling. Her husband probably installed it himself over twenty years ago. A coffee table in front of the couch was covered in Hummel's, each figure tilted at an artistic angle. A cabinet TV stood under the window, across from a La-Z-Boy with a crocheted afghan in green and orange arranged over the arm.

Molly went to sit and jumped when a snarl came from the couch. A little chihuahua was curled in an afghan matching the one on the chair. The dog shook with each breath as it delivered a raspy bark.

"I am so sorry, Precious, stop that. Enough already." Betty snatched up the dog. "That's about enough of that." She sat on the chair, and Precious was content to curl on her lap while giving Molly the stink eye. "I'm so sorry. She's a little firecracker today."

Molly cautiously sat on the edge of the couch. No more miniature canines went on the attack. "Spunky little thing."

"Do you have a dog? They are great company and better security. No one comes near this place without me knowing about it." Betty smiled at her.

"You're right about that, Ma'am."

"You look familiar. Of course, I saw your picture in the paper. You're the new Police Chief. Back in the day, I dated your grandfather, but I won't hold that against you." She laughed. "I'm kidding, of course, I mean, I did date him, but he was lovely. I've known your grandmother since kindergarten, and they were better suited. Trust me. I found my love. My Mac was a good man. I'm going to give you a tip. Marry a younger man; they don't last as long as we do."

Molly eased into the topic of her visit. "Right. Good advice. Ma'am, were you aware that your neighbors the Wilson's were robbed last week?"

"I'm not surprised. They leave out of town and don't even stop their newspaper. Might as well put up a flag: rob me." Betty didn't seem very sympathetic.

"Did you notice anything odd last week?" Molly pushed on. "People you usually don't see, strange vehicles?"

Betty peered at her with watery eyes. *Not a very credible witness. Damn.* Molly waited to let her have time to think. A low growl emanated from Precious.

"I don't think so, well, wait a minute. I thought it was odd that the security company did a check of their house when they clearly weren't home. They didn't stay more than fifteen minutes. Myself, I don't waste any money on those fancy electronic systems. My sister has one and the cops keep getting called out for false alarms. Makes a hell of a racket, too. Oh, I'm sorry. A heck of a racket."

Molly hoped her expression was stoic. "How did you know it was the security company?"

"The van had their goofy logo on the side, the one with the burglar in a window. I only saw the passenger, he had on a light blue jacket. Bald guy. The driver was shorter, but I didn't get a good look."

That was obvious. Molly smiled at Betty. "Did they carry anything?"

"They had a big toolbox, yellow. That's all I saw them carry. Funny, they both had to carry it out. Maybe the bald guy had a bad back. Me, when I get the lumbago, I can hardly feed the dogs. You might find me someday flat on the floor, with the dogs eating me for dinner." Betty laughed.

Molly coughed to cover her smile. "I sure hope not, Ma'am. Do you have any security concerns I might answer for you?"

"Nope, I went to Kroger and got my VCR marked. I doubt anyone wants the rest of my junk. And my babies are on patrol." Betty hugged her little dog, who then growled.

"All right then, thank you for your time." Molly went back to the patrol car and made a few notes. She drove around the neighborhood, and all seemed quiet, unoccupied as most people were probably at work.

She drove back to the station to change into her formal uniform. After a glance at the clock, Molly quickly changed. She didn't mind wearing the skirt so much as the dang pantyhose. The high heels did make her legs look longer. She rubbed a smudge off of her brass nameplate and slid on the jacket. She looked in the mirror in her wardrobe. Not too shabby. Some people hate to work a crowd, but that is where she excelled. She was a social butterfly, and chit chat was as easy as breathing on a cool spring morning.

As long as she didn't have to talk to Amy or any of the Gilberts. Any of them. The whole stinking family of mechanics. Souping up engines. Racing around town. Wait a minute. Nascar and more? *I'll be damned.* Uncle Yancy was correct. It's the family business all right. Call it what you want, but it was the mob. Her grandfather was a fricking rum runner. Right here in Diamond Lake.

She looked once more in the mirror. The funeral would at least keep her mind off the humiliation at the softball field, and hopefully, the lesbian gossip circles didn't expand to the whole town. Probably not. They would out themselves spreading rumors. *I am just being paranoid.* No one else probably even remembers what was said. Amy really had me fooled. Forgive and forget. Ha. *I don't have to forgive her. I really liked her.* Forgetting wouldn't be that easy, either.

CHAPTER 27

The light shining from inside the garage shouldn't have been on. Frank sat his coffee cup on the counter and flicked off the kitchen light, the darkness hiding his movements as he slipped out the back door and headed toward the shop. He stopped at the steel door and listened to the sounds inside the body shop. His palms felt sweaty against the jamb, his heart pounding. *What the hell is going on?* It was his shop, dammit. He twisted the knob and the door resisted. Locked. He pulled a key from his belt ring and eased it into the lock.

Opening the door, he saw the blue light from the back room, and a radio played some heavy metal crap. He watched the shadows move across the back wall until he was certain that it was Donny. He stepped back into the doorway and pulled the knob to shut the door. He strode across the room and put his head into the booth.

"What are you up to this late? Pet project?" Frank asked.

Donny startled and pulled the door panel from the metal frame of the Cutlass.

"Dude, you surprised me. Sorry to bother you." Donny reached down and flicked off the radio. He eased from the door of the car toward the frame, blocking the view of what was inside the car. "I guess time got away from me."

Frank looked suspiciously at Donny. Walking around the car, he peered into the window to confirm that there was no shop tag hanging on the mirror.

"Special project for a friend? I don't remember you having a Cutlass." Frank touched the hood of the car. "I don't mind you helping folks out sometimes, but you need to write a ticket, you know, for insurance and that kind of thing."

"Yeah, I know, I just have this one little project. I'll have the car out of here tonight." Donny pulled the ball cap from his head. "I've been your son-in-law a long time, I figured you would think of this as our family shop by now."

"You know I think of you like a son, Donny. I just think you're hiding something from me." Frank rubbed his chin. "What do you say you show me what you're doing on the inside of a door panel in a body shop?"

"Let's say I don't." Donny folded his arms across his chest.

"Son, this is my shop. My reputation. My business." Frank reached for the car door handle.

Donny blocked him and hissed, "My mistake thinking it was a family shop. But I'm not *familia* am I, Francis?"

Frank pushed him aside and swung the door open. A jean jacket and a cigar box were on the front passenger seat, otherwise, the car appeared empty.

"We maybe ought to talk about this tomorrow, with clearer minds." Frank clenched his fists.

"Pops. Really," Donny said. He smiled like a Cheshire cat. "You're like my father. You can trust me."

"I think you're cheating me, boy. The only reason I don't fire your ass is my daughter. It would kill her to know you're taking money away from our business."

Donny glared. "How dare you call me boy!

Donny swung a fist and Frank grabbed him into a headlock.

"I suggest you put your ass in this car and go home. We will talk about this tomorrow."

Frank watched as Donny slammed his hand on the car hood before he got in. He hit the button to open the overhead door and watched the tail lights as the car went through the dark street. He hit the button to lower the door and turned off the lights. He limped into the office and picked up the phone.

He thought about all the reasons he shouldn't call. After a moment longer, he punched in the numbers.

"Hello. I'd like to leave a message for the chief. Yeah, private." He waited while some clicks and Muzak played on the line. Finally, a voice instructed him to leave a message after the tone, and he spoke again. "This is Frank Gilbert I think my son-in-law is up to something with that van we talked about. It's gone, but he left the shop driving a green Cutlass. Tag 6710-GW." He hung up the phone and pinched his nose. *Please let this be the right thing to do.* He locked the back door when he got in the house.

"Honey, what was going on in the shop?" Rosie asked.

"Nothing." Frank sagged into his recliner and picked up the remote.

"I made a video recording. You missed Jeopardy."

***

Amy snapped her head upright when the boat shed door banged open. The bright daylight reflected off the metallic paint on the boat, the front windows reflecting light onto the ceiling, and then suddenly the space went dark as the door slammed shut. She squinted as her eyes adjusted to the changes. Don stood, hands on his hips, surveying the scene as if something could have changed with her strapped to the chair.

"Boy did you miss a big shindig, finally got around to burying the chief. At least what's left of him." Don walked around the narrow dock. "I wonder if they get a discount from the funeral home if they don't have enough left to embalm."

Amy felt nauseous. She hadn't known the man well, but she went to school with his son. Poor guy. One time a car went off the bridge into the Little Diamond Creek, and his dad made him get up in the middle of the night. He had to dive into the frigid water with a hook from the tow truck and attach it to the bumper. And still had to go to school the next morning. Amy had to do the family business too, of course, but it didn't usually involve night duty. Or jumping into icy water.

"You know what I don't understand? Why are there always bagpipes at police funerals? And on TV shows they do it too. The man had on the full regalia, with a plaid kilt, I mean, it was a Catholic church. Aren't Scottish people Presbyterian? I'm pretty sure he even had a knife stuck in his sock. Did he have to wear that ridiculous costume? A nice dark suit would be fine, wouldn't it?"

Don pulled the tape off of one of her arms, and then off her mouth. He handed her a can of Coke. "Don't be funny."

Amy eagerly sucked down the warm pop, grateful for the liquid. "You still could just take me back to the garage, you know."

He took the can and grabbed her wrist. He tightly wound it with duct tape. "I think it's gone a little far for that. I guess you didn't figure out who killed the chief? No? And no one else will either." He ripped a short piece of tape from the roll, holding it in the air for a moment before covering her mouth again.

"I make excellent plans." Don waved his arm across his chest. "That one fell right in my lap. Charley said that he'd been getting a little close to our set up, and then I was out hunting and there he was. Tottering old idiot, asleep at the base of a tree. I pushed him in the creek and he washed all the way to the lake. I'd have thought the fishes would have cleaned him up, but it's of no never mind. They'll never figure it out." Don smirked. He added a layer of tape to each of her legs. "And after tonight, no one will know what happened to you either."

The yell caught in her throat, and just a muffled noise came from her neck.

"Now, now, don't get all worked up. It's just part of doing business. Nothing personal." He opened the door and whistled as he walked out.

Amy looked around the space, desperate for a way loose. She pulled on her arms until her hands went numb. A sliver of light shone in as the sun went down, and she watched the reflection on the water. She thought about her brother's funeral, her father swinging the censer, wafting the smoke from the incense as he passed. The frankincense and myrrh had blended in a familiar scent, not unpleasant, yet not comforting. Her parents walked like zombies, their eyes red-rimmed and flat; her father swinging the chains as he walked their miserable procession. She couldn't remember anything else about the service.

At the cemetery, she and her sisters walked toward the burial site behind her parents. Their mother collapsed and had to be carried to the chairs waiting on the green AstroTurf that covered the legs of the support rack that would hold the coffin until it was lowered into the cement vault. The only thing that had given Amy comfort was the lineup of cars behind the hearse. The funeral home had run out of those little orange flags, so only every third car had one. Her family was devastated, but they didn't grieve alone. The weather even shared their grief that day, gray with spritzing rain off and on.

Amy jumped when a fish splashed next to her. What if they never find me? At her most dire hour, the teachings of the priests brought her no comfort. It reminded her why she didn't attend services unless coerced by her mother for a major holiday. What if her parents couldn't do her funeral there? They would be so embarrassed. They should be mad. Most everyone she knew was a cafeteria Catholic, taking just what they wanted and leaving the rest. Somehow her sexuality was too much for the church, and she was reminded regularly that she was acceptable to God only if she stayed celibate. What utter bullshit. Priests maybe shouldn't even have to do that. Why should she? Amy realized she had drifted to sleep. How much of the night is gone? She listened intently, hearing only insects and the slap of water on the boat.

CHAPTER 28

Molly tapped her pencil absently. The VHS tape from the Wilson house set-up had been delivered first thing and she'd watched it twice. Two of her guys were in the film, and she wondered if every damn one of them was involved.

The second delivery of flowers wafted a fresh scent across her office. Lily of the Valley. Fragile. Delicate. Like a new relationship? Easily crushed. She had read this card. *What did Amy mean about her ankle? Was she the one I pegged at first? I'll be darned.*

Molly tackled a pile of paperwork on her desk. It threatened to swamp her and she planned to clear it all out before lunch today. Most of it related to Human Resources stuff, vacation requests, and training schedules. It was easy for her to arrange things, and it let her mind work in the background to figure out a plan of action to clean up this department. She hummed to herself. So far her 'out' basket was bigger than the 'in' basket. Her phone rang. "Molly Gorman."

"Chief, this is Mrs. Gilbert," Rose said.

"From the garage, yes. What can I do for you?" Molly answered.

"Well, two things really. I wanted to let you know that we did an inventory of the vehicles in the back lot, and we did find that there was a white G van with a tag that was not in the series."

"I don't follow."

"The tags come in order, and right now we are into the 900's. That tag was from way back in the 600's, I think. I mean, it was our tag and all. But it was really old. It wasn't even in the computer system as a work order."

"And every car gets a tag?" Molly asked.

"Yes, of course, or we can't keep track of the vehicles or the work orders. Even in a small shop, things get a little crazy sometimes." Mrs. Gilbert paused.

Molly just waited. People always say the important stuff last.

Rosie cleared her throat. "And then another little thing. Amy hasn't come into work. I'm worried about her."

"When is the last time you saw her?" Molly asked.

"The day before yesterday, in the afternoon. She had some big softball tournament. We thought maybe she stayed out celebrating or something, but her roommate Robin said she didn't see her last night. I called her when Amy didn't come in. Amy always calls if she doesn't feel well."

Molly heard Frank's voice mumble something in the background.

"Frank says her car is out back, but her motorcycle is gone." Mrs. Gilbert paused. "Frank, anything else?" Another pause. "He says no."

Molly rubbed her temples. What fresh hell has Amy gotten into? Hungover somewhere? "Alright, I'm glad you called. It's a myth that you have to wait 24 hours. I'll start the search, but it would be helpful if you have a picture and could bring it down to the station."

Rose started to choke up. "Thank you, Chief."

***

With Amy's history of heavy drinking, she was probably sleeping it off somewhere. Or in a ditch. *Dammit. What do I care? I was just a notch on her bedpost.* Just like any other situation. Step one. Then step two. She pushed her phone buttons.

"Have dispatch post a bulletin, 30-year-old white female, last seen on a white motorcycle. Wellness check." She hung up. The white van. She picked up the phone again, and dialed. "Sheriff Reed, this is Chief Gorman. Can you meet me in Central Park by the picnic shelter in fifteen? Thanks."

Hanging up the phone, Molly locked her desk and headed for her car. She drove to the park by the river walk and waited. Sheriff Reed pulled up beside her car. When he stood up to his full six-foot-four frame, Molly was glad she had him on her side.

He pulled open the passenger door and compressed himself into the seat. His caramel colored skin nearly matched his shirt. His dark eyes looked thoughtful. "This must be serious."

"It is. And delicate." Molly exhaled, then took a quick breath. "I have enough evidence to link two officers to a number of burglaries. I need to make sure I get them all, and I want to get the fence, too. I need your help to find a green Cutlass." She handed him a tag number. "Quietly. These guys are brazen, but they've also been doing it a long time and are pretty smooth operators."

The sheriff rubbed his chin. "How deep do you think it goes?"

"Well, I didn't see you on the tape," Molly said.

"There's that," he said. He reached for the door handle. "Watch your back. It may go all the way to the former chief. And we know how that ended." He tapped her roof and she drove off.

Molly felt her headache getting worse. *I better eat something. That café is only a block away.* She pulled into the freshly painted lot and parked the car. The stench of the fresh sealer made her stomach roll. She stared at the door a moment, recalling her lunch here with Amy. *What a douche she turned out to be.* Molly opened her door and glanced around out of habit. All clear. She walked inside and sat near the door, her back to the windows.

Gloria, the same waitress from their lunch, walked past. "Be right with you." She plopped a menu on the table.

Molly was debating between the pecan waffle or the house special in a skillet when she noticed a shadow over her. She glanced up.

Robin said, "I've been looking for you for two days. Do you have a minute?"

"Have a seat." Molly folded her arms across her chest. *If I wasn't in uniform, I would have said no. Some nerve, chasing me down. Maybe she knows where Amy is?*

Gloria showed up. "Hey Robin, do you need a menu?"

"No, I won't be staying. How's Chip?"

"He's fine. What do you want?" Gloria snapped her gum.

"House special, bacon. Coffee." Molly handed over the menu. She took an even breath. "Have you seen Amy since the softball game?" *That hurt a little more than I thought it would.*

"Yes. The next morning, I got her some breakfast. Not since then. Why?" Robin asked.

"Her parents are concerned," Molly said.

Robin dismissed it. "I wouldn't worry. She can be a little impulsive."

"You don't say." Molly stared at Robin. "What can I do for you?"

"Funny you should mention the softball game. I'm sorry about what you overheard. Just hear me out." Robin looked Molly in the eye. "I am very sorry. I take full responsibility for what I said at the ballpark. It was hurtful." She blew out a breath.

Molly waited.

"I wish I could take it back, but I can't. Please don't be angry with Amy. It was my fault. See, I was trying to get her to ask you out."

Gloria dropped a cup of coffee on the table and a full carafe with it. "Food will be right up."

Robin held up her hands. "I know, it was a stupid way to do it. I suggested the bet just to egg her on, and Amy didn't want anything to do with it. It was childish. She was really happy when you guys went out. She really likes you."

Molly picked up a sugar packet, shook it, tore the corner and dumped it into her cup. She took a spoon, stirred and then sat it down. What do you say to someone who has no shame and tells all her secrets without a care for what anyone else thinks? Nothing.

She picked up the cup. "I appreciate you having the courage to talk to me." She sipped the hot beverage.

Robin blushed. "I can't undo what happened, but I won't ever do that again. I'm sure you were angry with us. I didn't think about your feelings, and I got carried away running my mouth." Robins' eyes appeared misty. "I was wrong and if you can't forgive me, fine, but please forgive Amy."

Gloria slung a plate on the table.

Robin snapped, "Gloria, Jesus, give me a break. Leave us alone."

"Alright, alright, crabby pants." She dropped the ticket on the table.

"I'm sorry, hang on." Robin picked up the tab and handed Gloria a twenty. "I should go and let you eat. Thanks for at least listening."

Molly picked up the fork and watched Robin leave the café. Robin seemed sincere. She wasn't quite sure what to think about Amy. Maybe she wasn't being deceitful. What if she does actually like me? She started to eat but had lost her appetite. She pushed the plate away and left a five-dollar bill on the table. She unlocked the squad car and slumped into the seat. She sat a few minutes to collect herself. She cranked the ignition and eased the car onto the street. A melody popped into her mind. She hummed and tapped the edge of the steering wheel in time to the music. She decided to take a swing through downtown and came up to a gas station intending to get a Coke and some aspirin.

At the light, she watched a white van run the red. She couldn't just let it go, not with the chance it was tied to the burglaries. If she called for backup, she'd look paranoid at the least, tip off the dirty cops at the maximum. She flipped on the lights and turned behind the van. At first, the driver sped up, and then he seemed to gain his senses and pulled into a parking lot. His backup lights glowed briefly as he shifted from Drive to Park. It didn't appear he was going to run.

Molly called in the stop. She waited until the tag came back.

Expired. *Great.* She stepped from the car and approached the side of the door. The driver grinned at her. "Sir, can I see your license and registration, please. You missed that stop light."

Donald Jenkins even looked cocky in his license picture. She carried the paperwork back to the car and began to fill out the citation. She called in the numbers, and his record was clear. She looked over the van. Something was off, but she couldn't put her finger on it. Walking to the van, she noticed that the plumbing logo on the side was fresh even though the rest of the van had faded white paint.

"You have a summons to the circuit court for careless driving, rather than reckless. You're welcome. Also, Mr. Jenkins, this van has an expired tag. You have two weeks to get it cleared up." Molly assessed his reaction.

His eyes flared with anger, but he spoke evenly. "I'm sorry, this is my aunt's van. She's getting older and probably forgot. I just didn't notice. Careless of me."

She knew he was lying, but his aunt probably had owned the van at one time. Molly stared at him as he took the paperwork. "Drive carefully."

"Yes, ma'am." Don tipped his head to the side. "You look familiar. Maybe you hang out with my sister-in-law. She's a dyke, too." With that, he rammed the gears into drive and jammed the accelerator down; the tires spun as he left the parking lot.

Molly watched him drive off, and her eyebrows furrowed over her face. *What a tool.* She slid into the car and put on her seat belt. She rubbed her temples.

Her radio crackled. "Chief, a white motorcycle is reported found. Downtown next to the Mane Thing."

She picked up the handle. "On my way."

Nancy and Winnie were both standing by a police cruiser when she pulled into the parking lot. Doug stood by a dumpster, his notebook open. The wheel of a motorcycle barely poked out from behind it.

Nancy clutched her hands as she approached. "Thank god you're here. I just know something awful has happened. You know we thought it was odd when we spotted this motorcycle this morning. I didn't know it was Amy's; it used to be candy apple red."

Doug looked at the Chief. "It's just parked, no keys, not locked. No riding gear."

"Dust it and have Pete come pick it up." Molly steered the women inside the hair salon. They both looked as if they might faint. "Did either of you see Amy in the last couple of days?"

"Yesterday. We both did," Winnie said. "I cut her hair, really short, for riding. You know, because of her motorcycle helmet messing it up, and then she went to get flowers." Her eyes welled up. "I fussed at her for treating you badly. She was really sorry and cut her hair in order to turn over a new leaf."

"Cut her hair for a new leaf. Right." Molly clenched her jaw. "What time was that?"

Nancy answered, "A little before five pm. She was in my shop just before close because I delivered your flowers myself."

"Did you notice anything unusual when you left?" Molly asked.

"No, I pulled the van up to load deliveries, and just went on my way." Nancy took Winnie's hand.

Molly wrote in her notebook. "So far you two are the last ones to see her. Do you remember what she was wearing?"

Winnie said, "Blue jeans and black combat boots."

Nancy added, "I think she had on a black t-shirt with some band? I'm sure she just got a ride or something." She turned to Molly. "Amy can be a little impulsive."

"You don't say," Molly said dryly.

Nancy said, "Oh, that's not what I meant. I gave her hell, and she cried. She was really sorry she hurt your feelings. You kids are more open about personal stuff. Never mind me, I'm just more old-fashioned. You kids wouldn't believe it. Winnie was the wild child back in the day."

Molly looked over at Winnie and raised an eyebrow.

"I am sure she doesn't need to hear all that, honey," Winnie protested. "Anyway, her hair is pretty short, blond spikes though. It's still cute. Or it was. Is." Her eyes misted up again.

"That will be helpful, thank you both. If you think of anything else or find anything else, let me know." She handed Nancy her business card.

Winnie burst into a fresh round of tears. "You two would have been so cute."

"I'm sure we will find her safe and sound." Molly slid her sunglasses back on to cover her eyes and headed out. *What the hell have you done, Amy?*

CHAPTER 29

Molly crouched near the dining room window and peered out into the street. Nothing. When they set up the sting, she knew it was not a sure thing that it would work. She crept back and stood near the china cabinet, her form disguised by the shadow.

It was lucky Sheriff Reed caught sight of the Cutlass parked at the Park and Ride. The list of items stuffed inside the door panels included mostly jewelry and other effects that were hard to identify and easy to fence. He'd been able to talk to the transfer truck driver that went to pick it up. He'd handed it off to the state police since it was headed out of the county. It might yet lead to bigger fish. Molly shifted her weight. She hated doing stakeouts. She had a hunch where things were leading, and she didn't like it one bit.

Molly was relieved when she finally heard the front door lock clank as it was bumped. She was starting to doubt they would take the bait. The footsteps across the tile echoed in the still house. She looked across to the sheriff deputies in the kitchen and held up her hand. She then put her hand on her revolver.

To her surprise, the burglars headed straight toward the stairs leading to the master bedroom. They must already know what they're here for. She knew another deputy was in the front bedroom waiting. By now, an unmarked car would be behind the van, blocking it in. She listened as they climbed the steps.

It sounded like only two sets of shoes. One person was heavier than the other. She waved her hand, and the deputies flanked the stairwell.

She scampered up the stairs. "Don't move." She aimed her revolver directly at the tallest man. He turned. *Dammit. It was Jeff.*

"Molly, Molly, Molly, welcome to our little retirement fund. The last chief just wouldn't take a cut, but I bet you're smarter and you will." Jeff pulled up his shirt revealing his holster.

Molly stared at him. "It's Chief, and that sounds like a threat."

"Oh no." Jeff smiled. "It's a promise."

The deputy stepped from the next room. "Don't count on that. Put your hands on your head."

The toilet flushed in the master bath and the rookie Tracy walked out, still zipping his pants. "Sorry, I didn't know there was a lady present."

"No, I'm sorry Tracy. Hands on your head." Molly flicked out her handcuffs and locked one wrist, then grabbed the second hand and secured it.

Jeff said, "Why the triple-A with guns? Dougie couldn't make it? Ah. You still don't know who is involved. Dude, don't say anything."

***

Sheriff Reed pulled in behind Molly as she approached the tidy cape cod. A kid's bike was in the driveway and several skateboards were in the front yard. A row of petunias cheerfully fluttered in the light breeze.

Charley opened the door before she could knock. "Chief, come on in."

The officers stepped into the modest home, a TV played in the background.

Molly said, "Charley Hansen, I am really not sure how it all came to this. You are under arrest. We can do this the easy way, or the hard way." She nodded toward the wall that was Sheriff Reed.

Charley at least had the decency to act surprised. "What are you talking about?"

"We've got film of you in the Wilson house," Molly said.

"Shit," Charley said.

"Yeah. And we just picked up the rookie Tracy and Jeff this morning. They didn't give you up. I was surprised Doug wasn't involved?" Molly said, fishing.

"That tool. I always sent him to investigate. He couldn't find his ass with both hands." Charley stopped talking. He looked at the floor for a long time. "I know how this looks."

"It looks like you're a thief." Molly shook her head.

"It's just, well, these are good guys who got caught up with what's been going on around here for a long time. They all have watched criminals make more in a month than they earn in a year." Charley splayed his hands out. "Have you tried to take care of a family on our salary? It's not easy."

Molly scoffed. "The way I see it, the new guys learned from the masters and you killed the chief because he got too close to the truth."

"Me kill Barry? He was like my own father; I wouldn't hurt a hair on his head." Charley pleaded with them, "You have to believe me."

"I don't know what to believe," Molly said. "I see crooked cops stealing from the people we're supposed to protect."

"That's all. We'd lift some small stuff, fence it, no harm. The insurance paid for it all, and we know those guys are a bunch of thieves." Charley stood rocking on one foot to the other. "I really thought Barry had a hunting accident."

"Do you want to wait until you have a lawyer?" Molly asked.

"I'll have him meet us downtown. Can I ride in the front of the car?" Charley asked.

"Sorry, no. I'll cuff you in the front, though," Molly said.

Soon they were pulling in by the police station. He hadn't said anything all the way to the station. Charley didn't resist in any way; he strolled next to Molly like he was arrested every day. She cuffed him to the table in the interrogation room and left him.

While the sheriff was talking with Charley, Molly sat at the table in the breakroom. Something still wasn't adding up. She scooted the chair back and headed to the interrogation room. She tapped on the door.

"Did you get a full story?" she asked.

Reed nodded. "Yeah, the security place would call in a system breach, probably caused by these guys, and then they would hit the place. They had a fence hide it in cars and run it around the state."

"Did they give him up?" Molly asked.

"Yeah, a mechanic at the Gilbert garage." Reed flipped through his papers.

Molly felt her throat turn dry.

"A Donald "Big Don" Jenkins." Reed handed her a paper. "This is his address, and my guys are on their way there."

"Is this up by the state park?" Molly asked.

"Yeah, his family owned it for eons. Big old farmhouse. Probably a view of half the town," Reed said. "What are you thinking?"

"I think he has something to do with the chief's murder, and now I think Amy Gilbert is in grave danger." Molly rubbed her forehead. "Do you know any of his family?"

"No. Ask Charley." Sheriff Reed opened the door behind him.

They headed into the small room. Molly leaned over, putting her hands on the table. "I think Don has Amy Gilbert. Where would he go?"

Charley said, "No way. She's his sister-in-law. Family before all others."

"Where would he go?" Molly repeated. "What do you know about him?"

"I recommend that you use this to bargain," the lawyer said.

"Dammit, Charley." Molly smacked the table. "I get protecting the guys you work with but this guy gave you pennies on the dollar and you won't give him up?"

Charley fidgeted. "I've only known him from doing business. He was a football star in high school. Too little for college ball.

He was still pissed about that.”

“And,” Molly said.

Charley shrugged. “He grew up in the Little River trailer park and married that Gilbert girl. Not the lesbian. The redhead.”

Molly rolled her eyes. “And?”

“And he inherited the family farm when his aunt died. And her cottage. He lives in a big place on the lake. It’s pretty sweet. We went fishing a couple times.” Charley leaned back. “I don’t know what that would have to do with anything.”

Molly pulled Reed into the hall. “I’m guessing that he won’t be home. Can you get an address? I’m headed to the cottage. Send another car if you have one.”

“I’ll be right behind you,” Reed said.

Molly rushed to her car, buckled in and hit the ignition. She scribbled the address down on her notepad with one hand, while driving with the other, her knee on the steering wheel. She flicked on her lights and headed around the east side of the lake and turned onto a washboard road. The car bounced across the dry earth. She was mad at Amy but certainly didn’t wish her any harm. *She noticed me at the first game she saw me at? Where the hell is she?* Only a few places looked occupied, but that would change once school was out. She slowed at a stone place that looked out over the lake from a low ridge. The address was on the mailbox. She spotted the white van and parked behind it so that it couldn’t be moved. *The dumbass should have at least hidden the van in the garage. Maybe it’s keeping the door from opening?* The overhead garage-style door on the boathouse looked rusted into place.

She hesitated. Then she picked up her mic and reported the location and tag. She rolled down the window to listen, waiting for the backup. The drone of insects and the lapping of waves on the lake edge were the only sounds. She flicked on her mag light, and then pulled her gun out, just to be ready. It seemed to take forever. *Amy, dammit, I really did like you. Do, not did. I do like you, even if you’re an ass. What is taking him so long? Amy, where the fuck are you?* As soon as the sheriff’s car slid in behind her, Molly popped out of the car.

Sheriff Reed came along her side, and she shined her light into the van. The two seats were empty, only wooden planks laid on the floorboard. The hood was still warm, but the engine was silent. Not too recently parked. They crept around the van to the side door of the boat dock. They made eye contact, and Molly grabbed the knob, yanking the door open.

The boathouse was empty. The slack ropes to the dock indicated where a boat had been secured. There was a smattering of fishing and boating paraphernalia hung on the rafters. Molly shined her light around the walls and settled on the water's edge. Two other officers joined them in the boathouse. An office desk chair bobbed with the wave motion, and gray duct tape contrasted the black arms. Reed used a boat oar to lift the chair and set it on the dock. Tape residue was along both front legs.

He studied the chair as if it might speak. "Where next? Any ideas?"

Molly nodded. "Yes."

***

Burglaries Solved *Police found their own responsible for multiple burglaries in the Diamond Lake area. Prosecutors say they caught them on video committing a burglary.*

Sergeant Charles Hansen, 41, is a 20-year veteran of the Diamond Lake Police Department. According to the state's attorney court filing, Hansen led the thieves who even targeted his own neighbor. More charges are pending.

Also charged are Jeffrey French, 34, a ten-year veteran of the Diamond Lake Police Department, and Tracy Smith, 25, a one-year veteran of the Diamond Lake Police Department.

According to court documents, "There were search warrants that were executed and based on the evidence and items recovered in those searches."

Police Chief Molly Gorman said, "I've dedicated my car-

eer to law enforcement. It's devastating to think that your own committed these crimes, but I try to think of the victims, the people who have had their homes burglarized. I think about them and the feelings they must have. I'm much more concerned about that."

CHAPTER 30

"Wakey, wakey." Don kicked her foot and Amy jerked upright. Her limbs were free from the chair, but her arms were now taped together. "It's time for a little boat ride." He pulled her up by an elbow, her legs tingling as blood began to flow. He pushed her along the edge of the dock, the water dimly lit by the moonlight from the front of the boat shed.

With one hand, he flicked up the latch on the railing gate, which swung wide open. The water smacked onto the hull when Donny stepped onto the AstroTurf decking inside the boat. He leaned across and pulled the rope to slide the boat closer to the dock.

"Watch your step. I wouldn't want you to get hurt." He laughed a throaty chuckle. "See, that's funny because I do want you hurt. I want your family hurt. I want that bitch cop hurt. And best of all, I get to see your smart-ass self out of ideas."

Molly? What did he have against her?

He reached out to hold her elbow and tugged enough to pull her off balance, forcing her to step. It seemed her choice, into the water, or into the boat. She quickly decided that wet or dry, she was going to ultimately end up in the boat. Timidly, she edged a foot between the boat rails, then fell to the floor, the boat rocking harmlessly on its tie lines. She could hear the sound of duct tape ripping and then Don was wrapping her ankles. She tried to kick, but his grip was too strong and from her stomach, she couldn't tell exactly where he was.

"You see, the problem with most people, they don't think things through. If I had untied the boat, I might be bailing instead of getting ready to launch. The most important part, follow the same steps every time. Then you don't miss something. Like life jackets."

He buckled the yellow foam across his chest. He threw a ski belt onto the floor. "This doesn't meet current boating regulations, but I doubt anyone will notice."

Don turned on a small flashlight and aimed it at the controls of the boat. He opened a cover with a snap, then flicked the switch. A green glow filled the boathouse. He flicked another switch and a white light popped on at the rear of the boat. "Safety first. Wouldn't want to get in a wreck."

He stepped to the back, nudging Amy toward the middle with his foot as he passed. He used the flashlight and hopped onto the deck to unhook the moorings. He leaped back in and pulled the last rope, coiling it neatly. As he went by, causing the boat to rock slightly, she could see his grin. She shifted her weight and could hear the motor fire behind her.

Cold air blew her hair as the craft slid out across the still water. Amy twisted around and was able to sit upright on the floor, even with her feet and hands taped together. The boat controls glowed casting a green shadow on Don's face as he captained the boat. On the disappearing shoreline, the twinkle of a few cabin lights flickered in the distance. She scanned the lake, knowing that there would be no other craft out. It must be the middle of the night. There was no sound but the motor and the water falling into the wake behind the boat.

Abruptly, Don yanked the tape off her face. "No one's going to hear you anyways. I'm bored. You might be entertaining, begging and all."

Amy blinked back tears from the sting on her cheeks. Her mind went a hundred miles an hour. She put her head on her knees.

"Oh now, I know what you're thinking. People never change. You think I should feel bad."

"Asshole." Amy clamped her mouth shut. He seemed content to wait her out. With no landmarks, she had no idea where they were on the lake, with all the inlets and bays, the waters could be confusing even in daylight. She slammed her feet into the bench seat, a bang echoing across the water. As she kicked it a second time, she felt the boat slow as he left the steering controls. Hands grabbed her arms and she jerked backward. She could feel him over her, still and silent. *Will he hit me?* She closed her eyes anticipating a blow.

The boat rocked as he walked back to the throttle. She tipped as the boat surged forward. Eventually, the boat slowed. The white light cut off, and the boat coasted to a stop. With a lurch, the boat rolled to the right and she fell backward, striking her head on the cold aluminum. A metallic taste filled her mouth from where she bit her lip. She stared up at the stars, the same constellations that sailors used to navigate for centuries, useless to her. The sensation left her hands, pinned tightly together. *He wanted her hurt. How hurt? After god knows how many days in the boathouse, he is going to kill me.* She felt her head spin. She forced herself to calm down.

"You can just let me go," Amy whispered.

"Four, three, two, and one." Don flicked the motor off. "I've made this trip every day this week in anticipation. Planning ahead. I know exactly where we are. In a few weeks, you're going to float up, and another Gilbert will be found dead in this lake."

She immediately knew where they stopped. They were outside the park beach. Her throat tightened. Donny was completely mental. And she had no options. He pulled a bowie knife from his belt, the blade reflecting in the moonlight. A set of headlights crossed over the water as a vehicle pulled up to the shoreline. They were definitely at the park beach. Donny looked toward the shore. If the arrival of an audience concerned him, it didn't show. Don turned, then calmly flicked his fishing pole, the line casting out smoothly. He sat back, slowly cranking the handle, winding the wet filament back around the spinner. Amy could hear him start to whistle.

"You have to stick to the plan, or you make mistakes." Donny sat the pole into a rod holder. "It has to look like an accident." He calmly opened a pocket knife and then cut the tape from her legs and yanked it off her pants, tossing the sticky clump into the dark water. She tried to move her legs and they tingled from hours of stillness.

She saw the flick of amber emergency lights reflect off his white jacket stripes as Don stood over her.

"You know, I really was rather fond of you. I hope you don't think poorly of me after this." He pushed her forward and flicked the blade between her wrists, nicking one as he did so. Blood dripped down from her hand.

"Dammit, now I have to wash out the boat."

He pulled the tape, wadded it and tossed it down. With a quick motion, he grabbed her up like a rag doll and flipped her over the side of the boat.

***

The shock of the cold water made Amy exhale before she knew what happened. She struggled and took a big breath as she bobbed above the surface. Her limbs were stiff from hours taped together and her soaked clothes pulled her down. *I can't be that far underwater.* She kicked her legs and waved her arms to no effect. She struggled to lay flat, the weight of her garments holding her down below the surface. Bit by bit the air in her lungs bubbled out of her mouth. She fought the urge to inhale. Her body slid vertical and she began to sink. Her lungs burned.

She thought of her parents, their bodies huddled together as they saw her brother brought ashore. *Not again; this time for me. When is the last time I said I loved them?* She would miss them, and her sisters. Maybe Robin would find the woman of her dreams, even if she couldn't admit she wanted a lifetime with just one. And then Molly. Oh god, if she had just had more time with Molly. *I am so sorry, I never meant to hurt you. I love you, Molly.*

The impulse to breathe became too strong and she sucked in the cold water. The burning as it passed her throat was unbearable. She struggled to exhale, but only more water gushed into her mouth. The darkness around her faded to full black.

CHAPTER 31

Molly sped across the parking lot, blue lights flashing through the darkness, reflecting off the trees, the siren screaming. Behind her was another police car, and a sheriff. The DNR officer was out of his truck, his headlights shining across the parking lot as he untied his boat. She skidded to a stop and leaped out of the car. A white panel truck pulled beside her, WATER RESCUE painted in black on the side. A crew of frogmen jumped out and started pulling out an inflatable rubber raft.

The tires spun as the driver of another rescue truck jerked into reverse, the trailer carrying the speed boat splashing into the water. Two men leaped out and started to unhook the straps, allowing the boat to float up. They flipped inside, and the motor roared to life.

"I'm going," Molly yelled as she sprinted across the dock. The fireman at the helm reached for her arm as she approached, and she jumped the distance to the boat deck. The boat lurched back and around as they skidded across the blackness.

The searchlight on the front of the boat swept the water, and only a motionless inky surface appeared. Molly spotted a motor boat. The image became clearer the closer they got. Donny Jenkins sat apparently fishing.

The captain in the other rescue boat spoke over a loud-speaker. "Maintain your position. This is the water patrol. Do not move the boat."

Molly stood, hands clenched, scanning the image for another body in the boat. *Where the hell are you, Amy?* As they slowed down next to the fishing boat, she shined her light across the empty seats. The engines churned as they swung closer. She heard the engine of the other boats as they circled the fishing boat.

The rubber raft bobbed on the wakes of the other boats. All three crafts had lights sweeping the water as the red boat drifted. The captain blinded Don with the main lights. Don laid down the fishing pole and put his hands in his lap. The officer in the next boat pulled out a rifle and aimed it at him. Don smirked and raised his hands.

"She must be in the water," Molly said, aiming her light across the surface near the hull. *I never got to tell you that I forgive you.* "Move the beam light further behind the boat." *Come on, come on, where the fuck are you?*

"I got bubbles." The driver aimed the light about ten feet from the bobbing craft.

Molly ripped at the latch at her waist and the duty belt with her gun dropped to the deck. She took two steps and dove into the lake, the shock of the cold water taking her breath. In four quick strokes, she reached the point of the light. She took a deep breath and dove down, peering in the water as she moved deeper. *There she is!* Her lungs burned as she kept kicking, reaching out for the upstretched arms.

Molly grabbed the hands and turned up towards the surface. She pulled Amy hard and pushed her toward the air. *Please, please be okay.* With a burst, she blew out her air and kicked the last few feet to the surface. She felt herself become unfocused, the urge to inhale strong, burning in her mind. She forced herself to keep kicking, and a set of hands pulled her upward. The diver smiled as she popped up. Sucking in a large breath, she forced the air out and took another breath.

Amy was floating face up, another swimmer pulling her along the side of the rescue boat.

Molly started to swim, her clothing dragging her back. "Is she breathing?"

"We did a few blows, but we have to get her on the boat to start compressions." The diver adjusted his mask off of his face. "You'd make a good water rescue. Now let's get you out, too."

The man pulled Molly toward the railing, and a ladder hanging from the side. He pushed her up by her butt as she struggled up, the short swim taking more from her than she realized. She stepped over the top and collapsed onto the deck. She looked up to see Amy flat on her back, a fireman leaning over her, listening at her mouth. He turned his face, pinched her nose and blew into her mouth. A second officer locked his hands and began to press her chest in a slow rhythmic pattern. He paused and another breath.

Molly sucked in, watching in silence as the men worked, the boat drifting, chopping at the water. She turned when an engine roared beside them. Donny jammed the throttle and disappeared into the darkness. The police boat followed behind, a flashing light on the roof skipping across the inky water, a siren blaring in the darkness. Molly turned her interest from the shrinking lights and studied the lifeless form on the deck, the men switched spots and continued their compressions and breaths. *Come on, breathe.* She brushed her wet hair from her face, suddenly aware she was cold.

A dark figure spoke from beside her. "Do you need us to board?"

The man doing the breaths called, "Yes. Get Jimmy to drive us to shore."

A diver climbed the rail and commanded the throttles. The boat lurched forward, the raft following behind.

Molly clutched her hands into fists and bit down on her lip.

The fireman said, "Got a pulse. Got a breath."

Amy twitched and they turned her to the side and water dribbled from her mouth. She coughed and gagged, more water coming up. Molly pulled in air, unaware until that moment that she had been holding her breath.

Amy coughed up more water, this time sucking in a big breath.

Molly scooted over, grabbing Amy, pulling her nearer. "Oh, thank god. Are you okay?" She brushed her face with her fingertips.

"I think so," Amy said, doubling over coughing. "I dreamed that you saved me."

"You did?" Molly looked around at the crew on the deck. *Screw it.* She shifted closer to Amy and kissed her cheek. "That wasn't a dream."

Once they reached the dock, the EMT's headed toward the boat. Molly caught her balance and stepped off, a fireman on the dock grabbing a rope to steady the craft. Molly felt herself shiver and her hands shake. *Hold it together. Everyone is all right.* A frogman was pulling the raft out of the water. A small crowd had gathered on the shoreline and she could see Robin pacing back and forth.

***

Amy felt horrible. Her head was pounding and her chest felt like an elephant was sitting on her. She felt her body pulled up to standing and saw the EMT's waiting with a stretcher, presumably for her.

"We got ya, easy does it." The firemen lifted Amy, one under each arm.

"Okay," she whispered. "I'm okay."

She was thankful for their support to get out of the boat. She sagged between them, her feet scuffing the dock as they carried her to the stretcher. She could hear Molly's voice but couldn't make out what she was saying. Her feet swung up as the fireman flipped her horizontal.

"Eeek," she screamed.

"It's all right. We got ya." The EMT helped her lay down and tucked a blanket over her shuddering body. A plastic mask was placed over her face, the air blowing was cool on her skin. They buckled the straps and popped the handles up and began to roll her toward the ambulance. The wheels clicked at each gap between the deck boards and crunched as they resisted rolling on the gravel. Amy saw Robin's face above her.

"Oh Amy, what the hell? I was so worried. Your parents are on their way. What happened?" Robin asked.

"Donny pushed me in the lake," Amy answered softly.

"On purpose? Mother fucker. I will kill him. I really will." Robin smacked the gurney rail.

Molly said, "I did not hear that."

When did she get here? Amy said, "Where are we going?"

"The hospital." Robin asked the blond woman pushing the stretcher, "Is she going to be okay?"

"We will take very good care of her." She answered.

The rolling stopped and Amy heard the legs clack against the ambulance floor. She felt nauseous as the bed bucked upward and was horrified to be vomiting just as they slid her into the ambulance.

The white lights on the ceiling blinded her as the young man simply wiped her mouth and readjusted the mask. "You're going to be fine. Just relax and take a deep breath. You may have some cracked ribs."

The first deep breath started a series of hard coughs, which caused white spots in her eyes. Her chest burned, but the airline helped ease the effort to breathe.

Robin bobbed into her line of sight. "She has to be okay, she owes me a birthday bash. Right, Amy?"

"Where's Molly?" Amy looked around.

"Are you her girlfriend?" the EMT asked.

"Friend, yes," Robin said. "Not girlfriend." Robin gave her a sweet smile. "I'm Robin."

"Michelle. Nice to meet you," the EMT said.

Even now, Robin was flirting. *I might be sick again.*

Amy saw Molly climb up, her clothes still wet, her hair clinging to her head. *Why is wet hair so damn sexy?*

Molly nudged Robin over towards the open door. "After tonight, I think I get that title, thank you very much."

The EMT smiled. "Okay, then, Officer. You can ride with us in the ambulance."

She took out another blanket and held it up to wrap Molly. Behind her, there was a bang from an explosion.

Molly jumped to the ground and spun around. "Jesus, there's a fire on the lake!"

Robin looked across the water and said, "That's the dam. You don't think a boat hit it?"

Molly shrugged. "As long as it was Donny's boat, I'm good with it. Let's get this bus moving." She climbed back inside and sat down next to Amy, pulling the blanket around her shoulders.

Fire at Blocker's Dam A 34-year-old man was killed when a boat exploded early Saturday morning at Blockers Dam, according to authorities and a witness.

Donald Jenkins, of the 700 block of East 44th Road in Diamond Lake, was dead on the scene, according to the medical examiner's office.

Around 2 a.m., the roughly 22-foot boat burst into flames with Jenkins on board, according to Diamond Lake Fire Chief Dennis Worley, witness accounts and the medical examiner's office. Jenkin's body was removed from inside the boat's remaining structure.

"We've had fires in the lake in the past, but no explosions of this magnitude," Worley said.

Jenkins death was ruled an accident caused by multiple blunt force injuries from the boat explosion and drowning, according to the medical examiner's office. "It is possible he was under the influence and became disoriented as to his location. The boat approached the wall at a high rate of speed. All warning lights were functional at the time."

Anthony Kantrell, who lives nearby, said he was getting ready for bed when he heard the blast, which was so powerful it caused pictures on the wall of his house to shake. He walked over, as he peered down from his picture window, he could see the flaming remnants of the boat.

"Then (I was) just watching everything burn and sink. I didn't know anyone was on board," he said.

"The Fire Department will contact a salvage company to remove the debris from the lake and the state fire marshal would investigate the cause of the explosion. Preliminary findings suggest the explosion was caused by the boat impacting the dam at a high rate of speed," Worley said.

Interim Police Chief Promoted *Local officials have announced Molly Gorman is promoted to full-time police Chief of Diamond Lake.*

"Chief Gorman not only brings a vast breadth of experience, but her impressive detective work makes her well qualified for this position," City Councilman Yancy Wilson said in a statement. "Her expertise in community policing and predictive policing align precisely with the goals and priorities of our City Council."

Gorman earned a Business Administration Degree from Eastern Michigan University. After the police academy, she worked for the Detroit Police Department, earning the rank of Sergeant.

"I am thrilled to appoint Chief Gorman to be officially our next chief," said Mayor Cooper. "Throughout her time here, Molly has demonstrated the utmost integrity and professionalism in her approach to policing and true leadership in the department."

"I'm extremely excited to have this opportunity to serve the city of Diamond Lake and its citizens," said Gorman. "We have a great team of officers who are committed to their jobs and I look forward to building an even stronger

team."

Gorman said priority as Chief will be to thoroughly review the structure of the department, and fill recent vacancies in the department.

Gorman will be formally sworn in during a ceremony later this month at Old Town Hall. She will be Diamond Lake's first female chief and one of only a handful of female police chiefs in the state.

Murder Solved *According to Diamond Lake Police Chief Molly Gorman, the murder of Former Police Chief Barry Tristan was "not a random act," and the town of about 4,000 residents is safe.*

"There is no cause for alarm," Gorman said. "We do believe at this point that the perpetrator was fatally injured in a boating accident."

Sheriff Reed confirmed her statement. "We have given materials to prosecutors for any related charges, but at this time are closing the investigation. Before the incident at Blockers Dam, the deceased confessed to a credible witness. No others are implicated in the murder."

CHAPTER 32

Molly scurried around her apartment kitchen. She dialed the phone, holding it under her chin while she cooked.

"Nancy?" Molly said into the phone receiver, "Can you make a delivery to my place?"

Nancy said, "Anything in particular?"

"Yes, roses," Molly answered in a hushed tone. "If you have them, I'd like orange." *More than friends*.

"Do you want something on the card?" Nancy asked.

"Yes. 'Impulsive is good.'" Molly looked behind her to see that Amy hadn't wandered into the kitchen.

Nancy said, "How's the patient? I thought maybe I'd deliver them with Winnie in the morning."

"She's getting cabin fever, and I'm sure she'd like to see you both. Tomorrow is fine. Thanks." Molly hung up the phone and pulled the pan from the stove.

Molly arranged a bowl of the hot cereal, a small juice glass, and toast. She put a smiley face in brown sugar on the oatmeal. She carried the tray into the bedroom, careful to keep it level. "How's my little patient?"

"I am fine, honestly, you are so sweet," Amy said.

After spending a sleepless night in the hospital, with all the noise and chaos, Molly had brought Amy back to her apartment. Amy slept a good bit, and she was generally an easy going patient. She was also pleased to discover Amy didn't wear pajamas. Molly sat the tray on the side table, careful not to knock the clock off.

"You drowned. The only reason the doctor didn't keep you in the hospital any longer was that I said that I would take care of you."

"Mom isn't too happy about it."

"She didn't get much say. I pulled rank. I am the chief of police, you know," Molly said, a smile sneaking across her face as she sat down on the bed.

Amy gave her a kiss. Then reached out for a hug. A little orange flash leaped onto the bed.

"Nope. Cheeto out." Molly lifted the intruder, setting him out and shutting the door. She turned to Amy. "Come on. You need to eat."

"What is this?" Amy scrutinized the tray next to her.

"Oatmeal. It's good for you." Molly nudged the plate toward Amy. "Come on, just a few bites."

"I want eggs. And bacon." Amy pouted. "I'm calling Robin for takeout."

"Nope." *What a big baby.* "Nothing you could choke on. You need soft things. You could still come down with pneumonia." Molly stirred the cereal. "Don't make me feed you."

"Alright, it looks hot, so don't blame me if it falls on my boob and burns me."

"Eat. I'll sacrifice if it falls and lick you clean." Molly touched Amy on the nose. "Do you want help with your shower?"

"Not if you want to be on time." Amy ate a bite of toast. "We have to be there before Olivia brings Dad back from the movies. Mom wants to surprise him."

Molly picked up a bag decorated with 'Birthday Boy' across the front. "Shall I go load the car?"

"Please. There's a bottle of wine in the fridge I want to take as well." Amy pushed the blanket back and tried to stand, her knees buckling. "Maybe I should take you up on the offer to give me a hand."

Molly dropped the bag like it was on fire and went to the side of the bed. "Take my hand. Easy does it."

"I'm just a little light-headed, not a hundred years old," Amy said. She leaned onto Molly.

"Watch the door frame." Molly banged down the toilet lid. "Sit here and I'll start the shower."

Amy picked up a bottle from the counter. "Either you go to Winnie or you're holding out on some serious primping skills."

Molly cranked on the shower. "Both." She held her hand in the water and watched as Amy stood up and started to fall. *Oh shit.* She grabbed but missed the catch. Amy collapsed onto the ceramic tile floor. Molly moved her onto her back and automatically checked her pulse. It was rapid but strong. Amy's eyes fluttered open.

"Can you sit up? Did you hit your head?" Molly asked. She helped Amy sit upright.

Amy touched her temple. "I'm fine, I just got a little dizzy, and then I was down here and you are, too."

"How about we see the doctor on the way to your folks. They can start without us."

"No, really, I'll just use the inhaler and the oxygen."

"No way and no complaints." Molly helped Amy up. "Into the car, do not pass go, do not collect 200 dollars."

"What about my shower? I only have one set of clothes."

"So? You can't wear them twice?"

Amy frowned. "This from the woman I've seen wear three outfits in one day."

"Fine." Molly led her back to the bed. She rummaged in a drawer. "Here you go, honey, these should fit you ok."

Amy looked at the shorts and shirt. She lifted her arms up to put on the shirt and dropped back onto the mattress. Molly scooped her up and helped her dress.

"I'm starting to see a very nurturing side." Amy lifted her foot and Molly slid the shorts up her leg. "Getting dressed is almost as sexy as getting undressed."

"Uh huh. Sick as a dog and still frisky." Molly winked.

Amy kissed her cheek.

Molly pulled back. "Easy there, captain. Let's get you cleared for takeoff first."

Together, they crept along to the car, and Molly fired up the Mustang. She appreciated the benefits of being the chief in a small town. A doctor in a big city would never come in on a Saturday for a patient. They pulled into the clinic and only the doctor's Cadillac was in the paved lot. Molly tucked an arm under Amy and helped walk her inside. Molly spotted the light on down the hall.

"Right this way." Dr. Eastman directed them towards a small exam room.

Amy wheezed, "Sorry to be a bother."

"She fainted?" he asked. He slid the thermometer into Amy's mouth.

Molly nodded. "Twice, and she may have hit her head."

He flicked a flashlight over Amy's eyes. He pulled the thermometer out of her mouth.

He looked at the glass tube, squinting through his thick glass lens. "It's 102."

Molly sagged. *How could I have missed a fever that high?* "I should have brought her sooner."

"Oh, these things pop up quickly. She's here now," Dr. Eastman said.

He put in the earpieces and blew on the stethoscope end. He gently placed it on Amy's chest. He listened for a moment and then moved it. He turned toward Molly. "I can call an ambulance or you can take her in. She needs a hospital. She's gurgling. I want some x-rays and more oxygen than that little tank can push."

"I'll take her. I think I can talk my way out of a speeding ticket," Molly said.

"I'm sure you can; I'll call and authorize the admission. Go directly to the nurse station, not the ER desk."

Molly scooped Amy up, stood under her arm and they wobbled to the car.

"What about Mom's dinner party?" Amy said. "I have to…"

"You have to get in the car. Olivia will be our eyes and ears. Your dad will understand." Molly held Amy up, her elbow in one hand, her other arm around Amy's back. When they reached the car, she paused. "Lean a minute." Molly took her keys out of her pocket and unlocked the door. She tucked Amy into the car, putting a hand on her head out of habit.

At the hospital, Molly parked in the ambulance slot and an orderly rushed over with a wheelchair. She drove to park the car and hurried back inside.

"Ma'am, you can't go back there." A tiny nurse spoke over the counter.

Molly exhaled and took out her badge. "I'm looking for Gilbert."

"Oh, I'm sorry, of course, room two, on the left side."

They had already started an IV, and something made Amy drowsy. She took longer and longer blinks. *She looks pale.* She drifted to sleep, and Molly sat perched on the edge of a chair watching as a nurse made some notations on a chart.

"I'm Carol. How's our little VIP?" the nurse asked.

"Pardon?" Molly said.

"Dr. Eastman's patients are all VIPs. If we mess up, he could kill us and no one would ever know." The nurse laughed.

Molly didn't.

"Because he's the coroner, he would fill out the forms and lie to cover up…oh never mind."

"I'm sorry, I'm just a little worried." Molly tapped her hands on her leg.

Carol lowered her voice. "You two are cute together. How long have you been dating?"

"Dating? Uh," Molly stuttered.

"Oh sweetie, I've known Amy a long time. We go way back. It's cool. Your secret is safe with me." She mashed a button on the machine to stop the beeping. "These things are so sensitive. Drives me bonkers. The doctor should be here soon."

Molly watched the lights on the machine. A bunch of numbers flickered, some in red, some in green.

A doctor that looked fifteen walked into the room. "Are you her sister?"

Molly raised an eyebrow, opened her badge, and held it up. "No. Do I need to be?"

"Uh. Huh, it's usually only the family, but since you're an officer, I guess it's okay." He cleared his throat. "Well, I am following Dr. Eastman's orders. He says she had a near drowning, and they recently discharged her." He clicked his pen a few times. "I'm sorry she's had a relapse. It happens. They will take her upstairs shortly. The x-ray technician hasn't responded to our page yet, but we'll get screens as soon as we can, just to monitor things." He scribbled something on a clipboard. "Don't worry too much. I think a day or two on antibiotics and she will be in good shape."

Molly shifted in the chair several times, stood up and paced around. *Do I look worried? I must look worried.* Finally, the staff came to take them upstairs. Molly followed the orderly pushing the gurney, and once in the room, made herself as comfortable as she could on the boxy chair. It might be a long wait. *Good thing I have a badge. What do other couples do? Are we a couple? I think so.* She leaned back and rested her head.

Amy adjusted the air blowing in her nose. "Hi. I hope you haven't been waiting long."

Molly smiled. "Oh, maybe a couple of hours. How are you feeling?"

"Just tired. What time is it?"

"About seven. Can I get you another pillow?"

"No, but I'd rather sit in the chair. I just don't know how to get there without flashing you all my business." Amy lifted her arm with the IV and tugged at the blanket.

"Like this," Molly said pushing the nurse button. "I'm pretty sure I've seen every inch, but I'll step out. Your modesty is kind of cute."

She stepped out as the male nurse came in. She went in search of a payphone. She dropped in a quarter and punched in the numbers. Amy's parents weren't home. The quarter dropped out and she repeated the steps to reach Robin at work. After leaving a message with the hostess, she hung up and went back to Amy's room and quietly opened the door. She found Amy tucked into the chair propped up on pillows with an oxygen mask over her face, a blanket over her lap and her IV attached to a rolling pole behind her.

Molly looked around and spotted a folding chair behind the bathroom door. She opened it and dragged it next to Amy. Molly reached over and gently took Amy's hand. As they were sitting together in the now darkening hospital room, Amy smiled at Molly.

"You have the greatest smile." Molly kissed Amy's hand.

The nurse returned with a soft drink and some snack packs. Molly automatically pulled her hand back.

"These are for you," the nurse said. "If you want to stay the night, the chair folds out. I can bring another pillow and a blanket."

Molly looked away. "I'm not family."

"Darling, I don't care if you're the Easter Bunny if she says you can stay, you can stay." He left the room as quickly as he arrived.

"Do you want to stay?" Amy asked.

"Actually, uh, yes. I do." Molly moved closer and kissed her cheek.

"Then stay." Amy coughed until she gasped. "Just don't plan on me getting a U-Haul any time soon."

"Damn. I hate to hear that. I already had your name tattooed on my ass." Molly winked.

"Speaking of asses, can you call Denny's and let Robin know we're here?" Amy asked.

"I already did. Your parents didn't answer." Molly brushed some hair back from Amy's face. "Do you want me to try them again?"

"Not while they're watching Jeopardy," Amy said.

Molly wasn't sure if she was kidding or not. Molly felt Amy's head. "I was sure you still had a fever because you look hot."

Amy tipped her head. "With pathetic lines like that, I can see why you've been single so long."

"No, seriously, you look hot. Let me get a washcloth. Maybe I should just page the nurse." Molly started to reach up.

"They check my vitals like every ten minutes. It can wait."

"I'm keeping track of the time," Molly assured her, tapping her wristwatch. The phone on the table rang, so she handed the receiver to Amy.

Olivia's voice echoed, "Boy did you miss a good one; Tina brought a date. He's a dweeb. Well, he and Dad started arm wrestling. Knocked into the china hutch and broke a Hummel. Mom almost killed them both."

CHAPTER 33

Molly climbed the steps to Robin's house two at a time. She clutched the grocery sack with one arm and held a bag from McDonald's in the other.

Just as she managed to open the screen door, Robin yanked the oak door open. "Hi. I was just on my way out."

"Don't leave on my account." Molly held up the bag. "I brought hamburgers."

"Thanks, no. I need to run some errands. Amy's room is at the top of the stairs, right side."

Molly watched her form disappear through a back room. "Alrighty then." She headed up and paused at the top, turned right and called out, "Knock knock."

Amy was sitting in a disastrous orange flowered chair. She started to rise. "Hi, there!"

Molly sat the groceries on a low box and handed the bag to Amy. "I hope you like cheeseburgers."

Amy took the sack and peered inside it. "No happy meal?"

"Those are only for good girls. Have you been taking your medicine? Using your inhaler?"

"Yes." Amy pushed the door shut and turned the lock. "But I'm not really interested in the food." She reached for Molly and they fell into a hug.

"That's too bad since I got double cheese." Molly leaned in for a kiss. *I wonder if Robin is gone yet?* Right on cue, she heard the rumble of the sports car starting. "Do you want to watch the game? The Tigers are playing."

Amy pulled back and started to pull her shirt off. "Nope."

Molly felt her mouth go dry at the sight of her breasts. She started to reach for her belt buckle and Amy stopped her. Amy pushed her back in the chair and stepped back. With a steady stare, Amy slowly pushed her shorts down. Molly felt an immediate heat in her pelvis. Standing in her underwear and socks, Amy inched her finger urging Molly to stand. *I would follow you across the desert on my knees to hold that ass.* She obliged again reaching for her pants.

Amy knocked her hands down. "Let me."

Amy untucked her shirt, sliding her hands up Molly's back and pulled her into a kiss. Molly detected a hint of Scope and peanut butter. She opened her mouth, slowly exploring the wetness, touching her teeth. The kiss became harder, more frantic. Goosebumps popped up on her arms when Amy ran her fingers through her hair, their hips bumping together. *I think I soaked these pants already*. Molly gently touched Amy's hair, brushing the short strands back.

Amy pulled at Molly's t-shirt, flipping it over her head. With one hand, Amy unhooked Molly's bra and slid it off. Molly kicked off her shoes and Amy pulled her off balance tugging at Molly's belt. They fell onto the bed, and Amy shoved her hand down the front of Molly's open pants.

Amy smiled. "Somebody is glad to see me."

"Glad doesn't begin to cover it." Molly reached out and stroked Amy's breast. The nipple popped up under the touch. "I'm not the only one."

"You got that right." Amy planted her mouth over Molly's just as she plunged her fingers into the folds.

Molly lifted her hips and felt the moan in her throat. She massaged the fullness and pulled her mouth away to attend to the matching nipple. Amy shuddered as she circled, softly sucking the tender skin. The ache in Molly's hips increased as Amy stroked. *Jesus.* The pressure of her pants across her hips changed the sensations as she lifted to meet Amy's hand. *Not already. Four times seven...is...28, no 24, no it is 28.* Her breathing became faster as Amy nuzzled her neck. *Four times eight is 32. Four times...nine...is nine...four.* A white glow started deep in her pelvis and Molly bucked.

"Jesus, Amy...." Molly clamped her teeth together and shuddered as the orgasm blasted through her body. Her thighs shook. *She's going to think I'm a sex maniac.*

"Molly, you are so fucking hot. Damn." Amy slid her hand back out of Molly's pants.

"Are you okay? You can breathe okay?" Molly asked.

"The only thing taking my breath away is you." Amy kissed her softly. "You won't wear me out."

"Are you sure you're all right?"

Amy nodded. "You're overdressed."

"Right." Molly twisted and pulled off her pants.

"All of it."

Molly stood up and stripped off her underwear. "Socks too?"

"Of course."

Molly sat on the bed and took off each sock. She stood and turned to crawl up to Amy.

Molly said, "Here, sit up a minute." She grabbed both pillows. "Scoot back against these."

As Amy slid up, Molly hooked her underwear with a thumb. "You don't need these." She tossed them toward the floor. "Are you comfortable? Put your knees up."

As Molly moved to sit between Amy's legs, she cracked her cheek on Amy's knee as it rose. They both laughed.

Amy touched Molly's face. "Want me to kiss it better?"

"I have other intentions." Molly scooted closer, between Amy's knees, kneeling. She licked a finger and trailed along her inner thigh. "Ticklish?"

Amy jumped and wiggled her leg. "Yeah, a little."

Molly leaned forward a bit, and slowly slid her hand back. She circled her left arm through Amy's right knee and lightly kissed her thigh. Molly moved her hand, careful as she edged her way between the drenched skin. Her fingers slid easily, and she increased her pressure up and down along the full length. Molly looked up into Amy's eyes as she plunged two fingers inside her as far as she could. Amy's eyes fluttered and Molly felt a new gush between her own legs.

Molly whispered, "You are amazing." She twisted her arm and her wrist crackled.

Amy smiled and opened her eyes. "Am I breaking you?"

"Not so far," Molly said. She curled her fingers, stroking the wall firmly, and then moved her thumb in a little circle around her rigid nub. She smiled as Amy closed her eyes again.

"We may need to practice this one a lot until you get this right," Amy said. "Maybe for hours."

Molly grinned. *I love making her feel good.* "If you say so. Shall I stop?"

"Oh god no." Amy grabbed Molly's shoulders.

Molly turned her head and kissed Amy's forearm. She increased the speed of her thumb. *Shit.* Her arm cramped. *Just a little more…*Amy tightened around her fingers, and Molly froze them, pushing harder with her thumb. The soft moan started in Amy's throat, and Molly watched Amy's expression change into a look of almost anguish as a loud cry erupted from her mouth.

"God, you are so fucking hot." As she pulled her hand back, Molly tried to move her leg behind her and toppled into Amy's sweaty stomach. *Fucking A., grace.* Amy hooked her legs around her hips and rubbed Molly's ass with her socked feet.

Amy put her hands behind her head. "I think we better try that again."

"After cheeseburgers?" Molly asked. She slid up just a bit more and gently kissed Amy on the mouth. Amy wrapped her arm's around Molly's back, clutching her legs around her hips. "Is that a no?"

"I need a drink, too," Amy whispered and let Molly go.

"Right away." Molly popped off the bed and turned. "Are you sure Robin is gone?"

"Pretty sure."

Molly opened the door and headed down the stairs. She stopped at the bottom of the landing and locked eyes with Robin. *Oh, hell.* She continued into the kitchen, took a glass from the dish drainer, and filled it at the sink. She took a deep breath, walked through the doorway and back up the stairs.

"Here you go," Molly said. "And just so you know, Robin's home."

Amy's eyes bugged out.

CHAPTER 34

Molly revved the engine as they pulled onto the highway. "It's really pretty funny that we're having the party at Olivia and Donny's lake place."

"Olivia is so upset, she would let us burn the whole house down if we wanted to. Besides she has known Robin as long as I have." Amy touched Molly's arm as it rested on the center console. "I really appreciate you helping out. I guess I don't have to tell you how much this will mean to Robin. She does like you, you know."

"She's warming up to me I think," Molly said. She took Amy's hand and gave it a little kiss.

"You two got off on the wrong foot, that's all. Do you have a shirt to put over that tank top?"

"No, it's like ninety degrees out."

"Rats. I should have gotten you another shirt. That tank top is going to drive me crazy all afternoon." Amy ran a finger along Molly's arm.

"Really?" Molly flexed her arm.

"Stop torturing me. It also didn't hurt that you got Michelle's phone number for her. I never thought I'd see her gaga after someone like that since Rebecca. It's totally unlike her, I mean, she hasn't been brave enough to even call her." Amy turned up the A/C.

"Rewind. Who is Rebecca?"

"Robin's ex. She burned her bad. Robin didn't date for a long time and when she did, she kind of went a little crazy. I think she sleeps around so she won't get attached because she doesn't want to get hurt." Amy kissed Molly's hand. "I guess we all have crazy ex stories."

"You don't have to tell me," Molly said.

"Oh really?" Amy asked.

"Uh oh." Molly clicked her tongue.

"What?"

Molly said, "I hope it's okay that I called Michelle. She'll be at the party."

"Nice deflection. Robin will be thrilled, and I'm glad you invited her. I hope she's okay with alcohol." Amy laughed. "I bet Robin's tanked already."

"EMT's see plenty of intoxicated people."

"At least Robin's a happy drunk."

Molly said, "She'll be truthful. Drunks have trouble lying."

"Oh really? You better plan on some serious consumption, then Missy. I have about a hundred questions for you. Starting with your ex's."

"Hey, it's not my fault you're so sexy we are too busy to talk." Molly wiggled her eyebrows up and down.

Amy leaned over and blew softly in Molly's ear while reaching into her crotch. "This kind of busy?"

Molly swatted at her hand. "Do you want to make it to the party?"

They pulled onto the lake drive and followed the gravel path. A long string of cars led them to where the large fieldstone house stood, a wall of windows overlooked the lake. Every lesbian for a hundred miles was parked across the front lawn. A volleyball net was strung across the side yard, and around the back, a huge multi-level deck stepped down toward a dock that leaned out over the lake. The boathouse was topped with a blue slide curving toward the water. People were everywhere.

Molly held Amy's hand as they walked toward the door.

"Hey, look who the cat dragged in," Robin slurred. She wore a t-shirt that said 'I'm the birthday girl' and a lei made from plastic flowers. She held up the string. "I already got laid. It's a lei. Get it?"

"Yep, we get it. Laid." Amy gave Robin a hug. "Happy birthday."

"Yes, happy birthday!" Molly stuck out her hand, which Robin grabbed and pulled into a bear hug. Molly patted Robin on the back and extricated herself. "I'm going to get the bags from the car."

Robin put her hands on her hips. "Amy. Your girlfriend is ripped, man. I mean totally. Honest."

"Yeah. I know." Clearly, Robin was trashed. "And we wouldn't have been late except we had to stop at the liquor store," Amy said holding up a bottle of Chivas.

"Excellent because we just ran out of tequila," Stacy reported. She sat at a table covered with shot glasses. As if held by a string, her head slowly lowered onto the table top.

Robin put a finger up against her lips. "Shhh. No, we didn't, I have more in the trunk of my car. For margaritas. Later." Her eyes glazed over.

Molly came back into the house, carrying a huge load of groceries. "Only one trip!"

"You're a stud." Amy started to lay out assorted vegetable trays, a fruit tray, and cheese and crackers.

Robin looked at the table. "Where's the beef? I don't want this rabbit food. I want a fricking steak."

"And you'll get one, birthday girl. I just hope to soak up a bit of the alcohol these women are chugging down. Speaking of chugging, I need to check the keg."

Robin followed her outside like a puppy and continued wandering down toward the dock. On the first deck porch, Amy lifted the beer keg chilling in a barrel of ice and it seemed about half empty. She called out, "Molly, is there anyone else here sober enough to get another keg?"

Molly stuck her head out the door. "I think just you or me. Are you sure we should get one?"

"It's not even two o'clock. I bet that this will be gone in a couple hours."

"Because everyone is sleeping over?" Molly asked.

"No, but not everyone is hammered."

"Yet. I'll go."

Winnie drove their boat over, and I'm sure she's sober too. We can go skiing when you get back." Amy said. "Have you seen Olivia yet? I want to see if we need anything else before you leave."

At that moment some woman was chasing Robin up the stairs with the threat of a spanking.

Molly laughed. "This will be a most excellent day. It's too bad Robin won't remember any of it."

Amy went back inside and began to set up a side table for the cake. A tap at the front door caught her attention. Michelle was standing on the porch.

Amy waved her in and smiled. "I'm so glad you could join us. I hope you know at least a few people, but let me introduce you around."

The front screen slammed open and Robin skidded to a stop behind Amy. "I'll take her. I mean you. I mean around." Robin held open the door for Michelle and tripped as she followed her out.

Amy smirked. *She's got it bad.* Amy carried out a bag of charcoal to the middle deck where music blared from a boombox. After several tries with the starter fluid, the coals were finally turning gray on the edges. Olivia showed up beside her carrying a huge platter.

"I see you still have your eyebrows. You want me to begin laying out the burgers?" Olivia asked.

Amy nodded. As the smoke drifted across the yard, she was pretty sure she smelled the distinct scent of marijuana on the breeze. "Maybe I should have asked Molly her opinion on pot before the party."

Olivia teased, "I suppose you two rabbits don't take time to talk?"

As if on cue, Molly climbed down the stairs, seemingly unaware, and inspected the grill.

Flames shot up from the grill and Molly took a spray bottle and spritzed water at the coals. "I double as a firefighter."

"Good to know. Where's the other keg?" Amy asked.

"In the trunk." Molly leaned in for a kiss.

Olivia waved her hands. "You two get out of here, I got this covered."

"And leave you at the mercy of dozens of lesbian women?" Amy asked.

Olivia lowered her voice, "These women are lesbians? And me without any lip balm." She rolled her eyes.

Before she could give a snappy response, Amy was distracted when Molly leaned back on the rail, her muscles flexing as she put her arms out. Her tan almost hid the scar. Every woman within eyeshot stopped and looked.

Amy frowned. "I am burning that tank top."

Robin called out, "What's happening?"

Olivia answered. "Just started grilling. Do you need anything?"

"Nah. After my steak, we're going to go tubing," Robin answered, stripping her shirt off. Thankfully she had a bikini top underneath. She started to fish the lei out of her shirt and fell into a pile of floats. Michelle helped her get up. Just then Winnie guided the ski boat against the dock. Julie caught the rope and she and Nancy tied the boat. Winnie and Michelle each hooked Robin's arm and escorted her up the stairs.

"Tubing?" Molly paled. "Are you kidding me?"

Amy said, "Don't worry, honey. Winnie will make her wear a life vest. Just be glad she doesn't want to go water skiing barefoot."

"What? Can she even water ski?" Molly asked.

"Oh sure," Olivia said. "She can slalom starting from the dock, and usually land back on it."

"Usually?" Molly asked. She looked over her sunglasses.

"There was an incident. It involved splinters, a full moon

and the premature death of a swimsuit," Amy said while taking Molly's hand to distract her. "Never mind about that. Do you want a drink?"

"Just a Coke. Someone needs to talk to the cops when they show up." Molly accepted a quick kiss from Amy.

Gail walked out onto the deck carrying a large cooler. "I found it! Do you still want the kiddy pool? I can call my Dad."

Molly shook her head. "I don't want to know what that was for."

"The kiddy pool?" Olivia shrugged. "Maybe water balloons?"

The ladies reached the top of the stairs with Robin in tow.

Robin said, "I'm gonna get the to kill ya. Tequila. For the upside. Downs."

Winnie hung back. "Can anyone translate?"

"Upside down margaritas," Amy said.

Winnie tilted her head. "How in the world do you make upside down Margaritas?"

"It's the bomb." Stacy approached with an armload of foam noodles. "See, you lay down in the lawn chair, and people pour it in your mouth all at once, the liquor and the mixers."

Winnie shook her head. "And they say I was wild. Of course, we could always show them how to play blindfold body parts."

"Wait, what?" Amy said. "Spill it, Winnie."

Nancy nudged her. Winnie said, "Fine. So basically, it involves liquor and a blindfold."

Molly raised an eyebrow. "We managed to put that together all on our own."

Winnie pursed her lips. "Um, let's see. The main way is one person sits in a chair with a blindfold on. And two people come up and based on a specific body part that they feel, they have to guess which one is her partner. And if she's wrong, she has to do a shot."

"Rewind," Amy said. "Which body parts?"

Nancy put her hands on her hips. "Main way?"

Winnie said, "Well, the crowd sort of picks, but it could be any really. Trust me when I say it's awfully hard to tell ears apart. I'm just saying." Winnie began turning a deep red blush.

Nancy leaned in, and whatever she said brought peals of laughter from Winnie.

Olivia finished taking the first round of burgers off the grill. She yelled, "Come and get it while it's hot," and climbed up toward the house.

A steady stream of women trailed into the house, and laughter could be heard drifting down the hillside. Winnie and Nancy held hands and walked up the stairs.

Molly smiled. "You guys sure party hardy. Shall we join them? This time you go first."

Amy asked, "So you can look at my ass?"

"Of course." Molly grinned.

As they reached the top of the stairs, Robin came running from around the side of the house, screaming. "Hide me quick! They started the strip volleyball and it's not even dark out yet."

"Strip volleyball?" Nancy arched her eyebrows. "I feel old. I don't even know how you play that."

Winnie laughed. "I couldn't tell you, either."

"You know blindfold body parts but not strip volleyball?" Nancy pulled Winnie into a hug. "Good." She kissed her cheek. "Let's go find out."

Molly went to follow them, and Amy stopped her. "Where do you think you're going?"

"I have to go. It's my training. I'm going to investigate. Besides, what if someone gets hurt?" Molly asked.

Robin said, "Oh don't worry about that; Michelle is playing."

Julie stuck her head out of the cabin door. "Amy! Olivia says to tell you that the stripper just canceled. She wants to know if Molly brought her uniform with her?"

Amy blinked. Her mind raced back to the story when Robin said that Molly should wear her uniform on dates. And the handcuffs. *Oh shit.* She put a hand on Molly's arm. "I'm sorry, I don't know what that's about, please don't be upset with Olivia. She's just kidding."

Molly grinned. She put her hands on her hips, gave a little

shake, watching for Amy's response.

"I'm glad you're not angry. Wait." Amy squinted. "Molly Gorman. You wouldn't!"

Amy stared at the woman in front of her, and her heart skipped a beat.

Robin nodded her head up and down. "Come on, Amy. It's my birthday."

"No frickin' way. This one is mine." Amy linked her arm with Molly's. "You go find your own cop."

##

ABOUT THE AUTHOR

McGee Matthews is a writer and a Jill of all trades. Still searching for what she wants to be when she grows up, she and her wife raise goats, chickens, and humans on a farm in South Carolina.

This is her first self-published work.

You can contact her at:

Email mcgeemathews1@gmail.com

Facebook at McGee Mathews

Twitter @mcgee_mathews

Her web page https://mcgeemathews.wordpress.com

Spotify – Music has always been a part of my life, from marching band in high school and college to playing bass in a country band and an all-women rock band. As I write, certain songs pop into my head and end up the soundtrack to the manuscript. If you'd like to hear the songs for the book, here they are!
https://open.spotify.com/user/iegmytbkii4a6m47lctw7b3fq?si=48xb5pDwQduVD4N8JkalDw

If you have time to spare, a short review would be greatly appreciated.

What's next? You already know! Robin and Michelle... see you next book!

BOOKS IN THIS SERIES

Ladies of Diamond Lake

Exceeding Expectations

Michelle Brennan has known since childhood she was meant to be a doctor. She works hard every day as an EMT and saves every penny toward her singular goal of attending medical school. She'll be the first in her family to go to college, and romance is the last thing on her mind.

Everything Robin Barberg has struggled toward is coming together. Years of painstaking restoration have her century-old home nearly perfect. She and her business partners have acquired a building for the restaurant she's always dreamed of opening. And she's finally met the woman of her dreams: smart, athletic, and sexy.

When these two meet, Michelle tries to harden her heart against love but succumbs to temptation, wondering if something's been missing in her life and if, just maybe, there's a way to find some balance. Robin, suddenly beset by unexpected calamity, is forced to confront the reality that the very self-reliance which has gotten her this far could cost her the one thing she wants most.

Delivering Generations

The women of Diamond Lake continue their adventures in the

latest in the series, Delivering Generations.

The newest officer to join the Diamond Lake police force, Jackie Dupuis is a little eccentric. She finds deciphering people exhausting, which leaves her lonely in this small town. She isn't quite ready to say that she made a mistake taking this job, but she's close. If not for the success of her paranormal hobby in this extremely haunted place, she might have already left.

When Angie Stolmeijer arrived, she assumed she wouldn't be in town for more than a few months. A budding musician and a cosmetologist, she works at the hair salon of Winnie, her Aunt Nancy's partner. As her aunts try to help her find direction, they watch with knowing eyes as Angie develops an interest in a certain new cop. Even with their support, though, there are some journeys in life that you must walk alone.

Amy Gilbert and Molly Gorman enthusiastically prepare for their baby. Amy's footloose lifestyle is challenged while attending to a stubborn, usually self-sufficient, and now pregnant partner. To her shock and pleasure, her parents embrace the upcoming grandbaby.

Molly has her eye on the future, yet her family history haunts her. Her parents are opposed to her having a child. Molly's paternal grandfather was her hero, upholding the law. Small-town gossip has her wondering if it's true that shady characters are sprinkled on her family tree. When a body is found, the rumors gain traction.

BOOKS BY THIS AUTHOR

Keeping Secrets

What would you do if, after finally finding the woman of your dreams, she suddenly leaves to fight in the Civil War?

It's 1863, and Elizabeth Hepscott has resigned herself to a life of monotonous boredom far from the battlefields as the wife of a Missouri rancher. Her fate changes when she travels with her brother to Kentucky to help him join the Union Army. On a whim, she poses as his little brother and is bullied into enlisting, as well. Reluctantly pulled into a new destiny, a lark decision quickly cascades into mortal danger.

While Elizabeth's life has made a drastic U-turn, Charlie Schweicher, heiress to a glass-making fortune, is still searching for the only thing money can't buy.

A chance encounter drastically changes everything for both of them.

Will Charlie find the love she's longed for, or will the war take it all away?

Slaying Dragons

Can you find love after a tragic loss?

Andrea Fenwick is too busy coping with grief, isolation, and guilt over losing Dani Powell, her partner of five years, to even consider this question.

Grasping for relief anywhere she can find it–counseling, grief groups, church–she turns her pain into purpose when she helps start a youth center to address issues related to the LGBT community and mental health.

And then there's Tommie.

Tommie Andrews, a computer whiz and occasional dog trainer, discovers she's developing a crush on her friend and co-worker as they struggle to repair the hole left in Andrea's heart. The timing could not be worse. Or could it?

Andrea has bravely reached out for help through this tragedy. But will that bravery allow her to see a happy future with Tommie, or will the loss of Dani prove too painful to overcome?